MW00939338

Dream State

Book One of the Dreaming Detective Series

An August Chase Novel

by Charles R Hinckley

Mad Drummer Productions

© Copyright C R Hinckley 2016

All Rights Reserved

Edited by Bryony Sutherland

Cover Design by Clarissa Yeo

This is a work of fiction. Names, characters, businesses, places, events
and incidents are either the products of the author's imagination or
used in a fictitious manner. Any resemblance to actual persons, living
or dead, or actual events is purely coincidental.

"Though this be madness, yet there is method in't."

Hamlet

"We are such stuff as dreams are made on, and our little life is rounded with a sleep."

The Tempest

"We must be willing to get rid of the life we've planned, so as to have the life that is waiting for us."

Joseph Campbell

"It is thought and feeling which guides the universe, not deeds."

Edgar Cayce

DEDICATION

I dedicate this book to my wife, my mother and my family. "Blest be the tie that binds…"

Table Of Contents

1
PLAY BACK

Pablo Carrillo was killed in the same dream several times before I attempted to save him. The dream always starts the same way: I'm in the passenger seat of a large sedan travelling along a suspension bridge. Light flickers through support girders, creating a strobe effect on the faintly illuminated guardrails. Outside to my right, at least a hundred feet down, is black water. I turn to the driver. He's a heavyset man with a five o'clock shadow and thick, dark eyebrows. He's fishing around for something between his legs, his eyes darting from the road to the seat. I try to speak, but nothing comes out. Awareness that this is actually a dream begins to dawn on me. It's already set in motion. I'm only along for the ride. The car will crash, and the man will be killed. I dream this again and again. But this time I have the presence of mind to do something.

"Stop the car." My voice is slurred and low as I choke out the words. He glances in my direction and smiles, like I'd paid him a gentle compliment. I turn down the sun visor and gaze into the mirror. It's not my reflection I see, but a dark-haired woman sitting in the back seat. Her eyes are black and intense. She glares at me as if I'd robbed her. Her mouth moves, but I cannot hear her words.

Up ahead, in the oncoming lane, a large pickup truck swerves across the road, coming straight at us. I hear the piercing sound of tires skidding on cement, and shock reverberates through me. A slap to the head and we're falling off the bridge toward the river. My stomach flies around in my chest; my heart pulses hard enough to burst my veins. Then the guttural smack of hitting the water, the puzzled look on Bushy Eyebrows' face as his fat frame pushes into me, the crunching of bone as my cheek melts into the car door. His face is in front of me now. I see it in his eyes. He knows. All is lost. Death rears up and there is no escaping. It's happening no matter what I do.

Can I stop it; change the outcome? Stop time and see who he is? Start at the beginning, play it back? It's only a dream.

I'm in the car again. We've already turned onto the bridge. I unlatch the glove box and search for papers. Who is this man about to meet death? A name pops off the page and into my head as I try to read the registration. Then a flash of light, the smashing of bones as my cheek slams into the steel door. I'm in the water now, trapped in the car, helpless and sinking, the cold enveloping me. Bubbles escape my mouth as I scream his name, "Carrillo. Pablo Carrillo." Then I wake up.

That was the first time I manipulated a dream to see who I was going to save.

The dreams started about five years ago, around the time I turned thirty. I was walking home early one Sunday morning after a party in the East Village. I'd been drinking since about ten the previous evening while chasing a pretty girl named Sarah, playing a flirty cat and mouse game, trying to get her to come home with me. I failed in my attempt, and in the process had way too much to drink. I got sloppy drunk, maybe a bit obnoxious, and she ended the game. With time on my hands and little money for a cab, I began to walk the fifty-something blocks back to my apartment.

It was freezing. Anemic snowflakes fluttered through the air around me. After a while the snow grew heavier, stopped melting, and began a rapid accumulation. The light sputtering transformed into a white curtain and obscured visibility beyond a half block in any direction. The wind began to pick up and swirling blasts hit me in the face, numbing my cheeks and nose. I grabbed a newspaper from a nearby trash bin and held it over my head. I looked down to protect my face from the biting wind, and watched one foot methodically plod in front of the other.

That was when I saw the blood. There was a large drop of it on my shoe, then another on my knee. Putting a finger to my nose, it returned covered in thin red liquid. I collected snow from the ground and put it on my nose. My legs felt heavy. I was no longer capable of walking properly, and dragged my feet across the sidewalk as I fought the pull of gravity. Wooziness enveloped me, but I trudged on.

After what seemed like hours, I finally made it home. I unlocked the door, staggered into the building and fell to the floor. Fighting to get back to my feet, I grabbed the stair railing and tried to pull myself up, but hadn't the strength. I slumped back down, my head thumping onto the linoleum floor, and everything went black.

That's when I had the first of many special dreams, the specifics of which are not important now. What I didn't realize at the time is that the snippets of information I was acquiring through this Dream State would later enable me to save lives.

This life-saving dream data came to me in short black and white images, similar to a video clip or micro movie, that I eventually learned I could play back in my head and try to comprehend, but only if I could wake up immediately. If I didn't wake up right after the dream, the information slowly dissolved from memorable pictures into a mist of crumbling gray dots.

I didn't choose for this to happen to me. I didn't believe in ESP, precognition, mind melding, kinetic energy transference, time travel, or anything else you can cram into that mystical category. I was just an ordinary guy.

Pablo Carrillo, the man I'd identified as the driver of the car, didn't realize his life was in danger. Nor did he think the gringo who knocked on his door that afternoon was anyone worth mentioning to his wife, Phyllis. It wasn't until the gringo started hanging around the corner deli near his apartment that he began to take the situation seriously, and not in the way the gringo had wanted, but in a way that could get him hurt. At least, this is the impression I had when Pablo grabbed me by the shirt and pushed me down in the corner of the bodega.

"Get out of my neighborhood, you understand me?" Carrillo said.

"I'm trying to tell you, you're in danger!"

Carrillo hauled back and held his fist above my head, ready to let loose.

"You think I want to be here? I hate this."

Carrillo lowered his fist, and sneered at the bodega guy watching us. "What are you looking at?" The bodega guy picked up a telephone and began to dial. "Now you get the fuck out of my face or I swear I'll put you deep in the ground."

"There's a bridge," I started, desperately trying to sound as sincere and foreboding as possible. "The Queensborough Bridge, you're crossing it. You have on a blue suit. A wedding? Are you going to a—"

The vision began to play in my head.

I see the truck barreling at us. I'm in the passenger seat and the truck is approaching so quickly there's no time to react. Impact. My chest heaves. I try to catch my breath. My body convulses and contorts as the car wraps around me.

Carrillo hesitated from pummeling my face, his fist still balled. A metallic taste filled my mouth, blood dripping from my nose down onto my chin. I was going into a Dream State.

"I didn't even hit you! You're sick, dude. Get yourself to a fucking hospital." Carrillo stared down at me in horror before running out of the store.

4

The pain in my head was overwhelming, and darkness took me.

I awoke on the sidewalk. I don't know how long I was out, probably not more than a few seconds. My face was cold. Numbness snaked up the side of my head from my right ear to the top of my skull. I sat up, brushed pebbles and dirt from my bloody chin and held my head in my hands.

I'd seen Carrillo crash and die, and there was nothing I could do to stop it. It had come in a vision so clear it was impossible to ignore. Like a ride in an amusement park, the dream had no feelings, no opinion of its own: it was just a cold hard fact on repeat.

I'd tracked him down for nothing. He and his wife were going to be mutilated on that bridge and fall into the river; their car would become a careening pile of junk. Perhaps they'd be on their way to a wedding or a funeral, I didn't know. But there was nothing more I could do about it.

I slowly turned my throbbing head toward the store. The bodega guy was looking at me through the window.

"And here I am on the sidewalk," I said to no one. No doubt Bodega Guy had dragged me outside and left me for dead, the empathetic fucker. I saw his little head darting back and forth, trying to get a better view of me from the window. "Yeah, I see you. I love you, too." I knew he couldn't hear me, and blew him a kiss. He turned away, busying himself with whatever bodega guys do.

Carrillo and his wife were killed in a fiery bridge crash a few days later. The paper said the truck driver had fallen asleep at the wheel and had somehow crossed over the construction barrier into oncoming traffic. It was a freak accident. They'd died instantly. Their bodies were fished out of the East River the following day. And that just plain sucks.

There had to be a way to channel this stuff, synthesize it into a form I could deal with, rather than chasing some guy until I was considered a nut job. Anyway, that's what I was thinking. That was the plan, until I finally got it down to a science.

5

You want facts and figures? I can give those to you. You want time and place? I can give you that, too. You want to know who? It's going to cost you, because that's what I do. Now I'm the Sleeping Detective, and if I dream about you and you don't listen to what I have to say, you're going to die.

2
IN CASE OF EMMA, BREAK HEART

The Carrillo dreams immediately followed another set of disturbing dreams about a young woman named Emma Donati. The dreams by this time were longer, more detailed. I began to see the time of day or night, the weather, what people were wearing. And if I awakened at once, a face might crystallize in my memory and be etched there forever.

In the case of Emma, I'd dreamed her death two times the first day, three times the second, then every night for the rest of that week. The dreams were vivid, violent and brutal. They'd become a torture I could hardly bear and were way too disturbing to ignore. Often they fell upon me like an avalanche, catching me unaware in the middle of an ordinary day.

Since Emma was one of my first Dream State experiences, I didn't yet connect the dreams to anything real. Nothing beyond enduring a recurring nightmare, and a slightly bloodied nose. I simply believed Emma was a mythical woman conjured from my imagination. After the dreams repeated several times, and the details became too numerous and explicit to ignore, I was inspired to do an internet search to see if there was anything on an Emma Donati. I found one mention on a social media account from a similar looking a girl in Manhattan, and as the dream took place in an alley near this Emma's midtown apartment, I decided she might be the girl in my dream. I had to warn her, not so much for her sake, but in the slimmest of hopes that the crushing dreams would stop.

"Hello?"

"Is this Emma Donati?"

"Yes, who's this?"

"You don't know me, but you see, I dream things, and well…your life is in danger."

Click

She hung up on me. Can you blame her? I was nothing short of a bumbling idiot.

I finally managed to track her down by staking out her apartment—I know, not cool—and I immediately recognized her from the dream. I approached her on the street outside in a cool, calm manner, with an empathetic smile on my face. But shit, how do you tell someone they're going to be violently murdered and still appear rational? I tried to have a serious conversation about my dream, detailing what she would be wearing, where in midtown she needed to avoid, that two men would be coming after her. Her face turned a ghostly pale. Her eyes grew huge, then squinty, before she bolted in the opposite direction. She was spooked. I did manage to slip a paper with my name and phone number into her purse as she scurried away, in case she changed her mind and wanted to work with me. Of course she never called; why would she?

I became obsessed with saving her life. I followed her to school, to work, to the dentist. I ran into her at a restaurant, in the subway, near a bus stop. Then one day, after a full seven days of shadowing her and feeling like a disgusting stalker, the dreams just stopped. Like a bright summer's day after a cloudy thunderstorm, I was unexpectedly and inexplicably clear of Emma. I was able move on with my life. Or so I thought.

A month later, I was having lunch at a local restaurant when I glanced up and noticed a poster featuring her photo tacked to the wall. Below her photo was a poem dedicated to her memory. My heart stopped when I saw that picture. Emma smiling for the camera, her clear, luminous eyes, her shoulder-length, bouncy blonde hair all caught in a candid, seemingly happy moment. She was wearing chef whites, just as I had seen her in my dreams. The text below the picture read:

Emma Donati: gone but not forgotten. Died on January 7th.
Victim of a mugging in midtown Manhattan.

I didn't need to read the details. I'd seen it repeatedly in my Dream State. Emma's brutal death was confirmation that even through all my insecurities, my nagging fears and frustrations, even doubts about my sanity, I was dreaming reality before it happened.

I began to think of myself as a reluctant traveler wandering the darkened halls of time, witnessing seemingly random events. But they weren't random in their descriptiveness. They always brought me to the exact moment someone was about to die.

Once I'd started to piece my thoughts together and figured out how I could harness my precognition, I placed an ad in the classified section of *The Village Voice*, under the heading *PSYCHIC DETECTIVE*. In it, I detailed my ability to dream the future and enlighten paying customers of what may come to pass. The only problem was that I didn't know if it was a lie because I'd never tried to conjure the future on purpose. My dreams had always brought me to a crime scene, as if guided by some unknown force, and it had invariably taken me days or even weeks to track down the victims. Each time, I'd ended up with nothing but heartache and pain for my troubles.

I was always shocked and amazed that I could track down the subjects of my dreams. I was turning into a pretty good skip tracer. But after all that work, invariably, they didn't believe me. Would you? So, the hell with it. I was going into the dream business for real to find people who wanted to believe and reward me for services rendered.

A little giddy and light-headed at the prospect of making some money and maybe even helping people, I pushed any potential incoming dreams out of my conscious mind. If I felt an unwanted dream beginning, I trained myself to become aware of the warning signs—a nose bleed, a vision forming in my imagination—and forced myself to stay awake, thus blocking it from taking over my mind, and clearing the way for paying customers only.

3
THE FAT MAN SINGS

My first paying customer came to me through a recommendation by a friend named Millar Milford. Millar and I had met at The Tavern, a run-down little bar that used to be a fairly nice British-style pub. Good burgers, fish and chips, shepherd's pie, soccer games continually playing on the television, wood shavings on the floor. You get the idea.

The bartender was a thirty-something Brit named Allen, who was skinny as a pole because he'd started a macrobiotic diet several months back. He thought he looked just peachy with two percent body fat. Allen had gotten mean in his skinniness, and acted accordingly, like he was above the lowly swine who haunted his late night establishment. For all I knew, he was a former Best Bartender of the Year award winner.

I was sitting in The Tavern, nursing a beer and trying to forget a recurring dream in which a girl named Francine's head was ripped off. She'd been out for a nice Sunday bike ride when a city bus cut her off at a street corner and crushed her to death. I'd heard of this type of accident before. In fact, it almost happened to me once. I was moving north along Third Avenue on my shiny red ten speed, lost in heavy traffic, mindful of the insane cabs coming at me from all directions. A city bus roared up from behind and took a right-hand turn in front of me. The bus covered part of the curb that I was trying desperately to get onto. I hopped off my bike and dashed up onto the curb just as the bus rolled on past me. If I hadn't acted quickly, I would have been sucked under that bus and my brains would have been splattered all over the pavement.

I was trying to get this nasty little image out of my head, thinking up ways to track down this girl and convince her she was going to have her head popped, when the bartender pushed a beer in front of me and nodded to my left. I looked over and saw a skinny guy with long, stringy hair and dark round-rim glasses held together with tape in the center. He nodded at me. I nodded back and thanked him. He smiled but said nothing. Then he bought me another round and another. A few rounds later, he sidled up next to me and began telling me about his pathetic life, how his wife was gone, and he was stuck holding the bill for an extended honeymoon she'd never intended to finish in the first place, blah, blah, blah.

Millar had created an app that allowed other apps to talk to each other. He was a computer tech millionaire, although you wouldn't know it to look at him. He also made a shooter game called *Killaz!* for the iPhone. It was all geek to me.

I felt sorry for him because he was one lonely, shy son of a bitch, who was a bit on the rude side and had the social skills of a wasp. Every other sentence he'd blurt out something nasty he'd seen or heard or noticed about you, or would fart, burp, tease, and generally distort the air space around him.

So, after hearing his heartache, I explained my special gift to Millar, who by then had requested I call him Mill. "Take control of this thing," he said. "Put an ad in the *Voice* and find some paying customers. You have a rare gift. You can make this pay."

At the time, I was an Exhibit Technician at the Museum of Contemporary Art, and not making a whole lot of dough. I assisted in the installation and de-installation of exhibits. I'd really wanted to be a writer, but that's a different story. I took him up on the classified ad idea: Psychic Detective for Hire. Why not make a little money?

Before I'd even processed the idea, Mill got all excited and poked me in the ribs, said he knew someone looking for a psychic, and could call him for me. He was some guy Mill had met in an online group of astronomy enthusiasts. I explained to Mill about the Dream State, how it just came to me, and how I couldn't force the dream subject. Millar was so enthusiastic—a rare thing for this guy, I later found out—that I agreed to meet Frank Cosh.

Frank "The Fat Man" Cosh inhabited a run-down, four-story walk-up a few blocks below Eighty-Sixth Street on the East Side of Manhattan. I knocked lightly on Frank's door. It opened immediately. A huge man stood staring at me with a goofy grin on his face and a knowing twinkle in his dark eyes. He cradled in his arms a large yellow tabby cat.

"August Chase?" he asked.

I nodded. "Frank?"

"Say hello to my buddy, Peter." Frank waved the cat's paw at me.

"Peter," I said, nodding at the cat. Probably in his early forties, Frank had a tarnished, uneven grin buried in a long gray beard. Thinning hair barely covered his head and assorted food stains decorated his tent-sized, button-down shirt. I stood nervously waiting to be invited in.

Frank turned away abruptly and the door started to close. *Was it something I said,* I asked myself, as I stuck out my foot to stop it, then cautiously followed him inside.

"Where do we begin?" he asked, as he huffed his three-hundred-odd pounds through the small, and by the looks of it, rarely used kitchen. I started to say something, but he continued walking down the darkened hallway. I followed close behind, past stacks of boxes crammed with old newspapers, books, magazines, and other assorted memorabilia. The boxes stood head high on both sides of the hallway. They swayed precariously as we creaked by on the old wooden floor. I could just see tomorrow's headline: *Phony Psychic*

13

Crushed in Hoarder Hallway Collapse.

We ended our little journey in a back bedroom that held the largest and blackest bed I'd ever seen. Frank gestured toward an uncomfortable-looking wooden chair at the foot of his bed. It was flanked on both sides by stacks of book-sized boxes, stuffed to capacity and tipping perilously inward toward the chair. I sat and smiled politely, hoping to give the general impression of comfort and ease, although I could feel a trickle of sweat on both temples.

Peter the cat lay at the end of the bed and stared at me as if I'd done something magical.

The Fat Man rolled onto the bed, which I realized was covered in black linen sheets, and laid his head on a well-troughed pillow. "I don't usually consult psychics," he said, "but I had a special feeling when Millar called me. And when I read your classified, I don't know. Something came over me. I'm worried about my sister, Kate."

"I see," I said. My peripheral vision was filled with lint floaters and boxes leaning in every direction. A strong feeling of claustrophobia began to writhe up and dance through me.

Frank smiled again, and closed his eyes, his face taking on a serene quality. Peter pawed at the sheets, then alighted on Frank's stomach.

"Tell me more about your sister," I said.

"Yes. You see, I think she's going to die," Frank said.

A flush went through me. The great oaf looked almost dead himself, lying there with his eyes closed and talking to me as if he was dreaming aloud. The corners of the room held remnants of stringy spider webs, apparently wrecked by a broom but left to dangle pathetically in tatters from the dark blue walls. I was two seconds from bolting. What was I thinking? I couldn't do this. He was talking about death. I couldn't dream on demand. I had to be under stress, physical stress, and then the dreams just...came. I had to be pushed to my limits, tired, vulnerable, and scared to have any kind of meaningful occurrence. Besides, hadn't I always been guided to these people by some unexplained, connective force?

"Okay," I said, trying hard to swallow. "Tell me about it. Her. Your sister, I mean."

"I'd rather you go into your trance and *you* tell me. I'm not going to feed you the information."

"But you know how this works, right, Frank?"

He opened his eyes and fixed them on me, then nodded his head yes, but had a blank look that said no.

"All right, let me lay it all out for you," I said, taking a deep, calming breath. "I have to get to know you, see? I find out the facts, your desires—well, maybe not your desires—but I get to know you, your essence."

"My essence? Sounds rather ominous, don't you think?" He squinted and slowly pulled at the back of Peter's huge furry head, making the cat's eyes look Siamese. Peter seemed pleased.

"I can't do anything here, Frank. I can't do a trance on demand. I have to dream it. I dream, then I tell you what I see."

"Oh." He sounded disappointed and let out a giant sigh. I thought the wind would unleash a barrage of dust mites. Peter looked at him thoughtfully, as if to acknowledge the pain of it all.

"You did read my ad, right?" I said, putting a finger under my nose.

"Yes, but I thought you'd trance sleep or something, and I could get the results right away?"

"Sorry, Frank. I know, in this age of instant gratification, that's what's expected, but it's not how this works."

There was a long pause. Peter purred blissfully while staring in my direction, apparently in some sort of cat bliss.

"Tell me more about your powers," Frank said.

I felt like an imposter. With super powers, yes, but super powers over which I had no control. I told Frank about my Carrillo dream and how I'd managed to track him down and warn him. He seemed impressed and we spent the next few minutes chatting about clairvoyance, ESP, and precognitive abilities. It became abundantly clear he was becoming a fan and was a true believer in precognition.

Frank appeared to me to be a quiet, intelligent man, trapped by many phobias and neuroses, living in a self-made tomb, surrounded by a lifetime of purchases. He was a hoarder, but a fairly neat hoarder, based on what I knew of the affliction. His only contact with the outside world appeared to be the internet, TV, newspapers, and the germs his cat tracked in through the window after a night out on the town.

His money, of which there was plenty, had initially come from a telephone answering service he'd started years before. Having briefly flourished in the early eighties, it died a quick, silent death in the early nineties when cell phones became readily available. Since then, he'd been living off an inheritance from his mother. That was enough information, I thought, for me to try to get a dream.

We walked back into the kitchen and stood by the door. "Here," he said, and held out two twenties. I hesitated, then took the money. "Take Peanut," he said, handing me a stuffed rabbit. "Been with me my whole life. I trust you'll be gentle with him. He'll bring you good luck." Along with Peanut, he handed me an empty plastic shopping bag. He gave me a hopeful smile and winked as he closed the door behind me.

In the hallway, I stuffed the toy rabbit into the bag. I decided to walk home instead of cabbing it, and pondered how low I could go before my need for integrity outweighed my need for money. Taking lonely hoarders for a twenty here or a fifty there was not my cup of tea, nor was it what I had in mind when I set out to help people.

Once home, I opened a beer and took a long swig. Peanut lay on the floor in the plastic D'Agostino's bag. I took out the toy and sat at the kitchen table, placing him in front of me. His matted head flopped to the right, like he was searching for something. "How you doin', buddy?" I asked. The rabbit wasn't talking.

I took a hot shower, changed into some sweats, and started to meditate. I wanted to clear my mind and concentrate completely on Frank's sister.

Sitting on the floor, I stared at the flame dancing above a large beeswax candle. After I had relaxed a bit, I took a firm grasp of the Fat Man's stuffed rabbit and lay down on my bed. I began a humming meditation, blocking out all else but the sound of my own voice. I soon felt myself drifting into a strange dream.

Images formed in slow, flashing pulses in my mind's eye: The Fat Man sitting on his bed, smiling; different angles of the bedroom; boxes toppling over; magazines spilling to the floor. I took control of my vision, and was able to zoom in on one of the magazines: an old issue of *Life*.

The pages flutter open to reveal blurred, color photos. One of the photos is moving. It resolves into an image of a young girl, then changes to a slender young woman. She's attractive in a nineteen-fifties kind of way. Her lips are full and bright red. Her hair is done up like something in a Jane Mansfield cheesecake publicity still. She moves in a staccato dance across the magazine's pages. I can almost hear a burlesque drum beat as she sways to its rhythm. Boom, bada boom, bada boom. She stops dancing and leans down to check out a fat little baby wearing nothing but a diaper, sitting on the floor next to her. The baby is goofing around with a pacifier, trying to stick in its mouth. She shakes her finger at it in a No, no, baby way. Don't cry, she seems to be saying. The Fat Baby crawls right off the photo, and I turn the page to follow it. On the next page, Fat Baby crawls over to another baby, a little Girl Baby, who also wears a diaper and some pink bootees on her tiny feet. She's lying on her back, pulling at her feet the way babies do, when Fat Baby pushes the Girl Baby off the page. She gets up, crying, and crawls off into the shadows of my bedroom. Then it all goes black.

I came out of the Dream State and looked at the stuffed rabbit in my hands. I swear he was smirking, like he understood what I'd just seen. His glass eyes were very realistic. "What do you say, Peter?" I said, mistakenly calling him the wrong name. The rabbit didn't seem to care. It was limp in my grasp. *Forget the rabbit,* I thought; I was encouraged to conjure up something, anything, by design, even if it was more hallucination than reality. I addressed Peanut again, "This is going to be one tough case. But the Fat Man is going to get his answers."

I flopped onto the bed to make some notes. *Two babies. Wonder if they represent Frank and his sister?* A realization struck me. Until *that* dream, the dreams had all been in black and white. This dream had been in vibrant color. Of course, *Life* magazine was known for its color photography. An inspiration, perhaps? There was something else in that dream I didn't quite see, but could feel. It was something just beyond my reach. I could sense its presence, like a shadow moving through a dark room. But I hadn't a clue what it all meant.

Climbing under the covers, I held the rabbit up to my face. "Give me a clue, rabbit. What's the Fat Man's game?"

My cell phone buzzed and rattled itself off the nightstand and into my shoes. I looked down and saw the name, *FRANK*, brightly lit on the screen.

"Shit!" I said aloud. "Give it a little time, will ya?" I rolled over to get some sleep.

This self-employment gig was going to be a pain in the ass. I mean, desperate people do desperate things, especially when they can transfer some of that raw energy onto someone else, like me. Frank was no exception. He called twice more in ten minutes, waking me up each time, no doubt wanting answers I didn't have. My head started to fill with wild ideas of things I could tell him. *Your sister is fine and will enjoy a long and happy life. Unfortunately, she will die someday. How, you ask? Why, at the hands, or rather the fangs, of an ill-*

tempered water moccasin down at the old retirement home in Florida. Or, *Your sister is healthy as a horse; it's you who has to be concerned, Fat Man.* Of course I wouldn't say any of that; it wouldn't be ethical. Besides, I hated to lead him on. I did, however, have a strong intuition I'd get some answers, especially if I looked through those boxes of magazines.

After a dreamless but fitful night's sleep, I finally gave up and turned over to glance at the time. My alarm clock burned an amber 10:00 a.m. I was wiped out, but it was late enough to return Frank's calls. I leaned over and pressed *RETURN CALL.*

"Frank!" I said, trying to clear the frog in my throat. "I just got out of the shower."

"I need to see you," he said, in his usual calm, well-mannered voice.

"Certainly. What time?"

"As soon as you can."

"Is anything wrong?" I asked.

"No." I heard his cat purring on the line.

"Okay, how about—"

"In an hour?" Frank asked.

"Very well. I'll see you then."

"And Gus?"

"Yes, Frank?"

"Bring Peanut."

"Peanut? Oh, the rabbit. I thought his name was Peter?"

He hung up without answering me. I looked at the rabbit lying on the floor next to the bed, his strange yellow eyes staring at me. "Peanut the rabbit?"

Before I could get up and hit the shower, the phone rang again. This time from *CALLER UNKNOWN.*

"Yes?" I answered.

"Hello, is this August?"

I cleared my throat and tried to place the female voice.

19

"August Chase?" the voice asked again.

"Who's calling?"

"You don't know me. My name is Carla Donati. I think you knew my sister?"

"Oh?" I tried to place the name, Donati. It was familiar.

"Her name was Emma."

My heart skipped a beat. Of course! The mugging, crushed in her head, Emma.

"Emma Donati. You spoke with her several times last month?"

"Did I?" Her death dream was suddenly racing through my brain like an emotional whirlwind.

"I need to see you," she said.

"The police cleared me of any involvement in her death," I said quickly, ready to hang up. "I have an alibi."

"I know, and I understand you were trying to warn her." Her voice was reassuring.

"Who told you?" I asked.

"I heard you're offering professional services now."

"You mean my ad?"

"Yes. I saw it and your name rang a bell. I put two and two together," she said.

"I'm offering limited services, yes."

"It's kind of awkward, but could you meet me at the Boat House Café in Central Park?"

"When?" I asked.

"About three o'clock this afternoon?"

"Oh…This afternoon?" I said, hesitating.

"I'm sorry for the short notice, but it's the best time for me."

"Okay. I guess. What's this about?"

"I think you know," she said.

"Is it about the mugging? Because really, I had nothing—"

"I just have to ask a few questions. Please, meet me?"

Her voice sounded edgy, like she was about to cry. I stared out the window and wondered if this was an extended Emma dream, a warped epilogue to her life story.

"I'll meet you, but I can't stay long. Got a lot of things going on today," I said.

"Thank you."

Out the bedroom window, I caught sight of a man across the street from my apartment. He was staring up at my window, seemingly looking right at me. The cell phone-camera he held toward me flashed a few times. I drew closer to the window and watched him as he walked around the corner. His dark leather motorcycle jacket and boots and black jeans were distinctive, set against his dark red hair, but I didn't see him mount a bike. A few seconds later, a black Harley knock-off came around the corner and barreled up the street.

"Hello? Are you still there?" I asked Carla, not aware she'd hung up.

What could she possibly want from me? Unless she thought I was some kind of deadly, prophecy-fulfilling stalker? She'd probably have the cops there waiting for me as I strolled up to the restaurant. Already things were turning to shit and I hadn't even had my coffee yet.

4

I CAN DO THAT

I stuffed Peanut into the plastic grocery bag but planned on removing him before I got to the Fat Man's apartment. I didn't want Frank to think I was disrespectful of his little buddy.

It was a relatively short walk, and just as I turned the corner onto Frank's street, I saw Motorcycle Jacket walking toward me. I stopped short and pressed my back up against the building as he was buzzed into Frank's building. A half-hour late and look what I found: Frank dealing in dirty secrets. He had his people spying on me. The Fat Man was starting to become *persona non grata* in my little world.

Stepping into a nearby coffee shop, I ordered a cup and sat at a small table near the window. I typed Frank's name into my phone's search engine to see what would pop up. *Frank Cosh* didn't show up anywhere. I typed in *Frank Cosh, New Hampshire*—his supposed place of birth—and came up with another blank. The hell with Frank and his scary motorcycle spy. The Tavern had a burger calling my name, and I had a few questions for my friend, Millar. Besides, however exciting I thought my half-dream of Frank's sister had been, I still had to lie about what it meant. I mean, *crawling babies*? How was I going to spin that?

Sitting with Millar at The Tavern, a few bites into my burger, I received a call from Frank. I apologized and told him I had cracked a tooth on some roasted peanuts I'd bought from a street vendor, and had to get to the dentist right away. There was a long silence, then a heavy sigh. "I broke a tooth two months ago." His voice was faint, like he was holding the phone away from his face. "Nasty business, the mouth. So many germs." After another heavy sigh, he told me he understood, and we arranged to meet at six o'clock at his place. I disconnected the call and looked at Millar.

"So you're telling me you only know Frank through this online astronomy site, *Manhattan Observers*, and you've never met the man, you don't know what he does?"

"He's just a name in a chat room, Gus," said Millar. "You think I'd subject a friend to your new venture?" A touch of sarcasm tinged the word *venture*.

"Come on, Mill, you think I'm a con artist? Haven't I proven to you this is legit? You've got me mixed up with a real freak, here."

"Hey, you're the damn Dream Detective. Just tell him you didn't dream anything and go on your way."

"I'll do that."

"Good." Millar took a long swig from his draught.

"Yeah, and thanks for believing in me," I said.

Millar put his beer down and touched my shoulder. "It's not that I don't believe you, Gus. It's just I don't believe in any of that voodoo shit. Don't take it personally."

"You're the one who told me to put an ad in the *Voice*."

"What can I say? I'm a capitalist. I see an angle, I go for it." Mill stared at me. "Tell me again about this dream thing you're into."

"Really, Mill?"

"I feel gluttonous today," he said and took a mouthful of his brew.

"What does that mean?"

"A glutton for pun—"

"—ishment," I finished. "Yeah, yeah, I get it. Well, if you really want to know."

"Not, *really* really, just a little really…"

"How many beers have you had?"

"Enough to make me listen. Go ahead, explain yourself."

I took a deep breath and began my rationalization. "Well, being what I consider a rational person and a believer in science, I have endeavored to understand how certain unexplained phenomena can actually occur, while other paranormal events are purely speculative and conjecture. In other words, how could I rationally accept my Dream State as being a real phenomenon while still not believing in other phenomena, such as ghosts?"

"I think Allen is a ghost. How do you explain him?" Mill asked.

Allen, the persnickety bartender, pricked up his ears and turned in our direction.

"I have absolutely no explanation for Allen," I replied, and took a sip of my beer.

Allen moved closer to us on the pretense of cleaning the bar with a damp rag.

"Anyway, precluding our...friend here," I said, surreptitiously nodding in Allen's direction, "I've had to think long and hard to come up with a theory involving time-space travel or ripples in the fabric of space-time. Because that's what I think is happening. Having had several precognitive episodes, some in great detail, I can't deny precognition does occur to certain people. Some are more sensitive than others, and therefore, some people have more detailed episodes. I call these *dreams* because they take me into a dream-like state and alter my physiology, resulting in the bloody nose."

"The bloody nose sucks."

"Yes, it does."

"My cousin used to get bloody noses," Allen interjected. "Turned out he had a tumor."

"How nice for him," said Mill. "Was it a girl or boy?"

Allen sneered at us and walked back to his spot.

I continued. "Some would argue these phenomena are the result of the brain remembering subconscious clues accumulated and

24

processed without intimate knowledge of the subject, until he or she becomes suddenly aware, and as a result, a conclusion, manifested by the subconscious, becomes apparent to the person in the form of precognition."

Mill looked at me through half-closed eyes. "Not a bad theory," he said, "but it doesn't explain the specific details you see."

"You're right. I see, feel, and hear during my Dream State. I see what the subject is wearing; I hear the occurrence, the gunshots, the screams, the crunching of bone. I see the results. This would be taking bits of information and transforming it into amazingly accurate speculation."

"Would be like a super power, don't you think, seeing all that shit ahead of time?" Mill looked at me suspiciously as he took a mouthful of beer.

"I mean, how could I possibly know Carrillo would be wearing a blue suit or that he'd be traveling to a wedding the day he gets killed? How could I have opened a glove box and read his name off the car registration, if I was working with data gleaned from mundane and common sources, when in fact, I had no idea who he was until the dream?"

"You say shit, and it sounds like big words, but really, you're just using regular words." Mill finished his beer and burped. "Say something again..."

"The same holds true for all my subjects. I'd never known any of them before I dreamed about them."

"On that basis, I have to reject the past information theory."

"Exactly," I said. "The only theory that makes sense to me is this: we are all emotionally linked. Each and every human is an emotionally complex being."

Mill looked at Allen and raised a skeptical eyebrow. "Hmm," he muttered.

"Look, I believe the depth of our emotional potential is seldom tapped, except in cases of rare and extreme stress—a cataclysmic event. In these events, that massive expression of extremes, a wave of human emotion creates a wake, a disturbance so profound, it transcends time and space, and ripples out, like a pebble tossed into still water, in all directions. This emotional wake is so clearly formed that those sensitive to it can pick it up, like a signal picked up by radio."

"We're all part of the fabric of time and space."

"Yes, precisely!"

"I think I'm feeling a ripple in my jeans," said Mill.

I ignored him. "The ripple of emotion moves out but can travel only so far before it hits a boundary and bounces back into itself, much like a ripple on a small body of water after reaching shore. It is this return wake, this ripple in time-space I pick up as the emotional signal in our present time. And that signal is transformed through our own emotion receptors into a reconstruction of the original event. Thus in many respects, we are the emotion receivers. We reconstruct a signal expelled in the future traveling back to the past."

"Like a radio picking up signals and transforming them into music."

"Correct."

He looked at me intently and said, "Why didn't you just say we're all radios and leave it at that? I have a signal right now. It's telling me to take a leak." He got up to go to the men's room.

"Hey, Mill?" I grabbed him by the arm and stopped him.

"Yeah?"

"I'm really glad you asked me about this stuff, because when I say it out loud it's cathartic."

He patted me on the back and walked to the men's.

After a few minutes of quiet contemplation, Mill returned, walked over to the jukebox and loaded it up with coins. The machine ate all of his money, but lay dormant. After kicking and almost tilting it, he shouted, "Hey! What the fuck, Al?"

Allen stopped wiping a mug, threw the rag over his shoulder and sauntered over to the jukebox. He fished around in the back of the machine for a minute, then pulled the plug. "Sorry, forgot to unplug it. It's been eating money all day."

"Thanks for the warning."

Allen strolled back behind the bar, slapped a few dollars' worth of quarters down in front of Millar and said, "Here you go."

Millar looked disdainfully at the coins. "I put at least three bucks in there."

"Well, this is all there was in the box."

"Well, maybe you should look again."

"I don't need to look again, because I cleaned out the box and got what was in there."

"You owe me two songs, then."

"Fine, I'll sing them to you as I put you to sleep. With my fist."

"Funny, Allen. I'm tickled down to my toes."

"I'm a funny guy." Allen stared at Millar, daring him to make a move.

"Fucking joint," Millar mumbled and backed away.

"Mill, I'll give you the fucking money. Be cool," I said.

Mill chuckled and sat down at the bar. He took a long swig of beer and called for another one. Allen walked over, dirty rag in hand and silently poured a new draught, placing it in front of Mill. Mill nodded and Allen returned to his spot.

"When are you two kids gonna get a room?" I asked Mill, smiling.

"We have. His dick's too small. Just a wee little thing." Mill raised his voice, "Hardly a mouthful."

I laughed in spite of myself. Allen glanced at Mill, then resumed watching the taped soccer game from 1985.

After a few minutes, when Mill seemed settled, I said, "Why do you think the Fat Man would be spying on me? Is he a writer or something?"

"How the fuck should I know? You're the Sleeping Detective."

"Is that going to be your retort to all things relating to me from

27

now on? Dream Detective, Sleeping Detective, Sleepytime Detective, like I'm a freaking herbal tea or something?"

"Got a nice ring to it." Millar smiled. "I gotta pee."

"Again? You've got the bladder of a squirrel."

When Mill got back to the bar, he sat down hard next to me and said, "I think Frank's got something to hide and wants…" He took a long pull on his beer.

"Wants what?"

"He wants you to find something for him."

"But he was so vague. Worried about his sister, whom I assume is still in New Hampshire. Not very specific," I said.

"Exactly! He wants to see how safe his secret is."

"What?"

"Consider this: he killed his sister, or *somebody* with the same name, and he wants to see if you can sniff it out. See how safe he is."

"Why would he want me to sniff him out? That's nuts," I said.

"Right. It's nuts. He's nuts. Get it? There're all sorts of nuts out there, Gus. You put an ad in *The Village Voice* for chrissake. Think of the calls you're gonna get. Every nut-bag in the city will be calling you, yapping about a ghost or dream…."

Allen snorted, giving Mill a knowing glance as he wiped a glass with the rag. Millar smacked his mug down on the bar, making a loud crack.

"Eyes, Allen," he pointed his fingers at his own eyes and then at the TV. Allen grunted and turned his back.

"But he was a referral from you!" I protested, ignoring the ongoing tiff.

Millar downed the rest of his beer, raised his eyebrows at me in a *what can I do* look and ordered a burger. Allen ignored him from his end of the bar.

*** *** ***

I was skittish meeting Carla, especially after seeing Motorcycle Jacket taking pictures of my apartment. I wasn't feeling overly brave while approaching the Boat House. Once there, I sat on a high wall behind the property and watched people as they came and went. Of course, I was a few minutes late, but hey, if she really wanted to see me, she'd still be there, right?

I was starting to feel guilty for standing her up as I walked sheepishly into the café and stood in the entrance. A dark-haired woman, about thirty-five and carrying two brightly colored museum bags, approached. I started to turn away, but held my ground at the last minute.

"Carla?" I asked.

The woman gave me a sad nod and kept walking out of the building. I followed.

"Sorry I'm so late," I said. "But I'm here now if you want to talk."

She walked briskly by me. I turned and chased after.

"Look, things are a bit messed up right now. I cracked a tooth! I'm sorry, okay? But I didn't kill your sister."

The woman half turned, a panicked look in her eye.

"You believe me, don't you? I wouldn't kill anybody. I'm not that kind of guy."

The woman slipped, almost dropping her bags, then found her footing.

"Carla?"

The woman was running now.

"Yes?"

A strong female voice came from behind me. I turned and saw a tall, light-skinned woman with shoulder-length dark hair, full lips and even, exotic features staring back at me. The other woman scurried off, her shopping bags flapping against her knees as she stumbled up the small hill in her high heels.

"You have a way with women," Carla said.

"Look, I thought she was—"

"Are you going to chase me up the hill, too?"

"What? No, I—"

Her smile stopped me.

"Okay, you got me. I'm a deranged stalker. You've nailed it."

"Mr. Chase, I wanted to talk to you about my sister…"

A look of sadness came over her. We stood in place, awkwardly avoiding eye contact for what seemed like five minutes as her eyes welled up. I couldn't help but notice how attractive she was.

"How did you know my sister was going to be killed?" she asked finally.

I looked away. What was I going to say? There was so much I could say, and so much I could never tell a stranger.

The hair on my head flopped around as the wind picked up. Autumn leaves blew into the corners and crags of the wall near where we stood. Her raincoat flew up in the back. I smiled slightly, hoping to break the ice as she twisted to push it down again.

"Let's get a cup of coffee," I said.

She nodded and we walked back to the Boat House Café.

I remember once a disc jockey doing his little spiel about women, his deep radio voice going on and on, saying, "She was a living doll but you, you know you're nothing to look at…" And, I remember thinking, *Really? Guys think that way?* Well, I don't. I'm a decent-looking guy and I know it. I've never been intimidated by women, taken off guard once or twice, but never really intimidated. I've always found something to say, plugging away in conversation until common ground is reached. If that's arrogant, then so be it. I just think of myself as confident with the ladies.

Only once did I stammer in the face of a beautiful woman. I was selling door-to-door subscriptions for my high school sports program back in Massachusetts. I came to a fairly nice house at the top of a cul-de-sac, and knocked, puffing myself up with false bravado to do my best sell. When the door opened, there stood the most beautiful woman I'd ever seen. I can't even describe her as looking like a real person. I'd say the closest thing I'd seen was a painting we had in the living room of a "gypsy girl." Dark hair, deep brown eyes, perfectly shaped nose and eyebrows. Curly locks pulled back just enough to reveal a large gold hoop in her ear.

Well, when the door opened, I stood there and couldn't even speak to this woman. Finally, after what seemed like minutes with my tongue tied in knots, I opened my mouth and out came something like, "You…buy…this?" I practically started scratching my armpits while grunting. Seeing Carla for the first time was like that. She took my breath away. And the suspicion she wasn't quite mortal crept up on me.

I got a regular cup of coffee and she a decaf latte. We sat sipping our drinks and looking beyond the large glass windows out at the rippling pond. Gusts of wind whipped through the trees around the back of the boat deck, adding to the coziness of being inside. A few boaters rowed to and from the rental area at a leisurely pace. I felt frozen in my chair, like I'd been dipped in dry ice and left on a pedestal for the chainsaw. Her eyes were clear and bright and radiated intelligence.

"My sister was murdered," she said, finally.

"I know."

"No, I mean it wasn't a random thing. She was targeted, and it was made to look like a mugging."

I slowly nodded in the affirmative.

"You knew," she said.

"Well…"

"I mean, ahead of time. And you tried to warn her." She looked out the windows at a couple strolling by arm-in-arm, then back at me. "Give me a reason how you could know that, or why I shouldn't have my friend over there bring you in?"

I followed her gaze to a man standing in the back corner of the room, staring at us. "What is this?" I asked, and I looked around the room for more men.

"This? This is a cup of coffee." She took a deep breath and added, "For now."

"Okay, so I'm supposed to be intimidated?"

"He's here for my protection." She nodded in his direction. He nodded back.

"You think you need protection from me? I'm gonna kill the whole family or something?"

"Who knows? It's a crazy, tough city," she said.

"But I'm not a tough guy."

"We all need protection," she said, smiling.

"Yeah, I could use some myself," I replied.

"Get a guy."

"How much do they cost?"

"I don't know, I ask friends for help."

"I don't have any friends I can trust."

"Too bad. But I can't blame them," she said.

We looked into each other's eyes.

"You really think I had something to do with your sister's murder?"

"Did you?"

"I just told you I didn't," I said.

"I didn't hear you say it," she replied.

"That's what I meant." I sipped my coffee.

She took her cup and held it in her hands, as if to warm them. "So do we keep on like this or do you want to tell me something?" She put her drink down and turned the cup handle in a forty-five degree angle in front of herself.

"You used to be a waiter," I said.

She smiled. "Clever. How did you know?"

"I'm starting to think I'm a bit of a detective."

"A detective? What was my sister wrapped up in?"

"I don't know."

"But you were on a case when you saw her?"

"Sort of. I do a lot of freelance work, on my own."

"And she came into your case somehow?"

I could feel the flop sweat starting to bead on my forehead. "Look, there wasn't a case, okay? I dream things and sometimes they come true."

She sat back in her chair. "What? What are you saying about dreams?"

"Didn't your sister tell you why I was trying to—"

"No," she interrupted. Her voice sounded strained, emotional. Her eyes glistened with moisture. I turned to look at the man in the corner and then back to her.

"Listen, you'd think I was nuts if I tried to explain what's going on. I'm not a cop; I don't have a badge. I'm just a guy who sees things and tries to help. That's all."

Carla looked crestfallen, her eyes darting to the man and back to her latte. I was hoping it wasn't a signal.

"Your sister was a sweet girl. I don't think she was mixed up in anything illegal, at least it didn't appear—"

"Of course not. But if you're not a detective, how would you know?"

I sat back, exasperated. She looked at the man again and nodded in his direction. This sent a jolt of panic through me. I started to stand. "Okay, call off your guy."

"I just did."

I turned and saw him walking out of the café. I sat back down in relief. "Why?"

She shrugged. "He had to go, and I don't think you're going to kill me. But I can get him on the phone right away." Her voice shot higher on those last words, and I knew she was still scared.

The young couple at the next table got up, leaving behind a copy of *The Village Voice*. I leaned forward, looking her straight in the eyes. "Okay, here's the deal. I'm gonna explain to you what I do. You're gonna have to trust that I'm telling you the truth. If you don't believe me, then I guess you'll never understand how I got involved with your sister. But if you do, we'll have it settled right here and now."

I grabbed the copy of the *Voice*, found my ad and laid it out in front of her. "Right here," I said, pointing.

She put her nose in the paper, read a bit and looked up at me. "Yes, I saw this."

"And this?" I asked, pointing to the word, *psychic*.

"Oh, I read detective and didn't realize…You're a psychic?"

"I hate that word."

"And you're telling me you knew this thing was going to happen to my sister?

"I did everything I could to warn her."

She sat back and stared at me, then turned to look out at the lake. "Weird," she said finally, throwing five dollars on the table and standing up.

"She just wouldn't listen to what I had to say," I said.

"A psychic. Oh my God. How much did she give you? That's what I want to know."

"What?"

"How much did you bilk out of her?"

"It's not like that."

Carla started to walk away.

"I'm telling you the truth! I saw what was going to happen."

"Pathetic," she said, half to herself. Then she stopped and turned to me, her eyes lit with sparks. "I can't deal with this right now, but know that I am aware of you. I am aware my sister was murdered and somehow you're mixed up in this." She secured her jacket belt. "I'll be in touch. Maybe." She shook her head, like I was a lost cause, and walked out the door.

5
THE BEAR CAVE

The door to Frank's apartment was ajar. He'd buzzed me in, leaving the door open for me to walk in. The kitchen was dark and stuffy, devoid of anything resembling homey or wholesome. It looked like a forgotten place. This time there seemed to be more boxes lining the hallway, making the path to his room even narrower. It gave me the sense of a dark, carnival fun house; cartons leaning and tipping in various directions, the floor creaking as I went.

I followed the faint light into his bedroom and sat down in the same wooden chair at the foot of his bed, flanked by twin towers, but Frank was not there. I called his name and heard a muffled reply come from what I assumed was the bathroom. I stood up and took the opportunity to look through a few things. In every box, old newspapers were folded and stacked neatly on top, except for the one stuffed with *Life* magazines.

I flipped through the first few issues and found nothing to catch my eye. They were dated from the fifties and late sixties. One had full-color photos from the battle of Iwo Jima. Next to the magazine was an old *Manchester News* from the early seventies. I reached into the box and pulled out three more of the same issue, all dated July 17, 1972. The same issue lay open on the floor at the foot of his bed. Four copies of the same newspaper? I stuffed one copy under my coat for later reading.

"Great stuff, isn't it?"

I was startled to see Frank standing in the doorway. I hadn't even heard the floorboards creak.

"Oh, yeah. Incredible detail in these photos." I picked up a *Life* magazine.

"That Iwo Jima photo shoot was something special. Printed in July 1968, I bet."

I found the date and he was correct. "I never asked. Are you a writer, Frank?"

"I am. Graphic novels, mostly."

He pointed to a poster of what I assumed was one of his covers. The title, *AUGUR,* was scrawled across the top of the page. Scratched out in blood-red ink, it was made to look like the handiwork of a big cat's claw. Below the title stood a dark, hooded figure with superhero-sized muscles, raising a massive wooden staff up to the sky. A flock of gigantic black ravens flew overhead and into the distant blue-black hills. Two names appeared at the bottom of the page. McNaughlty appeared on the left, and to the right, Finn. I shook my head in admiration and sat in my chair.

"Are you Finn or McNaughlty?" I asked.

"Neither," he said in an annoyed tone.

Not wanting to press the matter, I asked him if he liked to read, an ironic question considering his décor.

"I'm a voracious reader. I consume everything. But, as you can see, I can't seem to throw anything out. I'm always afraid I may need some reference or I may not finish a periodical and set it aside, hoping to return, but never quite getting around to it. But in my mind I know I will return eventually, so I keep it handy."

Looking at the stacks of newspapers and boxes, *handy* was not exactly the word I was thinking.

"They have computers for this type of thing now, you know. You can scan everything."

Frank's smile disappeared, and he flopped down on his gargantuan bed. "Where's Peanut?"

I'd forgotten the rabbit, or maybe I just wanted to hold onto it for a little leverage, in case of trouble. "He's safe," I said.

"Safe? What do you mean *safe?*" Frank's startled look caught me off guard.

"I mean, he's safe at my apartment. I had him in a bag ready to go, but I forgot to take him at the last minute."

"You have him in a bag?"

I gave him a gentle nod and said in a soft tone, "I was very careful with him."

"He's very old, fragile. I thought I told you. Be careful with him. And I thought you were going to use him to entice a dream?"

"I know."

"Well, I prefer Peanut to be here with me."

"Sorry, Frank."

My nervous squirming must have been apparent. Frank's perturbed look softened into a general calmness. He sucked in a deep breath and let it out slowly. "It lowers the blood pressure."

"The rabbit?" I asked.

"The breathing."

I decided to lighten things a bit. "I really like that rabbit. It seems nice. How long have you had it?"

"The rabbit seems nice?" he asked. Frank's eyes slowly moved in my direction, not quite finding my face.

I continued, "Nicely made, I mean. But its fur is a little matted. It's interesting the way it's not hunched up on all fours, the way you'd think a rabbit to be. It looks more like a teddy bear rabbit, except it has big rabbit ears…" I started to make rabbit ears with my hands, but stopped myself. He took another slow, deep breath. Weariness came to mind. I was making him weary.

"Good news. I had an interesting dream," I said, finally breaking down and deciding to tell him of the bizarre baby dream.

"Good. Tell me." He lay back further on his huge bed, gently closing his eyes.

"Well…" I started, but the words would not come. The dream played in my head, but I couldn't bring myself to describe it. I swear, a minute slowly ticked by and neither one of us moved, nor gave each other a look. Sweat dripped from my upper lip, and I tagged it with my tongue. My eyes wandered around the room, searching for a starting point. The dream I'd had just didn't seem useful or even something I wanted to share. Frank cleared his throat. I coughed. And it occurred to me he didn't get many visitors. Perhaps he was just enjoying the fact that he had company. That gave me the courage to start.

"Well, I saw something very interesting."

"Yes, go on."

"I have a few questions, though."

He sat up and looked at me. His large eyes appeared even bigger than usual in the darkened room.

"Your sister, was she your twin?" I asked.

"Not even close." His tone was a bit surly as he lay back down.

"Okay, then was she younger?"

"Yes."

"And you had a good relationship?"

"What do you mean, *had*?"

"Oh, sorry. How is your relationship now?"

"As opposed to…?"

"Before?" I asked.

"Before what?"

"You said *as opposed to*, and I asked, opposed to what?"

"As opposed to nothing. Move on, will you?"

I let a few seconds of silence go by to clear the tension a bit. "Yes. The room is dark now," I said.

Frank popped open an eye, apparently to check if the light was off, then closed it.

"So dark now, so dark. Oh look, a magazine. A woman in her thirties. She wears red lipstick and a kerchief on her head." I was studying an illustration on the back of a vintage *Life* magazine in the box nearest me. "Her lips are puckered and she seems acutely aware something is amiss."

Once again Frank opened an eye, and said, "What the fuck are you doing?"

"There's a baby boy," I said, and quickly added, "and I see a baby girl."

"Okay!" Frank sat up again. "Is this something you're seeing now or is this what you dreamt? You told me you didn't do trances, and there's nothing I hate more than a phony. You understand? You start making shit up, and I'll put you out on your ass."

Startled, I immediately went into recovery mode. It didn't matter that I was creeped out by this reclusive fatty, that he was sending people to my house to take pictures and had a strange affection for a stuffed rabbit named Peanut. All I saw was me losing a job, an employer, a gig. I was drenched in flop sweat. Being good enough to entice him further was my driving force, but little lies were starting to ensnare me. I had to untangle myself before I got wrapped in them. I didn't care about Motorcycle Jacket taking pictures of my apartment; I just didn't want to lose a customer.

So I decided to tell the damn truth.

I got up and paced the small open area in front of his bed, determined to lay it all out there. "Okay, Frank," I said. "I didn't want to tell you, but I saw you push your sister off the page of the magazine, okay? You were just babies in diapers. I would guess you were jealous and you pushed her off. Your mother was there, and yes, she did have red lipstick and a fifties-style hairdo."

After few seconds of silence, he asked, "I was in a magazine, you say?"

"Well, yes. I saw your baby pictures, and they came to life."

"In a magazine, not a newspaper?"

"A magazine. Full-color spread."

"And we moved around, like in a movie?"

"Yes. You moved in a cartoon-like movie. You crawled over to your sister—"

"How do you know it was my sister?" he interrupted.

"Well, I don't. I just assumed."

"Hmm. Yes, yes, go on."

"And your mother was there. Kind of an iconic female figure with a fifties hairstyle, I would guess."

"Yes, yes."

"And you pushed her, your sister, off the page."

"And my mother, what did she do?"

A good question. I hadn't noticed. "Nothing. That was the end of the dream."

"You're done?"

"That's all I have."

Frank closed his eyes. There was a thickness to the air, the pungent odor of anxiety. The pause seemed to weigh on my shoulders.

"Does any of it make sense?" I asked, finally.

Frank grunted and yawned, as if he himself was coming out of a deep sleep. "Interesting," he said.

Seemingly impressed, mystified and weary all at the same time, he got to his feet and lumbered toward the kitchen. I followed close behind. He stood at the open door, waiting for me to take my leave. I walked into the outside hallway and turned to face him.

"Dream some more," he said. "I'll call you. Use Peanut." He held out a fifty-dollar bill. I looked at it, not wanting to take it.

"What for?" I asked.

"I want you to come back."

My cheeks flushed. I felt like a prostitute. "I'll come back. I don't need your money." I choked on the last few syllables.

"You dreamed something interesting. Dream some more, that's all."

I looked at the bill he held out so politely in his pudgy fingers.

"Here, take it. You're making my arm tired," he said, finally.

Frank stuffed the bill into my hand, patted my back, and shut the door. And that was that. And I felt dirty all over. For the first time, I was making money with a gift I had no control over, and it didn't feel right. I stuffed the fifty into my jeans pocket. It was going to take some getting used to, accepting money for something I was still so unsure about.

6
GOT TO RUN

Allen was in one of his rare good moods. He greeted me with a wink and asked if I wanted my usual pint of ale. I nodded, gave him a half smile, and sat next to Millar, who evidently never left the place. He was just finishing another Tavern burger.

Wiping grease and ketchup from his chin with a crumpled paper napkin, Millar said, "I think I'll try another one, too."

I sniggered to myself. "What exactly does that mean? I'll try another one. Was the last one no good? Don't they all taste the same? Is one bottle of stout different from every other bottle of the same brand?"

Turning to me and with a slight grin on his face, he replied, "I've been trying to figure that out for years."

"Ah, research."

"Exactly. It takes years for a discerning palate like mine to adapt, conceptualize, catalog, and present findings on these matters."

"I'm so happy you're content in your work."

"Oh, don't be happy for me. I hate my work. It's a burden, but one I bear only so others may not have to."

"And when does this great volume, this tome, this wondrous work from the master of good taste come out?"

Millar's color transformed to a ruddy shade of crimson. "Ah!" he shouted, jumping to his feet, before bending over. "Oh!" he said, while holding a hand over his stomach. Stumbling a few steps toward the bathroom, he stopped and bent over again. "Oh!" He disappeared into the head.

I turned back to the bar and said, to no one in particular, "Now that's drama."

Allen stood at the far end of the bar, staring at a taped soccer game. Apparently, he'd missed the original broadcast of the 1982 soccer match between Scotland and Brazil and was ignoring all the fun at my end of the bar.

"Hey, Al, how goes it?" I asked.

"All right," he said, not turning away from the game.

"How about another beer for my friend, here, Al?"

"Right," he said, but continued to stare up at the game. I glanced at my watch and waited to see how long it was going to take his only customer to get served. After about ten minutes, Millar sat back down and said, "Whew! That was a close one. I thought I was gonna die and go to gastric hell."

"Spare me the details," I said, turning away from any trailing waft. "And order a salad once in a while, you might live longer." That must have shot over Mill's head because he didn't even acknowledge me. I tapped on the bar and said, "Al, how about that beer for my friend here?"

Allen grabbed a bottle, popped it open and slammed it down in front of Millar. He leaned in to stare at my face, his great buggy eyes bulging out at me.

"My name is Allen, not fucking Al! You hear me? Don't ever call me Al or tap on my bar again, you got it?" His emaciated face was scarlet now. Huge drops of sweat ran down the side of his face. Sweat stains outlined his armpits. The veins on his neck were popping out, making him look like a great snapping turtle, hissing and sneering at someone who'd just poked him with a stick.

I put my hands up in a conciliatory gesture. "Sorry," I said, and pushed the five-dollar bill on the bar closer to him. He stood in place, his crimson hue slowly resolving toward something human. I kept waiting for him to melt onto the floor. Finally, after a few simmering seconds of staring into my eyes, he snatched up the fiver, swaggered back to the cash register, popped it open, placed the bill neatly inside and slammed the cash drawer closed. Once again he took up his position beneath the TV, his foot propped up on a milk crate, elbow on bony knee, staring at the taped soccer game like nothing had happened.

"What the heck was that?" I asked.

Millar just shook his head. "Too many vitamins," he said and made a jerk-off motion with his hand.

"Got that right," I said.

Millar leaned in and whispered, "Don't worry about old Allen. I got a fix on." He winked and turned toward the kitchen doorway. Manuel, the day cook, looked over at Millar and nodded. He then carried a ramekin, perched on a small white plate, over to the bar.

"What's this?" I heard Allen ask.

"Chocolate pudding. Seventy percent cocoa. No sugar, no dairy. Just some coconut sugar. Made with soy milk, just the way you like it."

Allen managed a smug smile, nodded to Manuel and turned back to his game. Millar whispered, "I had Manuel put some laxatives in there. He gets a taste of it, he'll be cleansed for days." A rumbling chortle rose from his chest, followed by a coughing fit.

I squirmed on my stool. "Why would you do that?"

"The fucker deserves it. I've seen my cousin do the same thing to some asshole at his bar. It's funny."

I wasn't laughing. "How do I know you won't do the same to me some day?"

"You aren't a prick. Besides, Manuel can't stand him, either. He's nasty to the whole kitchen staff."'

"How has he managed to keep his job if he's so unpopular?"

"His uncle is the owner or something, I don't know." Millar lost some of his humor as he stared intently at the ramekin. "Just enough to teach him a lesson."

I took a swig of my ale. "It's only a lesson if he knows he's getting it and who it's from."

"You want me to tell him? Oh, I'll tell him, right after he turds up the joint. Or maybe we'll leave him to ponder why the Porcelain gods were so angry."

"That's cold, man."

"Yeah, ain't life a bitch?" Millar wiped the top of his fresh beer bottle on his sleeve and took a long slug. "I have half a mind to put some Saran wrap over the toilet bowl. See how he likes that."

We surreptitiously watched Allen and the ramekin of chocolate laxative for a while, but the bartender remained preoccupied with the TV.

I turned to Mill. "What else can you tell me about Frank?"

"I told you all I know."

"He's a member of an online astrology club, and that's it?"

"Oh, wait. I think I heard something about him being a druid, or something like that."

"What? A druid?"

"Yeah, you know. Some weird pagan shit he's into. I can make some inquires if you want. Ask some of the other members about him."

"That'd be good, Mill. This guy is turning out to be a freak, and I want to know if I should just walk away."

"Has he given you any money?" Before I could answer, Mill elbowed me in the ribs. "Oh, shit!"

Allen dipped a spoon into the pudding. Mill shook with muted laughter. I got up, took a last swig of my brew, put some money on the bar, and turned to Mill.

"Let me know what you find out about Frank, will you?"

Mill's attention shot back to me for a second. "Huh? Oh, yeah, the druid thing. I'll ask around."

I thanked him, and glanced at Allen just as he placed the empty pudding container on a kitchen tray. I shook my head in disgust and walked out of the bar.

Back at home, I sat on my bed and spread the yellowed New

Hampshire newspaper on the floor in front of me. I couldn't shake the image of Frank lying on his bed, his fat fingers joined over his bloated belly, eyes half closed as if he'd been saturated in opiates. Images of his room, the narrow hallway crowded with boxes, his fat cat rubbing on my pant leg, came flooding into my mind. Momentarily transfixed by these images, I was brought to awareness by the tinny sound of blood dripping onto the newspaper. As I put a finger to my nostrils, a sharp jolt of pain flashed through the center of my brain. I lost all orientation and was swept into a vision.

I am naked and alone in a darkened landscape. In front of me, long shadows extend across a grassy field on a moonless night. Trees frame a wooded clearing. The sound of children's laughter echoes through the field, then the sound of water splashing, feet kicking and another, louder, splash helps me to gain my orientation. I turn to my left. In front of me, a shadowy form moves against a dark gray horizon. A voice calls out, "Frank, stop it!"

Now I'm in a pond. The cool, rippling water touches my mouth and caresses my ears. A small face appears in front of me. Kate? I want to speak, but no voice will come.

"Frank, cut it out!" She sounds annoyed, her tone is firmer now, and then she's gone. I feel a terrible loneliness treading water by myself.

The girl emerges from the water inches from my face. She stares at me with huge wet eyes. She grins and I smile back. A black shadow rises up from the deep. I pedal backwards, frightened. It grabs hold of her legs and pulls her under. The water churns violently where she swam, then moves slowly in large circles round and round. The whirlpool expands until the whole pond is a churning vacuum. I fight to stay afloat. The girl bobs to the surface and screams, "Frank!"

The vortex pulls her under. She chokes, and coughs, fighting for her life. Her struggle and mine become one and engulfs me as I hold her. Briefly we are one, and everything she feels, I feel. Her panic ignites me. I open my mouth to scream, but water pours in and fills my throat and sinuses, drowning my screams and all my senses, except for the echoes of our struggle.

Quiet stillness envelops the pond, and I am alone, treading water. A dark figure is standing on the grass banking a few feet away. I struggle toward shore. I'm closer now, and he is there, at the water's edge, looking down upon me, but I cannot see his face.

Slowly, I rise above the pond, floating in air, far above the whole dark scene. Water gushes from my nose and mouth in a torrent, as I struggle to breath. The dark figure glares at me from below. His ruby-red eyes follow me as I rise above the trees, above the field, higher still, into the cold blackness beyond.

When I awoke and gathered my senses enough to function, I held a tissue to my bloody nose and opened the newspaper to the obituary page. There, I found mention of a young girl who'd drowned in a backwoods swimming hole near the town of Manchester, New Hampshire. The pond was at the end of a cul-de-sac, near a trailer park. It was probably where they lived at the time. She was ten years old, and her name was Kathleen Cosh. There were no other details listed, but at the bottom of the column it read:

She is survived by her mother, Janet, her father, Franklin, and brother, Frank, Jr.

Could this be one of Frank's relatives, or was this in fact his sister? And if she were already dead, why would Frank tell me he feared for her life?

The rabbit stared up at me from the bag on the floor. "What's the deal, Peanut? Is she dead?" But he had nothing to say.

Peanut bore no resemblance to an actual rabbit, beyond his

47

long elliptical ears and buckteeth. I wasn't even sure rabbits had buckteeth, but they fit his face rather well. I pulled him out of the bag and rubbed his very convincing golden eyes. They were smooth glass, solid and cold, secured tightly to his face with thick thread. The fur was matted on his belly and back, and almost completely gone on both sides. I searched the seams for any breaks in the stitching. On the back of his head, I felt for holes, rips or tears. I found nothing out of the ordinary. The rabbit was clean.

"I've frisked a thousand young punk rabbits," I said out loud, thinking of the line spoken by the corrupt policeman in *The Godfather*.

I held a cold cloth to my nose and wondered what had set me off. Had it been the newspaper? Or was it just Peanut doing his job, as Frank had almost predicted? Either way, for some reason unknown to me, I had been able to conjure a specific dream at will. Well, not really at will. The dreams happened whenever they wanted, but now I was certain I could influence their subject and focus.

That was a major breakthrough.

7
CARLA, CARLA, CARLA

Shortly after my first Dream State, on that cold and snowy winter morning in the hallway of my East Side apartment, I met a ravishing young woman named Diana, and the dreams suddenly stopped. And they had stopped just in time because Francine, the bike rider who'd been killed by the bus, had been haunting me. I literally thought I was losing my mind.

At the time, I was studying Creative Writing at NYU and working nights at a pizza joint on the Upper East Side called Delish. Diana was a vivacious, twenty-something, blonde waitress with large blue eyes and a smile that could light up any day. If somebody could have put together the perfect girl for me, it would have been her. She, too, was studying at NYU. The three years we spent together were the best and worst of my life. There's something to be said for getting lost in one's work, but when that work becomes an obsession, and when that obsession is focused on a woman, man, are you in trouble.

I was writing short stories at the time and they all revolved around our relationship. They usually featured an alluring siren beguiling a young male protagonist into some degree of psychological turmoil, thereby forcing him to think his way out of precarious and dangerous situations, but he was inevitably doomed to failure and despair. You know, classical shit.

Diana was a sexual intoxicant. My desire for her grew with each passing day, and it was more alluring than anything I'd ever felt.

Obsessive sex became the norm. After ravaging her for hours, I would lie with my head on her bare belly, taking in the aroma of her pussy, running my fingers over her soft skin, trying to find the fine, delicate hairs. I never tired of looking into her eyes, or watching her sleep. I wanted to live in her, breathe her, taste her, be a part of her, look into her eyes as I came, have sex with her always.

My schoolwork began to suffer. The writing became less focused and rambling as I attempted to capture elusive feelings I couldn't understand. Not only did I crave marriage, I wanted to crawl inside her womb and live there, poke my head out every so often to eat and maybe watch a football game, then crawl back inside.

I began eating compulsively whenever she was gone for more than a day, as if stuffing my face would fill the void I felt when I wasn't inside her. I gained twenty pounds in four months. Jealousy struck me whenever she answered her phone or had a friendly chat with a clerk at the grocery store. I began snooping into her computer files and monitoring her emails. I'd quiz her on old boyfriends and sexual encounters she may have had. I even considered tapping our home phone.

Then one day, my self-fulfilling prophecy came true. She left me. There was no drama, no long, dragged-out fight. I came home one day and her stuff was gone. That was the end. I didn't call her, look her up on Facebook, or otherwise stalk her. I knew why she left, and that it was my fault. I drove her away.

The fallout was immediate and devastating. I couldn't function at work or school. I became self-indulgent, narcissistic. It was all about me, me and me. What I was thinking, feeling and hearing were all that mattered.

I became susceptible to bouts of hypochondria. Did I have tachycardia or bradycardia? Why were my hands shaky? Did I have MS? Could I walk in a straight line? Was I having a heart attack? Was this all there was to life: to be born, grow old and die?

One day, love supreme; the next, desolation and despair.

A month or so later, while I was sitting on a bar stool in The Tavern next to Millar, listening to how awful his life was, I fell into a Dream State. Emma was being chased into an alley and killed. When I awoke from the dream, Mill was still prattling on, completely unaware of where I'd been in my head, but as if flipping a switch, I had changed back into my old self. Miraculously, the dream had transformed me. My inward spiral of self-loathing was lifted, and I was a useful, clear-thinking person again. I was free of Diana, and of course, quickly became the champion of trying to save Emma.

I still haven't figured it all out. Never before had I been so completely lost in another human being. Perhaps the precognitive dreams were a catalyst that pushed me into such a vulnerable and fragile state to begin with, and I disproportionately latched onto Diana for comfort.

Simply put, at first Diana had a grounding effect on me, and I responded as any drowning man would, by clinging onto her for dear life.

Recovery from past mistakes is what drives me now. Recouping the old self-esteem is a top priority. It's always at the back of my mind, that utter despair I felt when I lost Diana, and it gave me a newfound determination to never lose myself in another person or relationship again.

As far as women go, I'm no longer a sex-obsessed, dependent personality, but rather a passive worshiper of women. I empathize with their sensitive emotional state, finding it alluring, while being fully cognizant of the *sensuality* of the female mystique. I guess what I'm saying is, I'm still a sucker for a beautiful woman. Where a strong independent female may intimidate most men, I am invigorated. But I will never let myself get that close to oblivion again.

So, when Carla called the next day, all I could think about was her beautiful face, and I knew I could be headed for trouble again. Having never been a professional detective or precognitive seer for hire, I wasn't sure where the professional line was, and I didn't want to overstep it. That would be unethical, and probably drown out my focus.

Carla was brief. She wanted to meet me for coffee at a place called Beans, on First Avenue and Sixty-Seventh Street, near her work. I didn't bother asking what she did for a living. Actually, I didn't ask her anything. My mind drew a blank the minute I heard her voice.

I walked the thirty blocks down to Beans and waited outside. Cool autumn winds swirled up and blew dust around the corner of the building. I turned away to shelter my eyes and looked up in time to see Carla walking toward me. She was stunning in a short navy skirt and black, calf-high boots. Her skirt flew up in the wind and I turned away, not wanting to embarrass her.

When she saw the small crowd waiting to be seated at Beans, she changed her mind and we walked to a nearby French bistro called Cinq. The place was busy, but we managed to get the last window table. I ordered Café Américain and a chicken salad croissant. She ordered the same sandwich and a cappuccino. I was reserved and polite, not wanting to give her any impression other than a businesslike attitude. Once our food was ordered and our coffee served, she thanked me for meeting her, took a sip of her drink and started to weep. Quietly at first, then she had a few seconds of water works and nose blowing. She finally caught her breath and, with a heavy sigh, apologized to me.

"It's not often I talk or even think about Emma these days. Never mind think about the gory details," she said.

"Losing someone is hard."

Gathering another breath, she removed the black leather gloves from her slender hands and began to open up to me. "The reason I called you—and I'm sorry for the first time we met, but you know how it is…"

Actually I didn't, but nodded anyway.

"I wanted to see you again because the police, well, they're not getting anywhere. They have no leads, little evidence and I'm afraid my sister's killer will never be found." She lifted her eyes to mine.

Bloodshot and red rimmed, they looked tired, worn, but still had a spark.

"I don't know what I can do to help," I said. But that was a lie. I knew exactly what I could do, if it was possible for me to conjure that dream again. I just didn't want to face it. I could see remnants of it even as she spoke. Flashes of the crime scene shot through me like electric jolts. Emma, lying against a brick wall, her lips slightly parted as a last gasp escaped her body, her utter limpness, as life left her. And those pale, dead eyes staring up at me, seeing...What?

"I did some more checking on you," she said.

"Oh, where did you do that?"

"I talked to the detectives handling Emma's case. They seem to think you were legitimately trying to warn her, but they remain skeptical about you."

"I'm an open book, really. I've nothing to hide."

"Then one of them told me your story. About how you claimed to see Emma killed in a dream, or something."

"Yes."

"Are you really a psychic or a detective?"

"I'm really a detective," I said. It wasn't a total lie. I was trying to be one. "And I occasionally have these insights. I had one about Emma. I tried to warn her, that's all."

"But you didn't know her, did you?"

I shook my head no. She looked out the window, as if seeing something far away. Perhaps trying to make up her mind about something. "Still, it's impressive you managed to find her."

I gave a slight shrug. "It's what I do."

"I can pay you," she said. "I can't have her death become a cold case. I want her killer found."

I considered her clothes and purse. She looked nice, but I could tell they weren't exactly Fifth Avenue couture. "What do you do for a living?" I asked.

She turned away. I could almost see a cigarette between her

index and middle fingers as she rubbed her thumb between them. "What does that matter?" she asked.

"It doesn't. I just don't want to feel guilty collecting my check."

"Don't worry about the money. I can pay."

"I haven't said how much."

"You're not going to fleece me, are you?"

"Not the way I operate."

She sat back and looked at me. "How do you operate?"

"The other day I got the impression you thought I was a clown."

"I never said that."

"You didn't have to. I've seen it a hundred times. The cops, others. I tell people about my precognitive abilities and they laugh. When they realize I'm serious, they get strangely quiet, usually walk away."

"I'm not afraid."

"There's no reason to be."

She momentarily put the imaginary cigarette to her lips then let her fingers fall to the table.

"How long?" I asked.

"How long what?"

"How long since you quit smoking?"

She smirked and looked out the window. A very old man and woman hobbled by, tiny steps in unison, joined in each other's rescuing arms, hunched against the autumn wind.

"First, you guess I was a waitress, now a former smoker. I'm impressed." I shrugged. "I quit smoking about six months ago," she continued, then added quickly, "Can I ask you a question?"

"Shoot."

"In your visions—"

"See, I like that. You're already beginning to accept what I do."

"Well, you say you saw the mugging. How accurately do you see things? Did you report the mugger's face? Did they take you to the police station and fill out paperwork?"

54

"None of the above. I didn't go to the police. They found me."
She looked startled. "Let me start at the beginning. At first, I didn't
think there *was* an Emma. At the time, I couldn't accept what I was
seeing was real, you know, precognitive. As a matter of curiosity, I
became familiar with the area I kept seeing in the dream. I figured
she—the girl, Emma—might frequent the area, since that was where
the mur—" The vision of Emma lying dead on the sidewalk came to
me, and for a few seconds, it was all I could see.

"Go on," she said, in a strong voice, fostering new resilience. I
snapped out of it and smiled cordially at Carla. But Emma was still
there; I could feel her presence, almost as if she'd simply pulled up a
chair and joined us.

"Are you okay?" Carla asked.

"Yeah. So, well, after some random staking-out of the area," I
said, my concentration returning. "I ran into Emma going into the
subway near that very spot, where she was killed. I knew she was the
girl in my dream the minute I laid eyes on her. I had to warn her, but
wasn't sure how to make my approach. So, I followed her to a pub and
sat near her and her friends. She was popular, your sister: friends all
around her." I smiled at Carla. She smiled back, but said nothing. "I
watched them for over an hour. Eventually, I caught up with her at the
bar when she went to buy a round. I offered to buy her a drink. She
declined. I tried to use my charm, for whatever that's worth, which
apparently, isn't much. She rebuffed me. Finally, and foolishly, I took
her arm, like this." I grabbed Carla's wrist and gently pulled her
toward me. Her eyes grew large as she stared into mine. "I warned her
to stay away from midtown, not to go out at night alone. I told her she
was in danger and I wanted to help her."

My grasp on Carla's arms grew tighter as my story grew in
intensity.

"I told her I was a friend. Warned her something bad was going
to happen if she didn't leave town. She ran back to her friends,
frightened. They glared at me until I felt so awkward, I left the pub.

But I waited outside, not wanting to lose her. I tried to follow them when they left, but soon gave up."

I was squeezing both Carla's wrists firmly in my hands, lifting her arms up off the table as I stared into her eyes. She broke off, then yanked free of my grasp, frowning at me. I raised my hands in sudden acquiescence. "Sorry," I said.

"No need for theatrics." She rubbed her wrists. She was probably going to have bruises.

"I know, I didn't mean to—"

"It's contemptible and untrustworthy."

"Yes, it is."

She glared at me. I looked around to see if anyone was watching, embarrassed. Nobody seemed interested. I shook my head. "It's a gut reaction. Sometimes I get carried away. I see bits of the dream and I..." I made fists and shook my arms in front of me, eliciting yet another frown from her. I sat back and stared into my coffee. "I lived with it for months, the dream of Emma."

"And yet you never went to the police?"

"You know what the police do with someone who comes in and foretells a crime? After the crime is committed, he becomes suspect number one, and they arrest him."

The small tree in front shook in a gust and caught our attention as it released a few leaves from its spindly branches. The waitress brought our sandwiches and placed them down on the table. Carla thanked her, then her genial smile quickly faded. "I'm not sure why I called you." She retrieved her bag from the floor and placed it on the table.

"That's pretty much how you felt the last time we talked," I said.

"It's just too weird. I'm sorry. You're a stranger. Getting mixed up in my life in the worst possible way. There's nothing..." She paused, as though another disturbing thought came to her.

"What?"

"There's just no way to…"

"Make it better?"

"Yes."

I watched her absently rummage through her bag. "Look, I think I can help find the guy, if that's really what you want."

"Of course I want to catch him," she said. "Here's my idea. Take it or leave it. I'm going to hire a private investigator and have him pick your brains, follow any and all of your leads." She pulled out her cell phone. "I'm texting you his number."

"Oh, okay," I said, crestfallen she had no intention of working with me directly. "I'm sorry if I came on too strong. Grabbing your arms—"

"And I'll pay you for your time, of course, like I said."

"Of course."

She stood.

"Aren't you going to eat?" I asked.

She looked down at the food and said, "I'm not hungry. We'll call you."

"You do that," I said, wondering who the hell *we* was. "I'll get this." I pointed to the check. She nodded and walked out the door.

My nerves were tingling. I was high on adrenaline and caffeine. I didn't know her, but as much as I wanted to eat my chicken salad sandwich and chips, every cell in my body wanted to follow her. I threw some cash onto the table, and raced to the door.

As I turned the corner outside the cafe, I got a glimpse of her at the end of the block and jogged over.

"You'll be wasting your money hiring a P.I.," I said, once I'd caught up with her. She kept walking without turning to me. I kept stride. "You'd be paying someone for what I do anyway. Duplicating everything. Paying twice the money."

"Come again?" she asked.

"Look, I'm a detective. You're going to pay another detective to pick my brain and act upon that information when I can do it all."

She stopped and looked at me. "I just think you'd be paying out too much money."

"I don't even know if I can trust you, never mind hire you as an investigator."

"Fair enough. But I am licensed."

"You're a licensed detective?"

"Yes," I lied. "Well, almost. I'm taking the licensing exam this week," I lied again.

"What about your being a psychic? This is all very muddled."

"I hate that word, psychic, but yes, I am a kind of precognitive."

"And now you're a detective?"

"I'm going to be licensed soon, yes. Look, I've been tracking people for years. It's what I do." She looked up at the sky, as if searching for answers. I went in for the kill. "I recently had a big breakthrough. By experimentation, I was able to bring myself into a dream about a specific subject. That's never happened before. Usually, the subject just comes to me, and I have no say in who or what the dream involves, but now I have the ability to focus on an individual and see them in a Dream State."

"I have no idea what you're talking about," she said, and started walking. I stopped her with my arm and moved into her personal space.

"What I do is see things before they happen. Like in a dream, only I'm awake."

She looked doubtful. "How do you know this dream is what's really happening and not some fantasy?"

"Good question. I've never been wrong. I see it as it happens or will happen. Now, if I go back and look at a dream, sometimes I can gain control, freeze the images and examine them from different angles. Like looking at a photo. I can even identify faces, license plate numbers. Sometimes I see a date or a number jumps out at me, like on a calendar."

She sighed heavily and rolled her eyes.

"Okay, you think about it," I said. "I'm not going to force you to do anything you don't want to do, but really, I'd rather not go through another individual, least of all another private detective. A middle man will just muck up the works."

"I'll let you know."

"You have my number. Call me when you're ready."

She nodded and walked away.

"Okay," I said. "See you."

She didn't turn around.

*** *** ***

In our society, there are takers and givers. Nine times out of ten, it's a taker who snuffs out a giver. I didn't expect anything different in Emma's case. The deeper I looked into Emma's background, the more I admired her. She'd earned a degree in economics from NYU, and at the time of her death, was working toward her masters, while holding down two jobs. She'd been a teaching assistant at her alma mater. Because teaching assistants generally earn less than seventeen thousand a year, she'd been working part-time as a cook at Café Classic, hence the memorial poster I'd seen there on the wall.

I figured I'd start at the café and work my way over to the school. I wasn't going to wait for Carla to call, nor was I going into a Dream State if I didn't have to. I'd had enough bad dreams and bloody noses to last a while. Hopefully, when Carla did call, I'd have something to offer her by way of leads.

8

DON'T JUST CRASH THERE

By early evening, I was completely sapped of energy and ready to take a nap on the bar when Millar finally arrived at The Tavern. He walked in briskly, sat on the stool next to me and slapped a newspaper down in front of me.

"What's this?" I asked.

Millar called to Allen for his usual poison and turned to face me. I could still smell the onions he'd eaten at lunch. "This, my friend, is a mind-fuck," he said, smiling.

"As opposed to a mind-meld?"

Millar smirked. "You remember the dream you were telling me about? The one where the guy goes off a bridge? The same guy who almost smashed your head in when you tried to warn him?"

"Pablo Carrillo. Yeah."

Allen brought Millar his beer and looked at me. "You want another one?" he asked.

I nodded and picked up the paper. Allen grunted, ape-like, as he walked away.

The headline read: *Crash Victim Wanted For Questioning.* The story listed Carrillo as a "person of interest" in a fraud case that went south. Although Carrillo had been working as a night custodian at NYU at the time of his death, the article said his background was more complex and perplexing than authorities could have imagined. The article was strangely vague about the other activities in which Carrillo was involved. Apparently even the authorities weren't sure, but the investigation centered on illegal wiretapping and industrial espionage, and the story was as convoluted as his background. Seems he had many contacts in government and an honorable discharge from the Army. Intelligence Division.

I put the paper down and looked at Mill.

"Carrillo was employed at the same school as Emma."

"Strange coincidence?" Mill said. "You dream about Carrillo, then Emma, and they both worked at NYU."

I took that leap and suddenly saw Carrillo as a stalker of the highest order, a predator and cutthroat. He'd pursued Emma out of his dank, perverted world into the bright lights of mid-town, hoping to kill her. Rebuffing his sexual advances had cost her the ultimate price. Maybe he'd tried to get her into his car, and she'd run into that alley with him close behind. He pushed her down, and her skull shattered on the hard concrete abutment at the back door of a greasy spoon. That's how she died, in an alley, running for her life.

My mind traveled back into that bleak nightmare, and for an instant, I could see the pixelated contours of the murderer's face. Not clearly enough to be make an ID, but clearer than before. Could it be Carrillo? I never saw a connection, but my gut was churning now.

Images from the dream came back in waves of gray and black dots, washing over the blurred face of the perpetrator. Lights fluoresced, pulsing against the whitewashed brick of the alley and dark splatter on the wall, her dead eyes staring up at me. The murderer's face was now a heavy blur of hate, radiating pure evil.

"NYU. See that shit?" Millar said, pleased with himself.

My gaze went through Millar to the bloodstained wall behind Emma's head, her dead eyes staring back at me. Her expression, which I once thought said nothing and saw nothing, I now interpreted as questioning, almost pleading. *"Help me."*

"So what're you gonna do?" Millar kicked my barstool, and I

snapped back from the images in my head. I felt the blood drip from my nose, and I put a napkin there to stanch the flow.

"What am I gonna do? I'm gonna see if there's a connection, I guess."

"You guess?"

His cavalier attitude irritated me. Like a kid cheering on a prizefight, he had no idea how painful it was to be in that ring. "How the fuck should I know," I snapped. "What am I, a detective?"

A drop of the iron-tainted liquid trickled down the back of my throat. I wiped my nose clean, threw a few bucks on the counter, snatched up the newspaper, and headed for the door. Millar's querying voice was drowned out in my wake.

I hit the street, and was instantly slapped in the face by a cold gust of wind. My coat collar shielded me little, and I was chilled to the bone.

Real investigating wasn't my bag. This guy in my dream was beyond the mundane. There was an evil about him that unnerved me. I could almost smell death when I saw him. I walked along, my hands in my pockets, eyes watering from the cold. The Fat Man seemed tame in comparison.

I may as well call Frank back, I thought. *Make up a story about his sister.* All this Emma stuff was getting way too real, and my bravado was turning to jelly. A lot of good I'd do Carla now.

My apartment was dark and cold, the way things get at the change of seasons. I flipped on the heating and crashed onto my bed. I rolled into my blankets, hoping they would soothe my unraveling nerves. Eventually, the torturous image of Emma's death-stare was replaced by fleeting nonsensical thoughts. I momentarily drifted off, but real sleep would not come. The room grew darker as the minutes ticked by. Then I saw Carla's smiling face. It was a kind face, intelligent, warm, and caring. At last, a deep calm enveloped me, and I fell into a restless sleep.

9

THIS DRUID WALKS INTO A DINER

The next morning I bought a few books from a small bookshop near my apartment on Second Avenue. They were about detective work, tracking people, uncovering records, and other such nonsense. Stuff I would never normally go near. I figured I may as well learn something if I was going to pretend to know what I was doing. Maybe I'd actually apply for a Private Investigator license. That'd be a kick. I found the chapter on skip-tracing especially interesting. These days, with social media being so prevalent, and many websites dedicated to public records, it was much easier to track people down. It gave me hope that I may actually help to find Emma's killer.

The phone rang, but I let it go to voicemail. It was Frank, of course. He wanted to see me as soon as I was able. I'd forgotten to ask Millar what else he'd uncovered about Frank. I'd wanted more information before deciding how to deal with this guy. I dialed Millar, and my call also went to voicemail. I left a message asking about Frank, put on a coat and walked to Casablanca Café to get some breakfast.

It was almost noon. My nerves were still revved from last night's Dream State in the bar and from finding a possible connection between Emma and Carrillo. How could I have missed that? Or maybe they weren't connected at all. The dream images were vague.

Across the street from the café was a large, black motorcycle. I didn't think twice about it until Motorcycle Jacket walked around the corner. He was slick, didn't let on he saw me looking at him from inside the café, but we both knew. The bike's engine rumbled in my chest as he drove past me and down the street.

Shaking from a lack of food, I sat at my favorite booth. Connie, the regular lunch waitress, greeted me with a smile and took my order for the all-day breakfast special: two scrambled eggs, bacon, toast, and coffee. My cell rang. It was Millar.

"What did you learn about Frank?" I asked.

"You ran out of The Tavern without a word last night."

"I had to think," I said, and my stomach turned over at the memory. "That's a pretty serious coincidence, Carrillo and Emma working at the university."

"So, you think they knew each other?"

"I had a very strong reaction last night, Mill."

"Yeah, I noticed."

"It wasn't just that he worked at the university. I got a sense he was there when Emma was killed."

"Was he stalking her, do you think?"

"It has the earmarks. My impression of him was very dark."

"Warped. How dark?"

"Just thinking of him now makes me gag, how's that?"

"But you've met him before, haven't you?"

I thought about it for a second. When I tried to talk with him at the bodega, he had become violent. "Maybe seeing Carrillo in connection with Emma's death revealed things about him I hadn't seen before. Darker inclinations, perhaps," I said.

"You mean, 'It rubs the lotion on its skin...' That type of thing?"

"I don't know. Maybe he hadn't killed anybody before, but he certainly had peccadilloes. This type of guy doesn't just change overnight. I'm willing to bet he had a criminal record. The article said he was wanted in connection with another investigation. Question is:

how did he get that job at the university?"

"They don't hire dudes with records at the university?"

"See, that's the kind of thing I don't know. I assume not."

"Holy crap," Mill said, his voice gaining energy. "Crazy Carrillo stalking that chick, Emma, you dreaming about them both in separate dreams and not putting them together."

"Hey, I don't choose the dreams."

"Dude—"

"They choose me," I said, more firmly than I intended. "And I can't control everything I see. Some things aren't obvious, understand?" My face suddenly felt flush.

"Don't get constipated, okay?"

My stomach was in knots. Why was the food taking so long? I looked at my watch and saw it had only been a few minutes since I'd ordered, but felt like an hour. My head weighed a ton.

"Did you ask your online buddies about Frank?" I asked. Connie put a hot cup of coffee down in front of me, and I smiled and nodded.

"Guess what Frankie-boy's into?" Mill asked.

"Dead sisters?" I said, jokingly.

"How did you know?"

"What?"

Millar laughed, then snorted and a rumbling cough rose from deep in his chest.

"Mill, you've got to quit smoking."

"I'm trying. Believe me."

"Necrophilia?" I asked, getting back to the Fat Man.

"What? No, I was kidding. But, he is into occult stuff. You know, witches, druids, warlocks, crap like that."

A vision flashed through my head of Frank as a bearded wizard-master, sitting atop a bundle of dirty clothes on his bed and randomly waving a magic wand around. "Why am I not surprised?" I asked.

"He's in a few other online clubs, and I found out they have more to do with druids than anything else."

"Druids. You mentioned druids before. What does a druid do, exactly?"

"Those tree-worshiping pagans? Got me. Some form of ancient sorcery. Only these guys are called neo-Druids."

The waitress delivered my breakfast, and not a moment too soon. I smiled at her and took a bite of toast. "Neo, meaning what, exactly?" I asked Millar.

"Meaning they practice bits and pieces of some sort of bullshit, because nobody knows what druids actually were or did."

I laughed. "That's pretty funny. So they just call themselves neo-Druids and make up the rest?"

"I don't know. Hey, you coming to The Tavern tonight?" Millar asked, his interest in druids having run its course.

"I'll be there. You can tell me all about it then."

"Oh, can I?" Sarcasm dripped from the phone.

"And Mill?"

"Yeah?"

"You know any cops?"

"Oh, come on, man."

"What? I need a few questions answered. Thought a friendly cop might help."

"Well, my cousin's a cop. But he's on a leave of absence or something, I think. He might be able to help."

"Interesting."

"Yeah, head lice are interesting, but I don't want any."

"Why? Isn't he an okay guy?"

"He's a little fucking crazy if you ask me. Come to think of it, I don't talk to him much. So that's probably a no-go."

"How'd you like to get friendly with him again?"

"How'd you like to pay me a quadrillion dollars?"

I downed another piece of toast. "When I get two quadrillion,

I'll give you half."

"Funny guy."

"Well, the least you could do is show me a list of Frank's supposed online clubs."

"I'm your freaking secretary now, making lists?"

"You're not cute enough for that." I laughed.

"Chauvinist."

"I'm old fashioned that way. Sue me."

A heavy sigh came over the phone. "Will that be all, Mr. Chase? By the way, I'm pregnant. It's yours."

"Come on, Mill, I'm your best friend. Who else is going to listen to your happy horseshit and still buy you drinks?"

"You've got a point. See you tonight."

The phone clicked dead. I took a sip of coffee. It was hot and a tad bitter, just the way I like it.

10
IS IT JUST ME?

I decided to take a chance on seeing the Fat Man again and arranged to meet right away at his place. Once again, the door was ajar, and I wandered into the creepy apartment. Classical music echoed from the back of the place. I creaked my way past the mounds of stacked boxes and down the darkened hallway to his bedroom, half expecting Motorcycle Jacket to jump out at me. Finally, I stood in his doorway, looking in. Frank sat on the edge of his gigantic bed, like an enormous toad on a giant lily pad, floating in a black swamp. Around him was a fresh pile of comic books and vinyl records. A human skull, which I assumed was plastic but couldn't be certain, sat at the end of his bed, the orbital sockets pointing in my general direction.

I recognized Bach's *Cello Suite No. 1* as it rasped through the dark room. I could feel the slow musical notes unfurling like tentacles from around his bed, snaking toward me, Frank at the center, like a great octopus spreading his stealthy arms in search of prey.

"Come in, Mr. Chase. Sit." Frank gestured to my usual chair. I chose to stand at the foot of his bed. He turned toward me, his dark, inquisitive eyes searching mine.

"You like Bach?" he asked, and took a deep, soulful breath in through his nostrils. "So lonely, eh? Alive, yet alone in this world are we."

"Yes we are, Frank. Each of us."

"Things without all remedy should be without regard: what's

done, is done." He nodded slowly and closed his eyes, drifting off into deep, melancholic appreciation of the music. After a few awkward moments, his eyes popped open again and he searched for me, as if to be certain I hadn't left.

"Have you seen her?" he asked, a lilt of hopefulness in his voice.

"By her, you mean your sister? Yes, I have."

"And?" He sat up and stared at me. "Any hope of tracking her down?"

I shrugged, reluctant to go into detail of the odd dream I'd had.

"Come on, I can take it. Don't withhold anything."

"It was strange, Frank. I had a vision. It was cold, wet."

"Wet?" He seemed enticed. "Really. In what way, wet?"

"In the most direct way."

"Ah. The opposite of indirect, your chosen mode of expression." He seemed slightly perturbed. "You're a reluctant seer, aren't you?"

"You're a reticent client."

He looked down, examining his gargantuan, bare feet on the small rug at the side of his bed. "Where's the rabbit?"

I'd forgotten Peanut, again. I hesitated, remembering his infatuation with the toy, then said, "He's still safe. At my place."

Frank smiled. "Has something happened to him? Should I be worried?"

"No, he's fine. I just forgot to bring him."

"He's antique, you realize. Very fragile."

"I know."

Frank closed his eyes and listened to the music once more. I surveyed the room for further evidence of his druid leanings: a robe, a large wooden stick, incantations, a tree perhaps, and found a druid poster on the wall peeking out from behind the open door. I couldn't see much of it, just a hooded figure in darkened woods.

We listened to Bach's unsettling cello for a few more minutes before I broke the silence with a sneeze and cough. My eyes were beginning to fill from allergens. He turned toward me, to scold me, I thought, but was politely cagey.

"And now, we have Beethoven's later string quartet. No. 12, in E flat."

As if on cue, the music changed to the sprightlier quartet, and I realized this was him being sociable, sharing his moments. I nodded in faux appreciation, and took in a long, slow breath, letting the new sounds surround me for a moment. The odor of worn socks reached my nose. Opening my eyes, I saw there in the corner, to my left, a pile of dirty laundry. Sock mites! I pinched my nose to hold in another sneeze.

Returning from his immersion in Beethoven, Frank said, "So, getting back to your dream. It was wet, you say?" A mischievous smile crossed his face. "A wet dream. How lucky for you. I haven't had one of those in years." I admired the game he was playing, joking around, not rushing me. "Mind telling me what you mean, exactly," he continued, "by it being watery?"

"I think you know, Frank," I said, testing him.

Frank sat up. "So, you saw what happened?"

"You mean what I think happened about thirty-odd years ago. Does this really have anything to do with your sister?" I said, more loudly than I had anticipated.

He pointed a finger at me and said gleefully, "You're completely undone, aren't you? I may have to ask for my money back."

"I never made any promises, Frank. I told you I'd try. That's all."

My nerves were revving up and I started planning an escape from my new playmate. I could easily rush past him before he got off the bed, maybe push him back if he stood. Then I realized, if he accidentally fell to the floor, he probably wouldn't be able to get up again. He'd just lie there, silently dehydrating, wobbling back and forth like a turtle on its back. After a few weeks the authorities would find his rotting corpse, having followed the stench from the hallway.

"I need you to focus, Mr. Chase. Tell me exactly what you saw."

His demanding tone made me even more agitated. *All right, Fat Man*, I thought to myself, *let's play your stupid game.* I opened my mouth and a bundle of nervous energy spooled out. "A dead girl, that's what I saw. I felt her too. Her porcelain skin was soft and clammy, eyes dull, like a fish a few hours out of water. She had long brown hair wrapped around her throat and into her mouth. But she wasn't choking on it, because she had already drowned."

My repulsion of Frank grew stronger for having seen this gruesome vision. Another dead girl staring at me when I closed my eyes. He'd brought this nightmare to me, and I wanted to rub his face in it. "You want me to go on?" I asked, not waiting for an answer. "She was calling out to you, Frank! She needed your help, but you did nothing. You just stood there, a dark, dirty little soul, wilting in the shadows. She flailed and screamed and choked for air. And you could have easily pulled her out, taken her hand and yanked her to safety, but something held you back, something dark I couldn't see, dark as your soul, and it sickens me."

Frank pushed a button on a remote. Beethoven was finished.

A horn blared from the street below. It pulsed in steady rhythm to my elevated heartbeat. Frank cleared his throat. The horn stopped, but my heart pulsed on, harder and faster.

"You—" Frank started, but choked on his next words. His accusatory tone pushed me to my limit. I started out of the room. Frank leaped up, like a huge black bear. "Don't go!" He gasped, taking hold of my arm. "Please, stay."

I forced myself to look at his dark eyes as they searched mine, and they were kind, almost gentle. His pleading smile was cornered by his tears and they softened me. I relented, and slowly walked back into his room.

Brushing moisture away from his cheeks, and seemingly satisfied I would stay, he sat back on the bed. "I'm sorry if this makes you uncomfortable, but what you've revealed so far is quite intriguing.

You saw something…extraordinary, did you not?"

His statements surprised me, but I said nothing.

"I think your powers are nothing short of miraculous," he continued.

I mustered a slight nod, but the dark presence at the edge of the pond, the one I felt so acutely staring at me in the dream, was hovering nearby. I could feel it reaching out to me, like when I'd first emerged from that black puddle in the woods.

"Do you know what some people would give to have your gift?"

"It's a gift, is it?" I asked.

"You know it is. You have something only a few in this world are privileged to have."

"So, I take it this dream meant something to you, then?" I said, then immediately regretted leading him on.

"Historically, humans have developed various survival techniques," he said. "The spiritual world was a huge part of our past. But that world has been largely forgotten, and relegated to exploitative 'reality' ghost-hunting TV shows and ridiculous exorcism films. We've forgotten our past and built upon the false promise of technology."

"Huh," I grunted, hoping he'd just shut up, picturing him in his druid costume: a pointy-hooded white robe, strange earth symbols adorning it.

"But I promise you," he continued, "some of us have not forgotten our past. Some of us have honed those lost skills. The world is still a spiritual place, whether you want to believe it or not. Examples come to light every day: A mother senses her child is in danger and catches her before she falls. A brother feels the loneliness of a sibling and picks up the phone. A man decides he won't take a flight and changes planes, thus avoiding an impending crash. These are flashes of our intuitive lives."

I felt my ass melting into the hardback chair. Once again, I started planning my escape. Perhaps a pretend phone call or a powerful itch would do the trick, any excuse to get moving again. I could sneeze convulsively and beg to leave, but that hard chair seemed to have sealed my ass in place.

"Of course, we're more civilized now. The way we go about things today, there's generally a more peaceful augury. But there are those who would destroy us, have no doubt about that."

Us, I thought. Who are *us*? I scanned the room and found another druid poster I hadn't noticed before: A small, darkly robed person, hands outstretched, mouth opened impossibly wide, out of which flew a large flock of black birds, surging into the air.

On the bed, the human skull seemed to leer at me through its deep orbits. On the wall, slightly to my right, a detailed painting of a goat sacrifice seemed to animate out the corner of my eye. I turned, but it was still. How had I missed that one? I squirmed nervously in my chair.

"Are you uncomfortable, Mr. Chase?"

"It's getting late," I said, looking at my watch-less wrist. I tried to stand but my legs felt like rubber.

Frank relented. "I see. If you could just allow me," he said, and reached into his wallet, retrieving a few bills. He held them out to me between his thumb and index finger, like a dandy offering his date a scented snot rag.

"That's okay, I don't..." I didn't bother finishing the sentence. He knew I was repulsed.

"Oh? But, I haven't even made you a genuine offer yet. There are so many things we need to explore, and much more in-depth."

I sneezed, and could feel my eyes starting to swell. *I could climb through the window and down the fire escape*, I thought. I'd seen it done in movies; it couldn't be that difficult.

"I'm not much into the whole occult thing, Frank. Not my cup of tea, really."

He laughed heartily at that, raised a greasy pinky finger to his eyebrow and plucked at the thick hairs there. "Rather ironic, don't you think? Being an Intuitive, yet denying your gift?"

"I'm not comfortable talking about it. Besides, I'm a precognitive dreamer, not an Intuitive. And really, I'm not into witchery."

"Ah," he said. "That's what's making you so uncomfortable." He smiled and nodded toward the druid-bird poster. I smiled back. "I know it may seem foreign to you at first. The ideas are strange, not of our time, but if you're willing to focus, really concentrate your energies, you could be spectacular. I could help you with that."

"Nah, I'm good," I said, finally able to pry myself from the chair. I swear I heard a huge sucking sound as it let go.

He grabbed my wrist. "I have something to tell you." His clammy hand appeared to slide up my arm, but hadn't even moved.

"Okay," I said, swallowing hard.

"It's eating me up, Gus," he said. "My sister. You can't imagine what it's like." Huge puddles distorted his eyes, then tears began rolling down his puffy cheeks. "The pain of it. I can't sleep. She follows me wherever I go. She haunts my dreams. I can't rid myself of her, do you understand?"

A strong aroma wafted up from somewhere. His distress had stimulated an odoriferous biological response. I began breathing in through my mouth to avoid its rankness. Dead skin, old socks, rotting food, mixed with cat piss and body odor all converged in my sinuses and overwhelmed me, as if a veil had been lifted, finally releasing the decay of the room.

"To answer your question, yes, Gus, the dream has a whole lot of meaning for me."

"Great! Gotta go, Frank."

"I'll call you!" he called out, as I dashed down the crooked hall, through the darkened kitchen, and past his leering cat as it hissed at me from behind a curtain. I slammed shut the door and ran down the stairs to the street.

Once outside, I breathed deep the cool fall air. Out of morbid curiosity, I turned and looked up at Frank's window. A dark mass stared down at me, imploring me back into its grasp. It was the same *gloom* I'd seen at the pond. I turned and walked away as fast as I could.

11

GIVE THEM WHAT THEY WANT

"You see, the thing is," Millard paused and looked into his beer bottle, "the more I tried, the more she said no. After a while, I resented the rejection so much I didn't care anymore. Women and sex. They say the first thing to go in a bad marriage is sex. They don't tell you the last thing to go is your money."

"I think that's implied," I said.

I took a long slug of my draught, matching Mill's tug, and we both placed our glasses down on the bar at the same time. I'd never come close to getting married, so I just nodded in sympathy, not comprehending or even trying to comprehend the long-term significance of it all. I did, however, have failed relationships, and of course there was Diana, the one that almost drove me insane. She was the one, consciously or unconsciously, to whom I compared all other women.

"Mill, I don't get what happened, but if it means anything to you, fuck her."

"Fuck her!" he shouted.

Allen sent a sharp look in our direction and we took the rare opportunity to order another round. The happy bartender was gracious enough to break from the ancient game on the TV and take our food orders. A couple of Tavern Burgers with extra cheese, hold the mayo, with fries and a side salad for me. I try to get some greens in me no matter what.

"The first thing she did was hide all my stuff," Mill said. "I had a hat collection, on the wall above the bed. Didn't say a thing about it when we were dating. First thing after our engagement, she takes it down. Puts it in the closet."

"That sucks," I said.

"Never mind the hats, it's the baskets I can't stand. She's got a basket for everything. If I leave anything around the house, keys, keepsakes, bottle caps, magazines, into the basket it goes. She's got three of them. Or four. I think. The first one, she uses for stuff that's lying around. Then if it stays in that basket long enough, it goes into basket number two. That one is for the 'stale stuff', let's call it. Then if it stays in basket two long enough, it goes into basket number three, which she keeps in the closet. If I don't retrieve my stuff from there anytime soon, it goes..." Mill blinked a few times, then stared at me. "I don't know where it goes! Poof, it's gone." He waved his arms around, to simulate a disappearance. "I theorized a mythical fourth basket that lives in another dimension. If something goes into *that* basket, it's never seen or heard from again. Such is life with my wife."

"Sounds rough," I said.

"Oh, it is. I'm a guest in my own house. It's all her stuff. Her stuff that I can't touch. Try putting her shit in a basket! Huh! That's not gonna happen. It's her house now, anyways. Or it will be. Fucking divorce."

After he'd settled down, I leaned into Mill and asked, "So, you have that list?"

"List? What list?"

"Frank Cosh."

"Oh, yeah. Here." He handed me a printout of several links, but they had no descriptions.

"Is that it?" I asked.

"What do you want, a thesis? All the sites he belongs to are there, according to his web page."

"He has a web page?"

"Actually, it's a blog. You'd know that, if you'd bothered to check. Lots of links to friends. Freaks mostly."

"Druid friends?"

Allen slapped two pints in front of us and grunted as he took our money.

"Why don't you ever run a tab, Mill?" I asked.

"If you keep paying cash, eventually Allen will buy one back."

I nodded and drank some ale. "That cheap bastard will actually buy one back?"

"I'm hoping. It's only been two years." He gave me a doubtful look and I just had to laugh.

I was starting to relax after being held in Frank's grasp. I felt like I'd been held prisoner and made a remarkable escape, lucky to get out with my teeth intact. A fun house gone awry, was how I'd described it to Mill. He laughed and slapped the bar when I told him the story, loudly enough to elicit a sneer from Allen.

"Even the cat wanted a piece of you!" Mill said, and then added in a more serious tone, "Do you think he really watched his sister drown?"

"I have no idea." I shrugged, but deep down I felt his grasp, his unholy soul reaching out to me. "I know he did something he regrets. Not clear exactly what." I took a swig of ale and turned to Mill. "What do druids do anyway?" I asked. Mill surprised me with his studious response.

"Apparently, there are no real accounts or records of what they actually did. Julius Caesar wrote something about them being responsible for religious worship, sacrifices and some judicious matters."

"Like wise men or something?"

"A bit more official than that. They were trained holy men. Celtic myths and ancient Irish history reference them. And they believed in animism, human sacrifice, reincarnation…"

I frowned. Frank had said he was being tormented by something, or someone. "That is just too far out there for me, Mill. I'm done."

"That sounds funny coming from a guy who dreams about death."

"Yeah, but I feel like my dreams are related to some sort of time warp. Not supernatural spooks."

"What, you transcend time?"

"I transcend fucking time, Mill. And I'm done with the Fat Man."

Mill raised a glass and we toasted to being done with Frank "the Fat Man" Cosh. "Maybe my wife will marry a druid. He could charm her into having sex every night. But who the hell would want her?"

"Yeah," I said. "Who the hell?"

Two young women walked into the bar and sat at a booth near the door. I glanced over. Mill pulled at my arm.

"Don't even look at them. That's what they want. They sit there, waiting to be admired."

I laughed. He continued, his voice getting louder, "And they suck you in! Into that endless void of wanting and neediness. They train you to hate them, then they take your money!"

"Okay, okay, calm down," I said.

"Don't even look at 'em. Who needs 'em?"

I laughed again and said, "Okay, I think you've made your point."

Mill seemed to be getting drunker by the second. Allen shot us one of his nasty looks. Mill smiled at him, his voice becoming conspiratorial. "Hey, Allen, got any more of that delicious chocolate pudding?"

"Just what's on the menu. Now keep it down." His terse response begged no answer.

"Aw, no special pudding today?"

Allen turned away and started washing mugs. Mill cracked himself up, laughing loudly. I grabbed his arm, and told him to keep it down. I could see Allen facing front, but his eyes were scanning in our direction. His great, bulging eyeballs seemed attached to a 360-degree ball turret.

Obviously, Mill was still hurting from his divorce. The failure of the first significant relationship he'd ever had left him bitter, but he really wasn't as misogynistic as he sounded. "The only woman who'd ever put up with me," he'd said of his soon-to-be ex.

I was more than happy to play along, and slapped Mill on the back, hoping to get his attention away from Allen.

"He who hasn't gotten burned in love is either dead or a fool," I said, and raised my glass.

Mill raised his glass and loudly toasted. "To fools everywhere!"

Allen gave us a hateful sneer, retrieved the burgers the waitress dropped at the end of the bar, and plopped them down in front of us. Mill smiled at the juicy burgers, then at Allen. "That's a lot of red meat, Allen. Mine's particularly fat and red. Look at all that blood." Allen glared at Mill. "It's okay, though. Those cows were raised on a macrobiotic diet!" Mill roared with laughter.

Allen's face burned red. He walked away and turned up the TV sound with the remote. I had to admire his self-control. We regularly pushed all of his buttons.

Mill leaned toward me and said, "Ah, it's the little pleasures, Gus. The little ones."

We dug in to our meals. I glanced at the girls between bites. No sign of Diana there. The second time I looked, I caught Mill glancing at them, and we both laughed. I don't think they even noticed us.

12
THE EMMA CONNECTION

"I think Carrillo killed your sister," I said.

That got her attention. Carla wanted to meet with me. I said no to the Boat House. I wasn't going there again. We settled on a small café in the East Village that I liked. They served hot off-the-bone chicken breast sandwiches. Melt in your mouth good.

I got a little head rush when she walked into the restaurant. She looked gorgeous in a tweed suit jacket with matching skirt and those calf-high boots. The flutters in my stomach foretold trouble just around the corner.

We sat at a corner table near a small window overlooking a side street. It was just private enough to make me feel safe, and intimate enough for me to keep her focused on what I had to say. We ordered the chicken sandwiches and iced tea. I studied her face as she fished in her purse for something.

Real beauty has a surreal quality. She wore the same makeup, lipstick, base, eye shadow as any other woman, but somehow she was mystifying. I was suddenly ten years old and looking at my mother's make-up kit. Strange and wonderful smells filled my senses. This mysterious alchemy transported me to an emotional buoyancy and made me long for erotic fulfillment.

She sat upright, her hands near mine on the table. I wanted to take her hand and study it, let it tell me who she was. But I was no palmist, just another guy looking at a beautiful woman. She'd probably seen it time and again; another testosterone-jacked dude with the hots for a pretty face and looking to score. But it couldn't be like that for me. I was a professional.

"What can you tell me about Carrillo?" she asked.

"He worked at the college. I'm pretty sure he killed Emma. In the dream, I didn't see his face, but I could feel him near." That thought stopped me cold. Was he only nearby the murder scene? The idea rattled me. Could someone else have killed her, and he'd been watching?

"What percentage of accuracy are we talking about with these dreams of yours?" she asked.

"What do you mean, like a ball player?"

"Are you batting a thousand?"

"I don't know. I never thought of it like that. Maybe."

I took a sip of iced tea and looked out the window. My head was heavy, starting to spin. I could feel a Dream State coming on. I took hold of her hand. She pulled away but I couldn't let go. My head flew back and I was there on the street with Emma.

Concussive waves ripple through my chest, pale images of blood, her falling to the street, the bloody wall. I see a figure running, a mid-length, dark jacket flapping at his sides. It appears to be made of lightweight material. I see Emma in the alley, her dead eyes staring up at me. I feel a dark presence to my left. Carrillo is there, I can feel him, but is he the killer? I have doubts. The figure has disappeared.

I lurched back to reality. Blood trickled down my nose. I sat up, and was suddenly aware of being in the restaurant. Carla stared at me with what I can only describe as embarrassment.

"Are you all right?" she asked.

I put a napkin to my nose. "Yes. I'm fine."

She pulled her hand away from mine. "What the hell was that?"

"I'm sorry. Give me a minute, I'll explain everything."

Carla seemed hesitant, and looked at the door, as if measuring her options. She turned back to me and asked, "Are you epileptic?"

"No. I saw her."

"Just now? Was that it?"

"If by *it*, you mean a vision, then yes."

She sat back and stared at me for several seconds as if gauging my sincerity. She took a sip of her iced tea, then put the glass down. "That must have taken a lot of practice. Do you generally hit up widows who've got bank accounts or what? I mean, why are you hitting me up? I've already offered you money."

"Hey, you called me."

"After I took the bait."

"You think I can make my nose bleed on command?"

"Bite your lip and shove it back in your throat, who knows? Like milk coming out your nose from laughing."

I was stunned. We stared at each other in silence for a minute. The waitress brought our sandwiches to the table and asked if we needed anything else. I smiled and told her, no.

I was absolutely starving, so I ate. She watched me, but didn't touch her food. After a few big bites, I thanked her for her time and got up to leave.

"Sit down," she said in a conciliatory tone.

"Why should I?"

She looked embarrassed and looked around to see who was watching. "Please, don't make a scene. Just sit down."

"I don't need this. You think I want this?" I asked indignantly. "I've never asked you for a cent, never made a dime from this curse I've lived with for years, and you have the nerve to accuse me of a scam?"

"Please, lower your voice. Sit. You're embarrassing me."

I looked around the restaurant. A few people were staring. I sat down and took a quick gulp of tea.

She studied me for a few seconds. "Okay, I believe you."

"Oh, really? Just like that. Let's start the fucking parade."

"Look, I had to be sure. I figured if I called you on it...I don't know."

"I can't believe you still think I'm a phony. Why did you want to meet?" I took another bite of my sandwich, but my appetite was gone. I pinched some bread and rolled it in my fingers. "You've ruined a perfectly good sandwich for me."

"Hey, I said I'm sorry."

"I didn't hear you say it."

"That's what I meant."

"Be nice to hear it, really."

She scanned the room. We were no longer garnering attention. "Only if you tell me how you did the nose bleed trick."

I sat back. "Really? You're still going on? You just said you believed me."

"I believe your passion."

"My passion?"

"That will have to do for now."

"I still want to hear it."

"What?"

"That you're sorry."

She was nobody's fool and was determined that I was a huckster. The test of our wills had begun in earnest. She was a tough Bronx cookie. Breaking through to her was going to be hard. How could I ever get inside a head so walled up?

She smiled. "I'm sorry I doubted your sincerity, August."

It wasn't a full-blown apology, but I took it. "So, you don't believe I have visions, but you think maybe I can help. I get it."

"I may regret this, but yes. I want you to investigate Carrillo."

"Okay," I said.

"But I can't pay you a retainer."

I smiled at her. "That's fine. I'm not in this for the money."

She fought another doubtful look and said, "I can pay you after you get somewhere. And I mean progress, not some silly dreams."

"Silly—"

She cut me off. "That's not what I meant. Sorry, no offense."

"None taken. Happy to be of service." I smiled again and took a sip of my tea. If that's what it took to get her to trust me, then so be it. It was finally time to start working full-time on Emma's murder.

13
WHOSE CHECK IS THIS?

When your special calling becomes evident, you better be sure it's your real calling and not just a job. The boss from my day job had left two messages. A co-worker in my department at the Museum of Contemporary Art was in the hospital and another was out sick. Could I come in, even though it was my vacation? A traveling exhibit needed to be packed up and sent on the road. That was my job. I put artwork in boxes and shipped them around the world. I made platforms, wooden boxes, stands, and podiums. I cut wood and steel, made shipping crates, padding, and signage stands. In short, my day job had nothing to do with creative writing or detective work. I had been using my vacation time to start a detective business with the aim of not returning to the museum. Now they wanted me to end my vacation early. I sat staring at the machine. The little red light blinked death rays at me, and I thought, *I'm just unavailable. Sorry, out of town.*

I met Mill a little later at The Tavern. I'd asked him to run down more information about Carrillo, since my home computer wasn't working properly. The screen was black. I needed a new monitor, I guess. Mill never ceased to amaze me. He showed up with a manila folder full of notes.

"Mill," I said, crossing to the bar, "thanks for coming."

He had a devilish grin on his face. "Your burger is going to be mighty tasty, friend."

"My burger?"

"The one you're buying me."

We ordered the usual and sat at a booth. Allen especially appreciated that, since he didn't have a waitress at the moment. He tried his damnedest to act butch and obsequious at the same time. Mill smiled and watched, spellbound, as he ran from the tables to the bar, taking orders and drawing pints from the handful of customers, until I broke his trance. "How do you know he won't put something in your burger?" I nodded toward Allen.

Mill shot me a worried look.

"Hey, you did it to him," I continued.

"Yeah, but he never found out."

"How do you know your little kitchen buddy didn't spill the beans?"

"What motive would he have for doing that?"

"Motivation is subjective and infinite," I said. "Besides, I seem to recall you making a hasty dash to the little boy's room, just before Allen ate that spiked pudding. Maybe someone got to you first?"

Mill stared at me, then took a sip his beer and opened the folder in front of him. "I hate you," he said.

I shrugged.

Mill went through the notes, summarizing what he'd found. "Your boy, Carrillo, was not an ordinary guy. Like the article said, he had ties to the CIA or some secret crap like that."

"How so?"

"Field operative in the eighties. Overseas stuff. Foreign intelligence."

"But the newspaper said Army Intelligence."

"An oxymoron…"

"Yeah, yeah," I said.

Mill cleared his throat. "He started a small security firm here in the States with a partner, Jayson Bruno, also retired CIA. It started out pretty big, but his operation got smaller over the years. This last year he'd dropped completely off the map. No record of his keeping up his business license. No trace of Bruno."

"License for what?"

"Private investigation firm."

"So, was he was on the job at the college or really a janitor?"

"Good question, Gus. You answer that. Find out who he worked for and you're on your way."

My cell phone lit up. It was work. I cursed the day I gave them my cell number. I let it go to voicemail.

"You gonna get that?" asked Mill.

"I'm on vacation, Mill. Besides, I'm giving notice next week, if I can launch this business and make some freaking money."

"One way I see that happening…"

I looked at Mill's smiling face. "What," I asked.

"You still got the rabbit?"

"Peanut? Shit, I forgot about him."

"Ransom the rabbit!" Mill laughed and slapped the table.

Allen stood over us, lurched forward, and plunged the burgers down.

"Ketchup, please," said Mill, not missing a beat. Allen sauntered over to another table, swiped up the bottle in one clean motion and placed it in front of Mill, who smiled and nodded. Allen managed a sort of baboon grimace, then walked back to his spot under the TV.

Mill inspected his burger, poked it with a fork, smelled it, then smiled and said, "Fuck it," and took a big bite. "You can't be picky about choosing your clients. Generally, they choose you in the beginning. Only later can you afford to be selective."

I pondered going back into the Fat Man's lair. Shivers ran down my spine. My stomach tingled. Carla wouldn't give me any money, but the Fat Man was handing it out in hundred dollar bills. Carla was beautiful; the Fat Man was nauseating.

"No matter how crazy he is, the Fat Man pays," Mill said. "And think of the referrals he'd give. All those crazy-ass druid friends of his needing help with their crazy-ass shit." I tried to put that thought out of my mind. "Besides," said Mill, "he said he'd offer you more work, didn't he? Maybe then you can afford to get your computer fixed."

The truth was, I was starting to like not having a computer. It lent itself to a certain amount of freedom.

"Let's talk about the business at hand," I said, pointing to the folders.

We sorted through the data on Carrillo. One name that popped up as much as Bruno's was Phelps.

"Michael Steen Phelps, an economics professor at NYU," Mill said. "The professor and Bruno were linked indirectly to three companies outside of the school. Professor Phelps was listed as an adviser in two of the companies, and in one, Aphelion Energy Trading, as a principal adviser."

"What can you tell me about this company, Mill?"

"I'm sorry, how much is my salary?"

"Hey, come on. You know I haven't made any real money yet."

"How much you think I'm worth?" Mill asked.

"I don't know," I said dismissively.

"Better, yet, how much do you think you're worth?"

"Come on, Mill, cut the shit."

"No, I'm serious. When I had my software company going full out, I always asked prospective employees what they thought they were worth paying in salary."

"The point being?"

"Dude, if you tell me you're worth anything less than a hundred Gs, I'm not hiring you."

"Fine. Your salary is nothing. I can't afford you."

"I want a hundred and one thousand yearly, with bonus," Mill said.

"With bonus? What, ten, fifteen percent?"

"Up to fifty percent of annual salary."

I chewed my burger and took a sip of beer. We eyed each other for a minute.

Mill smiled and said, "I'm not saying you have to pay me, dolt. You can give it to me in deferred payment."

"Deferred until when?"

"Until you can afford it."

"That's more than I'll ever make."

We stared at each other again. Mill chomped a fry. "Read my lips," Mill said, "You don't have to pay me. Well, you do. Just write out a check and I'll take it. But I'll never cash it. Get it?"

"Okay," I said, shaking my head. "One hundred and one thousand dollars." I pitched my checkbook onto the table and looked at him. "You're serious. You really want me to do this?" Mill smiled and nodded. I wrote the amount on the check and scrawled my name in a flourish at the bottom. "Happy?"

Mill smiled as I handed him the rubber note. "Plus bonus."

"You're a piece of work, Mill."

"Yes, I am."

"Now, find out what you can about Aphelion Energy Trading."

"Fine, Chief, I'll get right on it."

"And Mill?"

We both said it at the same time, "Don't call me, Chief."

14
A CHOCOLATE FOR YOUR THOUGHTS

O ne of the great things about my cell phone is I'd installed an app that allowed the camera to zoom in several times closer than before. However, Motorcycle Jacket's face wasn't particularly clear in the photo. I must have jerked my arm when it was taken. He'd been snooping around the pizza joint across the street from my apartment. Since it's one of my favorite restaurants, I figured I'd scare him away.

He was standing by the side door when I caught sight of his motorcycle parked out front. Casually I strolled into the place, ordered a slice, and exited out the same side door. As I did, I flipped my camera at him and took the shot. He bolted inside the restaurant, exited out the front and set off down the street. I immediately walked to his bike, took a shot of the license plate, then casually returned to my apartment to call Mill.

"What now?" he asked.

"Is that any way to answer the phone when the boss calls?"

"You gonna push it?"

"The ink's not even dry on our deal and you're wimping out on me?"

Mill took a deep breath and sighed into the phone. "Sorry, Gus. Bad day."

"Thinking about the ex?"

"I hate her. Just got off the phone with the selfish little thing. I can't believe I used to love her. Now she's raping me...or at least my bank account."

"I know. You told me."

"Yeah, but did I tell you I hate her?"

"You hate me, too."

"Yes, I do, but not as much as her." He gave a little chuckle. "So what do you need, master dreamer?"

"That's more like it. I'm going to send you two photos. One is Motorcycle Jacket, the other his license plate."

"Wow, you *are* a detective."

"And Mill, does that hundred thousand buy a reach-out to your cousin to run down that plate?"

"Okay, I take back what I said about you being a detective. Dude, you can look that up online."

After a slight pause, I said, "Yeah, I knew that."

"Like hell you did. Go to one of those spy sites and you can look up anybody you want, for a fee."

"Right. I didn't think that applied to license plates."

"Nothing is private anymore. Pay the fee, any public record is fair game. Death, birth, marriage, divorce, licenses…"

"I'll try it on my phone. I'll talk to you later, Mill." I started to hang up.

"Wait! Send the pics. I belong to a site."

"You belong to a spy site?"

"It's a public records search engine. You sure you want to be a detective?"

"Not really."

"Then don't waste the fifty bucks membership fee."

"I'm sending the photos now. And Mill?"

"What?"

"You're my hero."

"Lovely. I hate you much less now."

"Later."

"And Gus?"

"Yeah?"

"Call the Fat Man. Make some money."

Those last words echoed in my head. I turned to Peanut, the ratty little rabbit. His funky ears protruded from the plastic bag like a dying wave hello. Guilt washed over me. Perhaps I was holding him hostage.

I pulled Peanut out of the bag and sat him on the bed. A stale odor wafted up from the toy. I reexamined the matted, faux fur and stitching, imagining all the hair dander, dead skin, and general disgustingness that clung to it.

"You're a dirty little beggar, aren't you?" I said aloud.

I picked up the phone and dialed. It rang several times before I got the Fat Man's recorded message: "This is a private line. If you're selling something or want me to take a survey, kindly choke and die. Otherwise, you know what to do."

I left him a sweet message about Peanut missing home, and said I'd drop by with him. I also suggested he give me a call as soon as possible.

I felt like an ass for the pandering tone I'd used. What was I thinking? Each time I'd conjured a Fat Man dream it got worse. My anxiety toward him grew to the point of hindering function. He rattled me to my soul. Being in the same room with him made me feel infected with creepiness.

Had he done something horrible to his sister, or was it just my religious upbringing coming back to haunt me? As a wayward Catholic, I'd forgotten most of what I'd been taught, but somehow the really scary stuff, the stuff that stays with you until you die—concepts like the devil, hell and eternity—no matter how you feel or believe objectively, these fears can be raked up like smoldering coals in long forgotten ash. Frank's witchcraft leanings had set off this unease in me. I didn't want to involve myself with him. Somehow, I felt vulnerable to psychological misfires just being around him. I think it was the possibility of living and dying alone, surrounded by crumbling cardboard boxes of forgotten memories, that frightened me the most.

My fear of Frank was spurred on by a certain logic: Accepting that I could see the future, then surely he could conjure spells, or worse. He could use his magic spells to control me, voodoo me, bewitch me, charm birds into attacking me, whisper sacrilegious obscenities into my ear, and send my soul packing to the great darkness below. Superstition and paranoia wafted through my emotional psyche. These were the things he brought out in me, and why I was reluctant to go any further with his case.

I had to figure out a way to make money at this detective gig, and there stood the Fat Man, with his fist full of coin. There had to be a better way. Was this going to be the detective's lifestyle? Maybe I was being absurd.

My emotional pendulum was still swinging back and forth between the spiritual and logic when the phone rang. It was work again. This time I answered.

"Augustus, thank God. I need you to come in to work."

It was my boss, Lillian Campbell. My name is August, but I let that slide. Her conciliatory tone and promises of an abbreviated schedule convinced me I should go into work. The exhibit was already cut into labeled sections, I just needed to customize the shipping crates for three pieces, and I could take an extra two days of paid vacation. I told her I absolutely had to stick to the plan and not work a minute extra, and she agreed.

After she hung up, I felt a huge let down. I was so involved in my new venture, my old life seemed stale, archaic, almost a relic of the past. In the evolution of my immediate life, it held no meaning.

At one time, I'd considered a degree in Conservation, but the politics at the museum had turned me off. Who would have guessed all that wonderful art could inspire so much petty bickering?

Now, after the prospects of going back to my regular job, all I wanted to do was to track down Carrillo's contacts and indulge myself in the pursuit of Carla's affection, and maybe, if I felt brave enough, earn some more of Fat Man's money.

I promised to be in at work by 9:00 a.m. the next day. That left me with the rest of the afternoon and evening to indulge in my new pursuits.

*** *** ***

I stood outside the Fat Man's apartment and waited. He didn't answer the door and I assumed he was still out, although I also had a nagging feeling he may be lying up there, helpless, his bacon-saturated heart having finally exploded under the weight of his crushing bulk. Or worse, he was futilely waiting for help, mere feet from a telephone that, ultimately, was unreachable.

I moved to a front stoop a few blocks away from his apartment. If Motorcycle Jacket was around, I didn't want him to see me.

I'd been waiting twenty minutes when a cab pulled up to the curb and Frank stepped out. With several grocery bags in hand, he managed to pay the driver and waddle up the front steps. I caught up to him in time to hold open the front door. He seemed surprised to see me, but didn't stop to chat as he strained and huffed his way up the stairs.

In the kitchen, he unloaded the grocery bags, consisting of several cans of cat food, frozen dinners, microwave popcorn, assorted canned stews and meats, and a bottle of malt liquor.

"How are you, Frank?"

I pulled the rabbit from the plastic bag, and held Peanut out to him. Frank paused, as if seeing an old friend after years apart, then gently reached out and took him from me.

"Thanks for returning him. Like I said, he's an antique."

"No problem," I said. "He's a good boy. Rather quiet."

Frank smiled, and gave me a knowing, if not embarrassed, glance. After closing all the open cabinets and folding the plastic bags into a larger plastic bag that hung from the back handle of the pantry door, he let out a soft, contemplative grunt, and drifted off toward the back bedroom without saying a word. Whether Frank was conscious of it or not, I realized he grunted as a sort of shorthand. Why say, "Follow me," or, "Come here," when a nice little grunt would do?

With some reluctance, I followed him to the back bedroom and sat on my usual chair. He untied his black walking shoes and lay back on the huge bed, exhausted from his grocery trip. After a moment of watching him rest, I said, "I'm sorry, should I leave?"

"No, no. I just need a minute." He smacked his full lips and rubbed his stocking feet together.

On the wall, to the right of his bed, stood a small table with what looked like a recently built altar of framed articles, candles and ashtrays with partially burned incense inside. Upon closer inspection, I realized it was a collection of graphic novel covers, one of which had been cut out and placed in a small gold frame, the centerpiece of the shrine.

"That your graphic novel?" I asked, pointing to the framed cover.

Frank sat up, leaning on his elbows and gave me a cold look. "You ran out of here rather hurriedly the other day."

My nerves immediately revved into high gear. I stammered a bit, then shrugged my shoulders. "Someone's been spying on me, Frank."

"I know what I look like. You think I want to live this way? I can imagine what this looks like to you."

"No, really, I—"

"You turn your back. You don't accept my money. Why are you here? Now, I mean?"

I slouched back in the chair. He'd completely ignored my reference to Motorcycle Jacket. I had to think before I spoke. My thoughts were not succinct. Something wasn't right. Then it enveloped me, the sequence of the dream I'd had with the girl drowning, her cries for help, and the evil blackness by the water—it all came flooding back.

My nose dripped blood.

A dot matrix of gray, wispy lines dances in front of my eyes. The lines widen, flatten out and become the pond. Cries for help stab my ears. I see Frank now, a smaller, younger version of him, running back and forth on the shore. He's holding a long stick in his hands, and trying desperately to reach the girl, but the stick is too heavy and long. He can't control it and she's too far out in the water. The evil darkness, like before, hovers just offshore. I can feel it coming toward me, a blanket of cold fog.

Her screams pull me into the water, across the rippling pond, closer now, her mouth open wide, hair and water rushing in, the awful gurgling as water cascades into her throat.

"Are you all right?" I yell.

A faint voice echoes in my head and pulls me back into Frank's bedroom.

Blood dripped onto my lap. I wiped my nose with the back of my sleeve. Frank held out tissues. I took them and jammed them into my face, embarrassed.

"Did you dream just now? Were you there?"

I nodded. My eyes were wet, blurring my vision. I blotted them with the back of the bloody tissues.

"I didn't mean to kill my sister." Frank's voice quivered and died as he said those words. I barely heard the word *sister*, but what he'd just said was unmistakable. He stared off, over my shoulder, toward the window.

"You didn't kill her," I said. "I saw what you did. The tree branch was too long, too heavy for you to wield, and she was too far out."

97

"I can't swim." Tears rolled down his cheeks.

"You didn't kill your sister."

"I let her drown."

"You tried to save her."

"She just…fell away into the deep water."

"You were a kid. She was too far out. It wasn't your fault."

"Is that what you saw?" He dried his eyes with a huge, navy blue hanky, then blew his nose into it. Frank smiled through red eyes and yellow stained teeth. His stringy hair fell into his face and he swept it back.

A flash of insecurity ran through me. What was he asking me? "Should I have seen something else, Frank? Am I missing something?"

He closed his eyes and was silent for a few seconds. "I don't know," came his thin, innocent-sounding voice. "I tried my best to save her but she just kept going under. Give me a minute."

We sat in silence. I could feel the afternoon shadows closing in on the street outside, but in this room, time seemed to have stopped. I squirmed in my chair and cleared my throat. Frank finally looked up at me. His irritated eyes were glazed. The large irises sat deep behind red-rimmed lids. A crooked smile curled his lips. "Yes. Yes, yes, indeed," he said, as if replaying what I'd just seen.

My heart pounded. My legs wanted to move. The powerful smell of his stale lair fought to devour what little oxygen there was. I looked out the window. Shadows filled the street below. It suddenly seemed very much darker than when I'd arrived. Frank took a deep breath and slowly let it out.

"Of course I must pay you." He fished in his wallet and pulled out two crisp one hundred dollar bills. "I trust this will cover it?"

"Is that it, then?" I asked.

"Is what it?"

"Are we resolved?"

"Finished you mean?"

I nodded in the affirmative.

"There is one other matter that I may need your help with. It's related to the last."

"I see." The reluctance in my voice was not hindered by my acceptance of the bills.

"But, that's something for another day," he said, and sat up, smiling broadly and took my hand. "For years I've..." His eyes drifted away from mine.

I waited uncomfortably for him to finish his thought, his hand, warm and clammy in mine. He took another deep breath and let it out through his nose. "For years," he repeated with special emphasis, his gaze coming back to me, "I haven't been able to shake the belief that I killed her. I killed my sister..." He smiled again and let go of my hand. Pity rose in me for this lonely, broken man.

"I'm amazed you carried that with you all this time, Frank. I feel for you."

"Don't," he said, and abruptly stood, towering over me. "A great burden has been lifted. I feel better than I have in a long time. What you saw, I envisioned also. At the same moment as you, as if our minds' eyes were connected." He tapped the side of his gargantuan head. "I was there with you, Gus. I saw what happened."

I suddenly realized why he creeped me out. Could the dark evil lurking in all of the Frank visions actually be him, now, as he was this very minute? The Fat Man, skulking, watching my dream unfold, with our minds linked in a bizarre fusion of psychic energy. Could his presence actually be seen and felt in my visions?

"You were there how?" I asked.

"I was there in every way."

We locked eyes. A chill ran up my legs and back down my spine, fluttering on my skin like a thousand moths. His gaze dug deep into me. I could feel his will attempting to strangle my soul. I swallowed hard, and pushed myself to ask the next question.

"When we first met, you said you were worried about your sister."

He nodded slightly.

"But if she's dead..."

He stared blankly at me. "Yes," he said, and offered no explanation.

I took his silence as a caution not to go there, but I chanced it anyway. "I can't tell where she is now, Frank. I can only see what may have happened in the past." Again, he made no effort to answer, but kept that blank look on his face. "I understand you're into the supernatural. Witchcraft and all that..."

Shrugging, he pointed to the framed picture of the druid graphic novel he'd penned. "I'm not really into that stuff. It's just for research."

I nodded, but didn't believe a word he said. About anything.

We walked into the kitchen, past the tools of his strange research, the conjuring wand, the carved cane, the pile of black laundry, the books on Wicca and neo-Druids, and he stopped me by placing a hand on my shoulder as we reached the door.

"About your talent. I need to know what you're capable of."

I could ask the same of you, I thought. I muttered an affirmative under my breath and shrugged.

"What I'd really like to delve into is your power within in the vision. I mean, are you all-powerful, omniscient in the visions? Can you manipulate time, stop and start things, be in control? Just what can you do?"

"I'm not sure," I lied. "I've never tried to do any of those things." Except for looking in the glove box and reading the registration of Carrillo's car, and reliving Emma's death over and over from different angles, and, well, you get the idea.

"I may need you to...There's a vexing problem I need your help with."

"Yeah?"

His belly shook with quick, hollow laughter. "Another time, Gus. Soon, but not now."

I nodded at his odd outburst. He was obviously still buoyed by our little breakthrough. I found myself out in the hallway looking at the two crisp one hundred dollar bills in my hand, and wondering how doing something so odd, so chilling, could ever be worth it to me.

When I reached the street outside Frank's apartment, my cell phone rang. It was Mill.

"I've got the dirt on the Motorcycle Jacket."

"That was fast."

"Hold on to your stuffed rabbit, you're not going to believe this. He worked for Carrillo."

"Holy shit, Mill."

"His name is Justin Colling. He was an associate investigator at Carrillo's company. There's still a photo of him on Carrillo's old website."

"You know what this means, Mill?" I asked. "The Fat Man didn't send him after me, someone connected to Carrillo did. And he'd tracked me to the Fat Man. Motorcycle Jacket is an agent for Carrillo and now probably works for his cohort, Bruno."

"That about sums it up," Mill said.

"Any mention of Bruno?" I asked.

"No. He seems to be out of the picture now."

"Well, I'm not ruling anything out at this point."

"Absolutely. Better to be thorough."

"We'll talk later." I disconnected the call.

This blew everything wide open. The surveillance by Motorcycle Jacket had absolutely nothing to do with the Fat Man, and everything to do with Emma and her connections. Looking back, I suddenly realized Justin Colling, AKA Motorcycle Jacket, had shown up before I talked with Carla that day in the park. That didn't make any sense. How had he known? The connection was not apparent, but I felt that someone from Carrillo's world was locked in on me before Carla had even reached out to me. How long had they been watching me? Paranoia began creeping into my thinking. Suddenly, Frank felt like a warm, fuzzy teddy bear. And now I knew that Carrillo had definitely been involved in Emma's death, and whatever motive they had for wanting her dead was still a weakness they needed to protect.

I turned around and walked back to Frank's apartment and knocked on his door. I wanted to ask him if Motorcycle Jacket had actually talked to him or had simply checked on my recent rendezvous, collecting information, names and addresses, perhaps. I knocked lightly a few times and then tried the handle. It was unlocked. I made my way through the kitchen and down the hallway, where I heard voices in conversation.

"I told you to leave me alone!" Frank's voice held a fiercely desperate quality I hadn't heard before. "Why are you doing this?"

The other voice spoke. "Because you have to pay."

Frank's voice again, only higher pitched. "I pay and pay! I pay every day!"

I cleared my throat to see what reaction I'd get. Silence stilled the atmosphere.

"Frank?" I called. No answer. Not a sound. The floorboards squeaked underfoot as I made my way toward the bedroom. "Frank?"

No answer.

"Frank, I forgot to ask you something."

The bedroom door was ajar. I slowly pushed it open.

Frank was shirtless, sitting up on the bed. His face and chest was smeared with chocolate, his eyes unfixed, staring at nothing. Candy bar wrappers covered his legs.

"Frank?"

Slowly gaining focus, he turned toward me. His hair was flying in all directions, his mouth and cheeks covered in sweet goo. He sucked and licked each of his fingers and thumbs.

"Are you okay?" I asked.

A wry, childlike smile broadened his face. Snorting, he ran the palm of his hand up over the front of his nose, pushing it into the shape of a pig snout, sucked in and let it go. His bloodshot eyes rolled toward me but didn't meet mine.

"Now you know my torment, Gus. You see how I can't go on like this?"

"What's wrong, Frank?"

"Wrong?" He looked at me, his eyebrows raised and twisted in a tortured expression of grief. "Everything."

"Okay, let's start at the beginning."

"We pay for our sins, Gus, one way or another, we all pay."

"I suppose."

"And each in our own way, we cope, make amends, regroup, and push on. We do what we can."

"Yes, we do." I said.

"And sometimes we have to think outside the box." I nodded. *The chocolate box.* "I hate that expression, Gus. I didn't know what it meant the first time I heard it. I suppose that means I can't think outside the box, huh? Or, that I was never in one." He smiled again. "Indeed. Never in one," he repeated, his voice trailing off. He took another deep breath and I sensed his focus beginning to wane, perhaps from all that sugar.

"Frank, I need to know if a guy in a motorcycle jacket came to see you a few days ago, asking questions. A skinny-looking dude, with red hair?"

"A dude?"

"It's important, Frank. I need to know what he asked you."

"The thing is, Gus, she never leaves my side. Always there, everywhere I go, she shows up to spoil it. Ridiculing me and taunting me. Second guessing my every move." He sighed.

"Frank, I'm talking about the Motorcycle Jacket man."

"Kate."

"Your sister?"

Quickly covering his face in his hands, he turned shamefully toward me again, as if to confirm I was really there. "It started in high school. She'd follow me in the halls, tormenting me, asking me questions. I managed to force her away through a series of spells I'd discovered in an old book on such things. She stayed away until my second year at Bard."

"Bard. Liberal arts school," I said.

"She came back with a vengeance then. It started one morning before early classes. I was on campus, in the cafeteria, fighting off a hangover of cigarettes, beer and pot. I sat quietly with my tray, trying to get myself motivated, when she appeared across the table from me. She was older than ten. She'd kept aging. You understand how grotesque that is? How that affected me? That told me, made it very obvious, that life did indeed continue after death."

I nodded slowly, wondering how a spirit could age when it had no body and, supposedly, was no longer tied to our world.

"She started out pleasantly enough, telling me I looked good, hoped I was doing well and all that, but I rejected her. I threw my coffee at her and made a run for the door. She followed me, calling me names, swearing, ridiculing the way I looked, walked, talked, my ignorance on so many matters, my ineffectual, indecisive nature." He looked up, a defensive sneer on his face. "You think I was born this way? Fat and ugly? I'm not stupid! I know what I look like. This is her revenge. It's what she's made me into!"

Tears ran down his cheeks and he smeared them with the bed sheets and chocolate. Pity rose in me and beat back my urge to run away. I sat awkwardly in the chair at the foot of his bed.

"As time went by, I realized she would never leave me. She's always around the next corner, in the next room, waiting for me. I began to avoid places she might be. Eventually, I learned to control her apparition by applying various incantations and spells. Keeping her at bay was my primary objective. She would haunt me otherwise, and I'm now convinced, she'll haunt me in the next life, too. But at least then we'll be on equal footing, and I'll have a chance to confront her."

"Frank, you can't actually believe…Your sister's a spirit?"

He slowly nodded. "Torments me to my soul."

"Why would she? What reason would she have?"

"One does not reason with the damned."

"The damned?"

"You don't know the things she did to me as a child. She died with evil in her soul, blackness has kept her spirit vital, expressive, her need to torture and ridicule fuels her being."

"She was ten years old. How evil could she be?" I said, wondering if I should even try reasoning with him. His madness was apparent, but I was not yet certain if I should call 911 or simply leave him to his self-imposed penitentiary.

"Evil rears up at an early age in us all, Gus. And if a person is not strong, cannot see past negative gratification, or cultivate or appreciate the good in people, they become lazy, indolent, possessive and manipulative in all things. Then that manifestation of evil grows, from a seed to a sapling, needing to be fed, and the child knows not but to replicate evil aspirations, garnering false climaxes, repetitively, exhaustively, concurrently, never achieving true fulfillment."

"You've thought this through. But Frank, really, I don't think I'm the one to help you."

He stared at me, his fat belly billowing with each tortured breath, chocolate smears spreading out on his skin like melanoma. "Oh, but you are the one, Gus. Your gift is the key to setting me free. You can go into your Dream State and reason with her, stop her, finally."

I shook my head. He was madder than I'd thought. I stood up to leave. He leaped from the bed with the agility of a bull moose, and stood next to me, taking hold of my arm.

"I have a plan," he blurted out. "I know how to defeat her. It will work!"

"What am I, Harry Potter? It's not going to happen, Frank!"

I turned to leave. He tore at my jacket, pulling my arm out of the sleeve. I struggled out of his grip, pushing my way down the hallway, toppling boxes in my wake.

"I know it will work!" His lumbering bulk cascaded down the

hallway like a herd of wild buffalo. I ran through the kitchen and slammed the door shut, bounced off the stair rail, and flew down the hallway and the steps below. I made my way to the outer door, shocked and amazed I'd gotten there without killing myself in a tumble. I heard his voice echoing through the halls behind me, "I'll pay! Gus! Gus! Come back! I've got money!"

I ran two blocks before I could look back to see if he was following me.

15
DESIRE IS A WONDERFUL THING

The next day, I called Carla and asked her to meet me at Delish, the tiny Italian restaurant across from my apartment. She wasn't overly eager to meet after our last chat. However, what I promised must have given her inspiration, because she was there in half an hour.

I was late getting there, and walked in to see her seated at a far corner table. I ordered a slice and a Coke, and sat down across from her. She was stunning, in an astringent sort of way. She wore green medical scrubs, and her hair was tied back into a short ponytail.

"You're a nurse," I said, as I sipped my drink.

"Nursing supervisor."

"Where?"

"Sloan Kettering."

"The cancer hospital?"

She nodded. Her slight, half smile contrasted with the seriousness of her gaze. Suddenly, the gravity with which she considered things made perfect sense. Here was a woman who emerged daily from the horrible drama of life and death, the almost matter-of-fact pain and suffering of the human body and spirit, providing comfort, lessening grief and sorrow, denying the human condition, knowing we are all dying a little bit every day and in varying degrees of suffering, and now at my beckoning has to sit in a greasy pizza parlor and listen to my theories about the Dream State.

Good God, no wonder she had little use for me.

"You look beautiful." Before the words left my lips I could feel my face flush, the rush of adrenalin course through my chest. My heart beat loudly in my ears. I immediately apologized, looking down at my soda, the pizza slice going cold.

She smiled. "No, that's okay. It's nice to hear once in a while."

I nodded and took a deep breath, trying to slow my heart rate. *God, had I just hit on her?* Nurses in uniform are walking angels, to be adored and lusted after, but mostly just admired.

"I bet you get that all the time," I said.

"Not often enough."

I smiled. She began to look nervous. "Tell me about your sister's connection to the college. NYU, right?"

"Well, she worked for a professor, as an intern, did most of his paperwork."

I interrupted. "His name was Michael Steen Phelps, PhD, professor of economics."

"Yes," she said, "how did you get that?"

"Pretty basic stuff. I have reason to believe someone at her job was involved in her murder. Or at the very least, this person witnessed her murder."

"Who?"

"A man named Pablo Carrillo. He worked at the school."

Carla wiped tears from her eyes. "I'm sorry. This is all still raw," she said.

"I know," I said, and I touched the back of her hand with my fingers. She gently pulled hers back, not wanting to insult me, but simply let me know she wasn't looking for that.

"I have a few leads," I said, "but Carrillo is dead. Killed in a car crash. Others, people who worked with Carrillo, may be involved. I can't go into details now. I just wanted to let you know." She nodded. "I need for you to tell me everything you know about the school and Emma's job there."

"How do you know about this guy?"

"Carrillo?" I asked.

"Yes. Was Carrillo there when Emma was killed?"

"Yes, I saw him there." I sat back, waiting for the fireworks.

"You mean, as in a dream?"

"That's right."

Her face grew tense, her lips pursed and she turned her head. "We could have done this over the phone," she said, finally.

I was startled by her response, but chose not to take it personally. "Of course, I understand if this is a bad time. You have to get to work. I just wanted to reassure you, in person, that we are making headway."

She nodded, and wiped her nose with the napkin.

"Did anyone from the school show up to her funeral?"

Carla thought a minute. "Several people. Co-workers, some strangers who had an affiliation with the school. A few others I didn't know.

"What about her boss, Professor Phelps?"

"I think he sent flowers."

"He didn't show?"

"No. We thought that was kind of strange. He was supposedly out of town on a business trip, or something."

I nodded, holding back a snide comment. She worked for him, yet he couldn't face the family or go to her funeral. It occurred to me that Phelps might have been wracked with guilt or fear.

"Did Phelps have any other contact with your family?" I asked.

"Not that I am aware of."

"Anything strange or out of the ordinary happen in your life lately?"

"You mean besides meeting a psychic detective?"

I smiled, acknowledging her little joke. "Like someone following you. For example, do you keep noticing the same person or face in a crowd? That sort of thing?"

She thought for a second. "Not that I can recall."

I nodded. "Well, a guy who worked with Carrillo named Justin Colling has been following me. I took his picture." I showed her the cell phone photo. Her eyes grew large as she stared, but nothing alarming seemed to register. "Have you seen him before?" I asked.

"I think I have, yes. Outside my apartment. He was hanging around for a few days last week, working on a motorcycle. Who is he again?"

"Justin Colling. He worked for Carrillo."

"And Carrillo is dead, right?"

"That's right."

"Then why would he follow me? What does he want?" she asked.

"I don't know. Loose ends maybe? Something to do with you and me meeting up? This all started just before you phoned me. Did you tell anyone you were going to call me?"

"No. I didn't tell anyone. Well, I did call my friend and tell him. The one who stood by at the Boat House."

"Right. I remember. Did this friend of yours have any affiliation with the school?"

"Who, Jim? None whatsoever. He's a nurse."

I showed her the digital photo again. Colling appeared startled, his red hair splayed out in all directions, his frown seemed menacing, but his eyes showed fear. "He's been made and he knows it. Now it's my turn to spy on him."

"Okay. So, why couldn't we do this over the internet?"

That question hit hard. *Why indeed?* I couldn't tell her that I just liked her. That she was beautiful and I liked talking to her, maybe wanted get to know her better.

"This type of thing, this personal connection with the deceased, demands we meet in person in order to gauge our trust. If you don't trust me, I can't do my job." It was a crock of shit, but I had to try. Then I added the *coup de grâce*. "Besides, I needed for you to see this

110

photo of Colling. Picking your brains on the phone or the internet just doesn't cut it." She looked at me with expressionless eyes, as if she'd heard it all before and wasn't buying. Or maybe I was just being too sensitive. I added, "How else was I gonna see if Motorcycle Jacket was still following me, or you? It's the way I work. I'm sorry if I dragged you all the way uptown to disappoint you."

"No, no." She shook her head. "I understand. You're right: it does demand personal attention to detail. I get it."

"If you see this guy, if he comes around, call me. Even if you only *think* it's him, call me."

"I will." She sat back, a blank look on her face. I could tell she was racing through the last few weeks, replaying any and all encounters. Had she really seen this guy, was he lurking somewhere and she hadn't noticed?

"It gets you thinking, doesn't it?" I asked.

"Yes. I'm pretty alert, raised in the city."

"But that may go against you, if you've become too blasé."

"I'll be more aware."

"The other thing I need to know is what Emma did, exactly. What was her routine, all her acquaintances, that sort of thing? You can call or email that info, but I need details."

"No, that's fine." She glanced at her watch. "I have to get going. I'm glad you called."

"Are you?" I asked.

"Yes, but I'm a little freaked out about this guy, Colling, hanging around outside my apartment. Should I call the police if I see him?"

"If it will make you feel better. I don't see how it would hurt. Just call me as well."

"I'm creeped out."

"Me too," I said.

Her furrowed brow betrayed the gravity of her mood. I walked her to the door. She hailed a taxi and turned to me. "I think you're starting to make headway, Gus. Thank you."

I caught a glimpse of a smile as she got into the cab. That slight chink in her armor made my head tingle. I watched her cab move slowly down Second Avenue until it disappeared in traffic. I casually scanned the area. Colling was nowhere to be seen.

16
A STRIPE OF ANY OTHER COLOR

S *oft candlelight illuminates her as I run my hand up her creamy thigh. The warmth of her skin radiates through my fingers, warming my hand. Her lush, complex smell, a mix of perfume, moist sweat, and shampoo is intoxicating. She gazes into my eyes as our bodies lock together. Diana's cobalt blue irises hold me spellbound, and I kiss her nose, her eyes, her chin. Oh God, it has been so long. Why have we been apart?*

A wave of mistrust runs through my gut. A little voice says, "Because she left you, fool." I look again into her eyes, and see no love there, only cold emptiness. Her sweet smile turns to choking laughter. Suddenly, I'm standing at the open door to my apartment, the cold wind howling at me, freezing me in place, naked, shivering and alone. A frigid gust rakes across my face, and my stinging ears ring in my head.

"Diana, don't leave me."

Her face draws close to mine and she hisses like a snake, opening her mouth. Thin, hollow fangs pop out from her smile and drip liquid poison. The voice is louder now, sounding like a parrot on a game show, "You're a fool! You're a fool!" Her laughter grows louder and harder until it turns into bells ringing in my ears, and I feel my head will explode.

I sit up in bed, gasping for air. Shivering. Afraid.

I opened my eyes to see a faint light illuminating just enough of my bedroom to realize I was awake, and had been dreaming. The covers were balled up on the floor next to the bed. I was buck naked and freezing. I grabbed the covers and wrapped myself back up. The amber readout on my alarm clock read 2:30 a.m. I sucked in breaths to calm the pounding pulse in my head. Then I realized the ringing of the telephone had awakened me. After several rings, the machine picked up. It was one of those old-fashioned message machines that comes built into the phone.

After hearing my voice telling the caller to leave a message, I heard this little gem: *"Waldo? Hey, Waldo? Where's my Waldo? Waldoooo? Ooh, I'm a psychic! Hey, what am I thinking? How about now?"* Then hysterical cackling until the line clicked dead.

Maybe listing my home phone number in *The Village Voice* wasn't the best idea I'd ever had. I made a note to torture Mill for talking me into placing that stupid classified. What was I doing listening to Mill, anyway?

17
ARE YOU SKITCHING ME?

I saw him in a nasty little dream that kept repeating at regular intervals. The kid on a skateboard had been haunting me for a few weeks now, and as much as I tried to put the dream out of my head and concentrate on Emma and the Fat Man, I just couldn't let it go. Probably because he was an innocent kid, around sixteen, and he'd gotten his head squashed under a city bus. At least in the dream he did. I was pretty sure he was still alive and maybe skated at Tribeca Skate Park.

Every few days, I tried to make it down to Tribeca to see if he was among the kids skating in the park, see if maybe I could talk some sense into him.

So, late one morning, I rode a bus downtown to see if I could find him. I was let off right in front of the park. A few kids stood around just outside the skate area, talking among themselves. I walked close to the fence separating me from the park and tried to make out a few faces. In the dream, Skateboard Kid had reddish brown hair, a ruddy complexion and a bad case of acne. He was skinny, and seemed a happy, gentle soul.

I wasn't having any luck finding him and was beginning to think I'd never see him outside of an obit in the *Times*. Aggressive action was needed, so I leaned into the fence and called to one of the skaters.

"Hey, kid. Come here."

Three teens stood talking to each other about twenty feet away, on the other side of the fence. Standing on their boards, flipping them, riding in little circles and talking shop, I supposed, all three casually looked at me, then turned away.

"Hey, I'm looking for somebody. Maybe skates here."

They looked at me disdainfully, then turned to chat some more.

"Hey come on, guys," I said.

"Fuck off," one kid said, and flicked a cigarette toward me.

"He gets his head bashed in hanging onto the back of a truck. You do that? Hang onto moving trucks?"

An older-looking dude flipped his board into his hands and walked over to me.

"I'm looking for my nephew," I lied. "Have you seen him?"

The guy was about thirty-five, round head, short black hair, and had a thick full day of growth on his face. I wondered why he was still hanging around skate parks.

"What's his name?" he asked.

"Ah, he's got red hair. Reddish complexion."

"His name?"

"Bad acne on his face. Skinny—"

The guy turned away in disgust.

After a few minutes, the cigarette flicker came over and stared at me through the fence.

"I'm worried about my nephew," I said.

He leaned toward me. "How about I shove this board through your skull and wear you on my board's deck?"

"Why would you do that? I'm only looking for the kid."

He took out another cigarette, lit it and blew smoke at me while giving me the stink-eye.

"He's about sixteen. Red hair, zits on his face. Skinny."

"What about him?" He took a deep drag and, in what I suspected was a well-practiced move, blew the smoke sideways from his mouth.

"He grabs onto cars and trucks, takes rides, you know? They pull him on his board."

"Yeah?"

"Isn't it dangerous?"

He shrugged. "Depends if you can ride."

"It seems nuts to me."

"Skitching is the bomb, man. We all do it. What's this grommet's name, dude?"

"Look, I just want to ask him something."

He took another deep drag and let it out, closing one eye from the smoke. Another well-practiced move. "Did he dent your ride, man?"

"No, I'm not saying that. All I need to know is if you've seen him around?"

The kid dropped his board onto the ground and flipped me the bird as he rolled away.

They must get a lot of perverts hanging around the park, I thought. That's the only thing I could figure. I looked around. There were no more kids on the street. I decided to wait for the next bus uptown. If Skateboard Kid showed in the next twenty minutes, I'd grab him and give him the talk. If not, so be it, I'd have tried.

Ten minutes later a city bus pulled up. As I waited for people to exit, the kid from my dream stepped off the bus. He was toting a black and red skateboard and a backpack, had on a red hoodie, tight black jeans and, of course, skate shoes.

"Hey!" I said, but it came out louder than I wanted. The few people getting off the bus, including Skateboard Kid, looked my way, then scattered in all directions, like I was a crazy person. A few of them walked toward the park, along with Skateboard Kid.

I ran to catch up to them and touched Skateboard Kid's shoulder. He turned to face me, a look of fear and anger on his face. "Hey, fuck off, man!" he shouted at me.

It was startling to see him in Technicolor. His green eyes were alert, intelligent. I could tell something was going on behind them. A silver labret piercing just below his lower lip looked new. The skin around it was slightly inflamed, as was the huge red zit on the end of his nose—the headless kind that really hurts.

"Sorry, sorry," I said. "I was hoping you could help me."

Skateboard Kid looked me up and down and backed away a few steps.

I held up my hands to show him I wasn't going to hurt him. I knew I'd already messed up by coming on too strong and held out little hope of salvaging the situation. "Listen, my nephew is coming to visit me for a few weeks. Is this the best place around to board?"

"Yeah, best place," he said, looking completely uninterested in having anything to do with the crazy asshole harassing him.

"Hey, don't I know you?" I asked.

"Don't think so." He kept walking, picking up a little more speed.

"Do any skitching lately?"

He stopped about ten feet away from me and squinted, as if trying to remember who he'd pissed off.

"No, no, I'm not a cop or anything. I'm just curious how you do it? Isn't it dangerous? Don't kids get killed doing that?" He made a move toward the park, then quickly turned back to me.

"I don't know you, man."

"Look, I'm a writer, for the *Voice*. I'm writing an article about boarding in the city. You know, a fun piece about the sport." A spark lit his eyes. "Yeah, my boss, the editor, what an asshole, he's been on me to get some stuff from the kids skating around here, you know? I mean, who says the West Coast has the best boarders, right?" He frowned and literally rolled his eyes at me. "Anyway, I was hoping you could help. What's your name, anyways?"

"Don't talk to this asshole!" Cigarette Boy strode over to Skateboard Kid and stood by his side. They bumped knuckles. "This perv's been snooping around looking to get some grommet ass. I've seen him here twice already."

"Hey, that's not true. I don't even know what a grommet is," I said.

"Fuck you, man," said Skateboard Kid.

Great.

They chuckled and high-fived each other and turned away. Then Cigarette Boy made a quick turn and lunged at me, jabbing at my stomach with his board, contacting me just enough to make it hurt.

"Ow! Hey, that's assault!" I yelled, surprised by his aggressiveness.

"So is taking it up the little grommet ass, douche." They snickered and walked into the park.

"Look," I yelled after them, "I know you guys grab rides on cars and it's dangerous! You got that? Kids get killed every day! Boarders like yourselves. Experienced boarders!"

The round-headed guy flipped his board up to his hands and walked over to me. I took a few steps back, putting my arms up to protect myself.

"I'm just trying to help the kid," I said. "I saw him almost get his head busted the other day. It's crazy."

"That's why they do it, fuckwad." He looked disgustedly at me then said, "Partly."

"Yeah? What's the other part?"

"Catch a ride, man."

We stood staring at each other. I began to feel queasy. The thought of Skateboard Kid sliding under a bus and getting his skull crushed nauseated me. But these kids had no interest in listening. How many times was I going to get the shit kicked out of me trying to save someone's ass?

"What's the kid's name? Can you at least tell me that?"

Round Head looked me up and down, and apparently decided I wasn't a perv, or maybe just a harmless one. "That's Luke." I noticed a slight accent. Eastern European, perhaps. "Now go. You make me nervous looking at the boys." He turned toward the kids hovering around the park, some talking in small groups, some riding tricks. I realized he probably worked there, maybe even ran the place. Or he just hung out to protect the younger ones.

"I'm not a pervert," I said. "I just—"

He balled his fists and stared at me. I could see the agitation rising in him and thought he was about to become violent or worse, call the cops, and I completely deflated. What's the use? Notch another failure on my belt.

"Thanks," I said and turned to head back toward the bus stop.

There's no way I could save everybody. I guess it was about time to learn that lesson. But it still hurt to let it go.

18
A TREASURE OF TALENT

We met at my favorite diner, the Blue Athena, on Second Avenue near Eighty-Sixth Street. It was a typical hole-in-the-wall featuring gargantuan breakfast platters, a smattering of Greek and American fare, and poorly painted murals of Mediterranean vistas. It was unique in Manhattan in that it was still open after five years. Most places came and went with the seasons, the rents too high for anything but instant success. Anything less and the doors closed within weeks of opening. It was a wonder any mom and pop stores still existed in the city. And that homey charm was part of the reason I frequented the Blue Athena.

Niko, the owner, was a short, middle-aged guy with a toothy smile. He bustled about taking orders and cleaning tables, an undercurrent of tension about him, making the rent probably not far from his mind. He greeted everyone with a warm, *How are you, my friend?* even though he'd probably never seen them before or, if he had, didn't remember who they were.

His daughter, Lucy—a pretty teenager with dark hair and olive complexion, fighting a bit of acne on her cheeks—was a part-time waitress and one of my favorite servers. Her sienna eyes were bright, her manner was charming, and if you were lucky enough to have a chat with her, you'd realize she was sharp as a tack. She was an honor student at some private school in the neighborhood.

I arrived early and sat in a small booth in the back. Lucy came over, offering her usual charming smile. I ordered a turkey club and coffee.

Mill had been very excited when he called earlier and insisted we meet right away. On the phone, he wouldn't tell me what it was about, other than to say he'd found buried treasure and wasn't sure what the hell I was going to do once I saw it.

"You spend treasure," I said.

"This type of treasure could turn to poison."

That piqued my interest, but he insisted on telling me the details in person.

Lucy brought my turkey club. I asked her about school and she blushed a bit, talking about soccer and choir, and her interest in going to Columbia next fall. I was warmed by her sincerity.

Halfway into my sandwich, I saw Mill snooping around outside the diner. He stood with his back to the front door, then turned quickly, cupping his hands on the window and peering inside. He caught sight of me, looked around outside again, then darted inside. He sat down hard, almost knocking over my coffee.

"Hey. What the hell, Mill?"

"Shit, man. You're gonna love this. Shit!"

"Stop saying that. I'm trying to eat."

He grabbed a fry off my plate. "Chicken salad?"

"Turkey. What have you got?"

"Only the whole freaking connection between Carrillo, Emma and the mighty Professor Phelps."

"You got all three connected? How?" I asked.

"I dug, baby. Dug for gold!"

I took a sip of coffee and stared at him. His face was flush and his eyes sparkled with excitement. "So? You're not gonna say something stupid, like you found the glory hole, are you?" I asked.

"You don't pay me enough for this shit."

"Again with the S-word."

"Sorry." Mill looked around nervously, squirmed in his seat, then grabbed another fry from my plate.

"Do me a favor, will you?" I said. "Just calm down. Relax. You look like a crazy person standing in the middle of freeway traffic."

He placed a small backpack on the bench seat and pulled out some papers. He spread them onto the table, like a winning poker hand.

"What's this?" I asked.

"Okay, here goes." Mill took a deep breath, like he was about to unload a mouthful. "Let's talk Cap and Trade scams, CIA money and secret files for dirty dealings in Central America."

I stared at him. "What?"

"A phony company used to raise slush funds. Let's talk the smoking freaking gun, baby!"

"You know who killed Emma?"

"No. Yes. Well, no," he said. "But I think I know *why* she was killed."

"Okay, start at the beginning, Einstein. Tell me all."

"I'm the freaking Hacker King, Gus. You know I'm the king. Say it."

I hesitated, then decided to play along. "Okay, you're the king."

"No, no. I'm the Hacker King."

"Okay, you're the Hacker King."

"And I command all respect from peons near and far."

"I think I prefer you as a disillusioned lush."

"Ow! My delicate sensibilities. Don't say things like that. I stopped saying shit didn't I?"

I dropped what was left of my sandwich, a few crusts with mayo, down on my plate. "Okay, Mill. What's the story?"

"Man, we got layers upon layers here, Gus. I don't think you're quite ready for this stuff."

"Just spill it."

"Okay." He blinked twice at me, like he was resetting his brain, then carefully began to uncover one printed page after the next. "Carrillo, your dead bridge accident guy?"

"Carrillo, yeah, go on."

"You remember he had a connection to Army Intelligence?"

"That's what the paper said."

"Well, it goes beyond that. I think he was CIA."

"Why do you say that?"

"Because, when the investigation into the phony energy company, Aileron Energy Trading, or AET, was being built by the Manhattan DA, Carrillo was about to be indicted as one of the principals in that company. But it was suddenly dropped. The whole investigation was dropped, for no apparent reason."

"Huh. No reason apparent to you. Could be a viable explanation for that. And?"

He looked down at the papers and back at me. He blinked a few quick, fluttering blinks, like he'd been rebooted, then grabbed another paper. "Okay, I found some investigative reporter stuff from a guy at the *Times*. His name is Guy Jackson. He's their White Collar reporter. He wrote something about the whole operation being a front for CIA funny money. CIA funds garnered from a front company in the Cap and Trade Energy market, namely, AET. That's the same company."

"CIA?" I said. "This is some crazy shit, Mill. Where did you get this?"

"I pieced it together from articles, and I got into the DA's computer files. I couldn't go very deep but I found a few emails an assistant DA had labeled AET."

"Holy shit. You hacked an Assistant DA's email? You can do that?"

He gave me blank look that said, *Who do you think I am?* "I went phishing and she bit."

I stared at him as he beamed. "Holy shit."

He frowned at me. "Now who's saying that word?"

I laughed and said, "I guess I'm starting to get the picture, although it sounds completely incredible to me. What about the professor?"

"What about him?"

"How does he fit into this?"

"Well, the way I see it, the professor was a front for AET, the phony energy trading company, and it was backed with CIA support. You see, they needed a front, someone with a legit connection to that game. The professor used to be in a company called EEG, Incorporated, aka Electron Energy Group."

"EEG," I repeated.

"Yeah, apparently there's a rule they have to use initials in the company name or something." He laughed and waited for me to react to his little joke, but I said nothing. "Anyway..."

Lucy poured me some more coffee and left the check. I smiled and thanked her. Mill stared at her butt as she walked away.

"She's seventeen, Mill."

He turned quickly back to the papers on the table. "Anyway," he continued, "our professor sold his shares in the old company and retired a while ago after making a killing, but got back into teaching last year. He was filthy rich, but lost a lot of it in a nasty divorce."

"Divorce will do that," I said.

He looked at me like I had three heads. "Ah, yeah, I'm gonna have that tattooed across my ass...So, now the professor is under a cloud of suspicion *and* he lost the rest of his money when the energy market crashed. They were overextended and couldn't pay off their debt in time. They went bust."

"So, the professor lost all his dough and now he's back teaching?"

"He may even lose that job if he gets indicted for fraud, which is what the DA is hot for."

"Wow. What about Emma? Where's the connection?"

"Oh, Emma, poor baby. The way I see it, the possibilities are A: She found out about the phony company being a CIA front and got whacked—"

"That would explain the Carrillo connection. If he was a trained killer for the CIA," I said.

"Yeah, nice guy, huh? Or B: she had an affair with the ol' professor and ended it; maybe she threatened to expose him. Either that or he's just a mean prick and killed her out of spite. You've got to remember, she was working for him during the heyday of this whole energy thing. She could have gotten caught up in some bad shit."

"Or it could have been a crime of passion," I said.

"Yeah. That's B. A crime of passion." Mill's voice trailed off as he looked out the window. I followed his eyes and saw he was staring at the mailman.

"I know that guy, Mill. He's okay."

Mill gave me an uncertain, almost helpless look for a second, then went back to his usual stare.

"I don't know, Mill, this is leading into some awful deep water."

"Tell me about it. I'm seeing CIA everywhere I go." He lowered his voice. "I mean, holy shit! I don't want to get whacked, you know?"

"They don't know what we know, Mill. We're not even a blip on the radar. We don't even know if there is a *they* anymore. I mean, the energy company is gone now, right?"

"Yeah," he said, nodding. "Defunct. All the principals are either dead, or about to be indicted, except for Bruno, who got a free pass. You can forget Bruno. He's long gone. I couldn't find anything about him." He grabbed a pouch of white table sugar and squeezed it between his fingers as he talked. "Look, the only reason we connected Carrillo to this is because you saw him in your dream, right?"

"Yes."

"A dream! Shit. Otherwise, I mean, from what I read, the cops have no leads in Emma's murder case and aren't even close to seeing a connection with Carrillo." I nodded in agreement. "Otherwise, it would be in the ADA's email. And now he's dead,' Mill continued.

"So we can't get to him. The DA, the cops, or whoever investigated Emma's death didn't find a thing. Called it a random killing."

"That's what Carla told me, too."

"Yeah, Carla." A twinkle lit his eye.

"She's just a client," I said.

"Yeah, of course she is," he said, with tongue firmly planted in cheek.

"Move on," I said, perhaps more sternly than I wanted.

He batted his eyes again then said, "Oh. Okay…So, either the professor did it, or had someone do it. Or the CIA goons found out she knew too much and they whacked her."

I nodded. "And in that case..."

Mill rubbed his face and took a deep breath. "We're treading on some serious ground here, Gus. Serious ground."

I took a sip of coffee and thought for a second. "Tell me about this energy Cap and Trade. What is it, exactly?"

"Okay. When the government decided it was time to reduce air pollution, it created these credits, these energy credits. Each polluter was allotted so many of them based on their annual production of pollution, what they produced in pollution by the pound. So, each credit represents a certain amount of allowable pollution. If a company doesn't use all their credits—let's say they are able to reduce the amount of pollution they produce because of improvements in equipment or whatever—they are allowed to sell off the leftover credits to another polluter, or even put them up for bid on the open market. Because of this, these trading companies were created, these energy trading companies—"

"Like the professor's first company," I interrupted.

"Exactly. These companies were like brokers, created to find buyers and expedite the credit transactions. With each sale, they got a commission, usually something like six percent of the sale price."

"So the professor made a killing doing this?"

"One trade could be worth hundreds of thousands in

commission." I whistled. "Then he got out when the getting was good," Mill continued, "but the old ball and chain took half of everything. So, he decided to teach again. That's how he'd started out, teaching economics at a university."

"I see," I said, trying to grasp the concept of selling allowable pollution. I sat quietly for a few moments, letting this information sink in. "So, then the CIA wanted to make some money, and somehow they got involved in energy credit trading?"

"That part I'm not too sure about. It was in the *Times* article. I tried following up on it and got nowhere. It appears the story was dropped, along with the whole case against the fraudulent company. But the DA is still investigating the professor and others for their role in the company."

"So, what you're saying is, someone got greedy, and they promised to sell energy credits they didn't have?"

"No, no, they didn't just promise. They *sold* credits they didn't have. They said they had them, but they shorted a few companies and got caught." I drank the last of my coffee and sat back. "The freakin' CIA, Gus," Mill said, his eyes again wandering to the windows, checking the foot traffic outside. "You remember that Robert Redford movie, *Three Days of the Condor*?"

I shook my head.

"The CIA shot up a roomful of people who found out about some of their funny business."

"That was a movie," I said.

"And we just found a CIA front."

I shook my head again and took a deep breath. This was leading to places I'd never imagined, and really didn't want to delve into. The issues at hand were sobering. Much more complex than I had ever anticipated. Best thing to do was to skirt the whole mess. "This doesn't have to involve us directly," I said. "We don't need to understand the energy trading business, for now. Is there a way you can send files to the DA, anonymously, showing a link between

Carrillo and Emma?"

"I suppose," Mill said, but he seemed unsure. "There's no guarantee those knuckleheads at the DA's office will even know what they have in their hands. Maybe if I spell it out for them..."

"Write them a nice note. Spell it all out in a letter."

Mill nodded.

I pointed to the papers spread out on the table. "Why don't I bring this stuff home and take a long look at it? Sort it all out. See where we want to head with it, then we can write that note together. Maybe we can work the system for Emma."

"For Emma," Mill said, and gathered up the papers into a neat pile and handed them to me.

Dig deep and weep, said a voice in my head. *Somebody's gonna pay for Emma.* "Meantime," I said, "I want to see what Carla is up to, make sure she isn't in any danger. Colling has been following both of us. You get anything on him, by the way?"

"Motorcycle Jacket? Nothing beyond him working for a security company tied to Carrillo."

"He's probably just a flunky looking for loose ends," I said. "I want to know why he's so interested in Carla. Why he follows everyone she talks to. And how did he know I was going to meet with her before I did?"

"That's a brilliant observation, Gus," said Mill. "Maybe he's got her phone bugged."

I looked at him. "Maybe. You're not rattled by this are you?"

He let out a laugh as he got up from the table. "Nah."

"Because if you are—"

"Shit," he interrupted, "If I can handle my ex's lawyers, I can handle this. What's a little CIA?" His feeble grin looked unnatural. I wasn't used to seeing him smile at all.

"Okay," I said. "Let's dig some more and make a move when the time is right. Meantime, I'm on Carla."

"Yeah," Mill said, with an even wider grin. "You're on Carla."

He winked at me and walked out of the restaurant. I sat back and looked at the stack of papers. Now my lack of experience seemed like a vast ocean of stupid. Who was I kidding? I'm no investigator. *What I am is a dream detective,* I thought. No, I wasn't even that. This business was getting serious. I had no business calling myself a detective at all.

I vowed that as soon as I got home I'd cancel the classified ad in the *Voice*. I didn't want any more strange cases, distractions, or late night crank phone calls. I was going to need to focus everything I had on this case.

And one thought keep going through my mind: How the hell was I equipped to go after these people, when I couldn't even get a teenage skateboarder to talk to me?

19

GHOST IN THE BOX

I spread the papers out on my bedroom floor. Mill had notes scribbled on almost all of the printouts. A smiley face he'd scrawled on a page grabbed my attention, a news column by *Times* reporter, Guy Jackson. The article read: *Numerous sources have hinted at CIA involvement and that the agency had used funds for clandestine missions, mostly in Central America.*

I wanted to get closer to this reporter and his sources. Emailing was an option, but I decided to go down to his office to see him in person, maybe get him to trade information and explain why the story was dropped. I doubted he'd made the connection between Carrillo and Emma, but I was willing to bet he knew who Carrillo was and maybe something more about his role with the CIA. I copied Jackson's phone number from the article and went to my home phone.

The message light was flashing on my answering machine. The first message was a click and screech. That's when they hang up and you get thirty seconds of blaring dial tone. The second message was from that same clown wondering where Waldo was and could I call him back. *Shit*, I thought, *now he's leaving messages.* Serves me right. Next came a wail that slowly turned into a sob, before Frank's unmistakable tenor rang out.

"Mr. Chase? Is that you?" A long pause, nasal breathing, cat purring. "Mr. Chase, are you there?"

"You said that already, Frank," I said.

"Mr. Chase, if you are there, can you please pick up? I have to ask you...Something quite disturbing happened today. Oh..." His voice cut out like he'd dropped the phone. The machine clicked off.

"Great," I said aloud. "The freak show continues."

The drama of the message was pitiful. Just what I wanted: A dependent personality, throwing money at me in hopes of solving a bizarre riddle he'd conceived years ago, culled from the bottom of that black lake in his head. I should have worded the *Voice* ad: *Freaks, mentally deranged and insecure, call me, give me your money. Lifelong relationships welcome.* I felt like Waldo all right, but only crazy people were searching for me. The irony of that statement being, the only paying client I had was a referral from Mill.

I tried dialing Frank but got no answer. *Shit.* I didn't want to return to that mausoleum of an apartment. Frank needed to be weaned. I had no use for his strange little game. Did he drown his sister? Did he have evil motives? Was he a druid? Was the shadowy figure at the lake truly Frank? I didn't care anymore. I had to prioritize. Carla was the main event now.

I grabbed my phone, opened the email and typed:

Carla, getting closer. More clues to run down. Hope you are well.

Gus

I hesitated for a moment before pushing the send button. I relished being able to communicate with her directly through email. To my surprise, I got an immediate response.

Thanks, Gus. Can we meet soon?
☺

Was she flirting? I almost sent her a smiley face in return, but thought better of it. Let it rest. These things have to gel. I sat back and stared my phone. In my mind, I told her she was gorgeous. That I'd have her on my mind twenty four-seven until the case was solved. I wrote back:

Yes. Be in touch soon.

My finger lingered over the emoticons for a few seconds, then I hit send. No smile for you today.

The day had begun to wear on me. It was only 3:00 p.m., but I was ready for bed. I dialed Guy Jackson's number. A recorded voice: "This is Guy Jackson. You've reached my personal, anonymous tip line. If you have a tip, leave a message and I'll call you back."

I hesitated, then said, "I've connected Carrillo of the CIA and AET Energy to a murder in Manhattan." I wasn't sure how detailed my message should be, so I ended with, "Call me." I left my cell number and hung up. "Shit," I said aloud. It was done. I was in it for real. Getting an investigative reporter involved was something I'd never considered. I was playing in the big leagues, now.

20
MAY AS WELL FACE IT

It was one of those early September evenings when the air is clear, the sun is still warm as it sets beyond the tall buildings, gilding the architecture of Second Avenue in warm hues.

As I crossed Eighty-Sixth Street from Second, I caught sight of a large person lumbering down the sidewalk. He seemed burdened, carrying heavy grocery bags, about fifty yards in front of me on the same side of the street. My first thought was that it was Frank. He was dressed in black. His sneakers pronated heavily to either side, similar to Frank's, but I decided it couldn't be him. Even though he fit Frank's description, I knew he'd never be walking all that way from D'Agostino's while carrying heavy grocery bags. That would be too much for him. He'd preferred his groceries delivered, or he'd call a cab.

As I gained ground on him, my stomach began to churn. The unmistakable gray, stringy hair and tufts of his beard became visible. It was definitely Frank, stopped about forty feet in front of me, wrestling with the plastic bags. Cans of soup and greens spilled out onto the sidewalk. He looked around, in what I presumed was a conscious or subconscious attempt to seek help. I dashed into a doorway and pretended to look at a bath shop window display. Bars of fancy soaps and back-washing apparatus filled the space. The young girl inside the store stood at the counter and glanced up at me. I nodded to her. She smiled and turned back to her duties.

A few seconds later, I cautiously peered out and saw Frank had resumed walking. I moved on toward The Tavern. A few seconds later, I again dashed into a doorway as he turned his head in my direction. His huge frame slouched to one side like a listing garbage scow as he stopped to rest for a few seconds, then he moved, wrestling with the bags. I said, quietly, "Stop calling me."

He dropped a can, stooped and started to turn in my direction. I bolted inside. I could feel his gaze like a laser beam tracking me, but in reality, there was no way he could have seen me. Maybe he'd heard my footsteps, who knows. I just couldn't face him.

Mill was seated at his usual spot at the bar, and was pulling on a mug when I sat down next to him.

"You want to try another one of those?" I asked.

He squinted an eye, looked at the bottom of his empty mug, thought about it for a second and said, "I think I better."

"Two more, Allen, please." Allen gave me a tart look and set about filling the mugs.

"Gus, I've been trying this brand of beer for a few years now."

"And?" I asked, exuding enthrallment. "What have you determined, doctor?"

"I have *deduced*," he said, looking at me so as to correct my wording, "that certain things are intangible. This chair, for instance, is tangible. Solid and scarred. Filthy actually. It's moldy and rotten with epithelial cells and has seated thousands of smelly asses. I can perch on it for many hours and feel its uncomfortable seat pushing against my bony ass."

I looked at the high-backed stool on which he sat. "Indeed," I said. "You do have a bony ass, requiring you to shift occasionally, no doubt."

"Yes. Shifting is key. However," he continued, "a mug of brew is not solid. It holds the shape of a mug, it can be spilled, swallowed and slurped, and, when you taste it, the result is mercurial. I cannot taste this beer for two long hours."

"Indeed," I said, feigning interest. "And?"

"And what?"

"Is that it? All these years of research and nothing more?"

"That's as far as my research has taken me. However, I am awaiting grant money."

"Ah yes, the grant money must come through."

Allen plopped down two mugs and looked at Mill. "I need grant money," he grunted.

"Oh, oh, Allen," Mill said incredulously. "You're not listening in on our conversations are you?"

"Fuck off," Allen said quietly, and gave us a sour look as he walked back to his spot under the TV.

"Well," Mill said. "That settles it. Allen is an eavesdropping turd."

I swigged my beer. "So," I said, "I called that reporter at the *Times*, and left him my number. And Carla wants to meet up soon. But first, I want to get to the bottom of this whole Professor Phelps connection."

"Ah," he said. "The professor connection. I'll tell you what I think. The professor is a puffed up scumbag. He got raped by his divorce, lost a boatload of dough, and when Emma wanted out, he killed her."

"We don't even know if she had a personal relationship with him," I said.

"But she could have."

"It's possible, but not probable," I said.

A sly smile widened his face. "Carla should be able to shed some light on that." Visions of the lovely Carla danced in my head. "As a matter of fact," said Mill, "I think she's withholding information from you. She would have known what Emma, her only sister, was up to. Emma *is* or was her only sister, right?"

"Yes, I think so," I said. My vision of the lovely Carla faded as

I took a taste of my beer.

"Sisters tell each other everything. Why wouldn't Carla know if Emma was fucking the professor? Why wouldn't she tell you that? Unless…"

"Unless what?" I asked.

"Unless she has a vested interest in you not knowing the whole story."

I thought for a moment. "She came to me," I said. "Why would she do that if she were hiding something? Why open the whole thing back up?"

"Why indeed?" Mill squinted in a conspiratorial gesture, then took out a bent up cigarette, popped it into his mouth, sucked long and deep on the twisted butt and then exhaled, as if smoking.

"You're taking me to a place I don't want to go, Mill."

"Exactly," he said, taking another long pull on the dilapidated cigarette.

"I thought you quit?"

He took another sniff of the white paper portion of the butt and put it back into his pocket. "Memories, Gus. Just stoking the flame of lust for the beloved evil weed."

"Shit, Mill. Why are you bringing up suspicions about Carla now?"

"Because, my dear friend, she is your evil weed. Your *Diana*. I don't think you're thinking clearly about her."

"Don't bring up Diana," I said. "Carla is not Diana."

"Nobody is Diana. Diana's not even Diana."

"What's that supposed to mean?"

"Diana was your mythical white whale, Gus. You were chasing an obsession, not a real person."

I thought for a second, feeling the insatiable craving for Diana twist my gut. I slapped it back into its hole and smiled. "True," I said, and took a sip of beer.

Mill squinted at me and sniffed the butt again. I turned and saw

Allen walking over to Mill. "No smoking," he said sternly.

"Am I smoking?" Mill looked at me. "You see any smoke? I don't even have matches."

"Well, just don't," Allen said.

"Well, I just won't," Mill replied in a mocking tone. They glared at each other.

"He's not smoking, Allen," I offered.

Allen's gaze travelled to me and then back to Mill, who had finally turned his attention to his beer. Allen slowly took a few steps back, keeping his eyes on Mill, then turned and walked away.

"Allen's been watching too many westerns," Mill said.

"If we weren't two of Allen's only regular customers, I think he would have kicked us out long ago," I said. Allen returned to his spot under the TV and stood his ground, like a dog guarding its rundown cage.

I didn't know what to say to Mill. Part of me was thinking he was just pulling my chain about Carla being my new Diana, but part of me had doubts. He was right about one thing though: she was clouding my thinking. And it was getting worse. Best be done with this case and move on. Maybe Carla would go out with me after it was all settled? The thought made me feel like a pathetic waif. The first attractive woman I meet on the job and I fall for her. Was she really so special, or was I that desperate?

"You want to pay a visit to the professor with me?" I asked.

Mill looked at me and then down at his mug. "Nah, I'm rooted here for the rest of the night."

"I meant in the morning, Mill."

"Morning?" He looked puzzled by the concept.

The paradox of the two Mills: Here sits the guy who invented phone apps and computer games, made millions with his innovative thinking, and yet seems content to be a sloth for the remainder of his life, spending most of his time in this dumpy tavern. Then there's the Mill who brought me the information at the Blue Athena—happy, enthused, intelligent. That's the Mill I wanted on my team.

"I'll meet you at the college at nine," I said.

He shook his head, no.

"Ten?" I asked.

Still no.

"Noon. Maybe we can catch the professor at lunch."

"Noon," he said, then put the tortured cigarette up to his nose and lovingly inhaled. "Noon I can do."

21
WANT A CHASER WITH THAT?

The part of NYU where Mill and I were to meet up was just a smattering of red stone buildings in the Washington Square Park area. Seems our beloved professor, Michael Steen Phelps III, PhD, was available only occasionally and taught just twice a week in person. His special emphasis was the economics of technology, productivity and economic growth, investment theory and modeling. Appropriate, I guess, for a guy who figured a way to make a small fortune out of the fledgling energy credits program.

It wasn't hard to track him down. A quick look on the NYU website, then over to the Department of Economics, to the People pull down, and there he was. A contact phone number and an email address were conveniently listed. I called the number several times but kept getting a recording. I finally reached his assistant on the phone, a master's student named Grant. He seemed like a nice guy. I'd read in one of the detective books I'd purchased that saying you're a reporter sometimes opens people up. It's a calculated risk, however, because they either get chatty and want to help you in any way they can, or they clam up and are useless. I pegged Grant as chatty, and was rewarded for my intuition. He told me all about the professor's schedule, lectures and online classes, and even offered to call the professor on my behalf to ask him if he'd like to meet me. I said sure, but had no intention of taking a formal meeting. I was going down to his stomping grounds to catch him off guard.

It was a little after twelve noon when I arrived at the rendezvous spot to meet Mill. I sat on a wooden bench under the shade of a tree in Washington Square Park. Twenty minutes later, I was beginning to wonder if Mill would show. But then, twenty minutes late to him was on time.

The park bustled with people, most of whom seemed to be students. I watched kids walking to and from school buildings, listening to music on earbuds, and for a while, was captivated by a dude juggling flaming pins. A group of what I assumed were students passed around a lit joint.

The students made me feel old, and doubly worse for not having continued my stellar foray into educational bliss. There was something about school that made me want to run and hide in a dark corner. Maybe a general distaste for authority figures, I don't know. It all seemed vague to me now, tied up with psychological motives from ancient times, when I actually cared about pleasing others with my life choices. I had nothing to prove anymore. I was doing what I wanted to do. School had served its purpose, and I'd moved on. Mill told me once that if I ever had a hankering to go back to school, to just read some syllabus books in whichever subject I was interested, and it would amount to about the same education. I think he missed the whole point of a diploma.

The Center for Research in Applied and Theoretical Econometrics (CRATE) at New York University was located on West Fourth Street, just a few blocks away. The professor was supposed to be there this afternoon, but only for a few hours.

I told Grant I was writing an article on Bounded Rationality in Burgeoning Economies—a theory that states we are all making boneheaded decisions based on our own limitations and the limitations of any information we have at the time. I looked it up and thought it was something he might buy into as an excuse to let me in to see the professor. Why we needed this theory and who thought these things up was beyond me. Observing the obvious and calling it a theory was part of the reason I distrusted the whole concept of school.

Here's a theory: We're a bunch of self-aggrandized apes floating through space on a rock moving at sixty-seven thousand miles an hour, and yet we've managed to create string cheese. That's my *String Cheese Theory.*

Professor Phelps proved somewhat elusive. I didn't want to miss talking to him, so I headed over to Fourth Street by myself. Mill could catch up later, if he ever showed.

New York University was unique in that, if not for the purple flags with NYU lettering flying out front, you couldn't tell it from any other office building. I waited outside the CRATE building and watched the doors, half expecting to see Frank come lumbering up the sidewalk and calling my name, "Gus, Gus!"

After a few minutes, I caught a glimpse of a little bald guy scurrying away from the building. Based on the webpage photo I'd seen, he could have been Phelps. I crossed the street and followed him a few blocks into the park. He disappeared into a swarm of kids and I momentarily lost sight of him, until they parted and he emerged out the other side, heading for Macdougal Street. I ran to catch up, then walked directly behind him.

He was short, about five foot five, in his late fifties, and wore brown shoes and a tan tweed suit. A smart brown leather satchel slung over his right shoulder looked like it held everything important in the universe in its many locked and secret compartments. Having had such terrible luck approaching strangers—albeit to tell them they would soon die—I was reluctant to touch him or say anything that might scare him off. I had to think of a way of contacting him, nonchalantly, without letting the proverbial cat out of the bag. A terrible feeling of doubt washed over me. What was I doing chasing down another guy I didn't know? Possibly not even the right guy. Shit. I had to do something, and quickly, as he scurried on his way. It was do or die.

"Hey, Professor!" I shouted.

He kept walking.

"Professor Phelps! Professor!"

He stopped and turned, one eye focused warily toward me. I was directly behind him now.

"Professor Phelps?" I extended my hand. His face went from frown, to concern, to utterly disturbed. "I'm sorry to catch you like this, Professor, but I've been trying to reach you."

"And so you have." His response was scholarly, cool, like I was one of his first year students.

"I'm not a student. I have something very important to discuss with you."

"Oh?" He looked me up and down, as if anything I had to say couldn't possibly concern him.

"The murder of Emma. Emma Donati."

His head sunk down for a moment, as if he was trying to remember an ancient theorem, then his eyes drifted back up to mine, distinctly watery. I'd struck a nerve. So he *did* love her, or at the very least, cared about her. I could feel that.

Instantly, I saw the crime scene. *Emma struggling to free herself from the grasp of a stranger. A man. A tall, strong man. She turns to her attacker, mouths what I assume is a silent prayer, then blood sprays the wall behind her.*

A wave of relief flooded through me, catching me off guard. *It wasn't the Professor.*

"Very upsetting that. A tragic loss." He rested his arm on his ancient shoulder satchel of wisdom and glared at me. "Who are you?"

My focus was gone, having been dissipated by the vision of Emma's death and the emotions that carried. I had to concentrate and present myself in a rational way. I cleared my throat and smiled, staring at his bulbous, acne-pocked nose.

"My name is August Chase."

"I don't know you?" His tone was questioning, like he feared I'd slipped from his memory. Perhaps he was thinking we'd met after the murder, which was probably a difficult time for him, blurred into a fog of police interrogations, memorials and, no doubt, intense personal grief. I could feel all of this.

"No, you don't know me," I said, assuredly. "I was hired by Emma's sister, Carla. Do you know her?"

He abruptly turned on his heels and walked away. "Please, I'm running late. Make an appointment with my assistant. I keep office hours."

I followed closely behind as he weaved through the pedestrians in our path. "I have only two questions, Professor," I shouted.

"Oh?" he shouted back.

"Did you love her?"

He stopped dead in his tracks and turned back to me, his clenched fingers squeezing the bag. "Why would you ask me that?"

"Because I think you cared deeply for her. Were you having an affair?"

Snorting, almost laughing, his eyes still glistening wet, he turned again, dismissing me a final time. "I have to run."

He walked faster. I ran a few steps to catch up and sidestepped in front of him. He nodded his head in affirmation of something, but I couldn't quite make out what it could be. I felt anger rising within me. I couldn't let him get away without talking to me further. A little voice in my head was screaming, *Let the man go! Make an appointment.* But I couldn't do that. My nerves were revving up into a fever of irrational compulsion. I felt like grabbing him by the throat and shaking him, screaming, *"Who killed, Emma? Who killed Emma?"*

I said, "You nodded in affirmation. Is that a yes? You did love her?"

"That was a nod confirming my initial impression of you," he said coldly. He held the bag up in front of his body to protect himself, I presume, and tried to sidestep me. I stepped in front of him again. "This is outrageous! How dare you assault me?"

He looked around to see if anyone noticed us or would come to his rescue. His frightened look deflated my veracity and reluctantly, I stepped aside to let him go on his way, but immediately began following, dogging his every step. I didn't know the person doing this. This aggression was foreign to me. And this certainly was not the quiet chat over a cup of coffee I had imagined.

"No one's assaulting you, Professor," I screamed much louder than necessary for him to hear. That sent him scurrying faster, still. "I've been hired to investigate this murder, and you and I have a lot to discuss."

Practically running now, his satchel flopping heavily against his side, he crossed the street and held up his hand to hail a cab. I dodged a city bus and sidestepped a bicycle messenger, catching up to him on the corner.

"This isn't the way I wanted this to go," I shouted over the bus noise, fumes pouring over us.

Holding a white hanky over his mouth and nose, he waved his free hand furiously to hail a cab, the dust and noise of the street conspiring to drive him further from me.

I grabbed his arm and turned him. "Can we have a cup of coffee and talk about this?"

The look of incredulity and fear on his face was priceless, striking me so oddly, I almost broke out into laughter.

"Listen, you little weasel," I said, clutching his arm. "Carrillo was there when she was killed! I saw him."

Phelps stared at me, the hanky still covering his mouth and nose, his eyes wet and burning red. "I've told the police all I know. Please, please leave me alone!" he yelled over the din.

I fought back the beast within and relented, stepping onto the sidewalk. A cab stopped and he quickly got in. A feeling of disassociation, of complete and utter disbelief over what I'd just done, rose up from within my gut and spread onto my palate. It tasted like bus fumes. I'd won the prize. All hail the conquering idiot. It's a wonder I didn't chase him with a stick raised over my head, yelling,

"Bounded Rationality, Bounded Rationality!"

As his cab disappeared into traffic, I pictured the beautiful, stately, five foot seven Emma with that weaselly little pipsqueak, and I had an epiphany of my own bounded rationality. *It never happened for you and her, did it, Professor? You loved her all right, but nothing ever happened. Not like you wanted.*

22
THE CAT AND THE PENDULUM

Mill was staring at me from across the street. He shook his head, cupped his hands to his mouth and yelled, "Nicely done! Good job," over the traffic noise. I pointed toward the park and he nodded. I crossed the street, thinking about the myriad of ways I had just fucked up my encounter with Professor Phelps.

Mill and I met a few minutes later in the west end of the park.

"I'm surprised you didn't beat him to death with his bag," Mill said, sniggering under his breath. A beat-up cigarette dangled from his lips.

"He overreacted," I said. "Give me that." I reached for the cigarette, but he turned away, taking it from his own mouth. Then he took a long, deep whiff of the tobacco rod and placed it back in his lips. I plopped myself down on a park bench and sighed.

"So, tell me what led to you chasing this guy into a cab?" Mill asked.

"How long were you watching us?"

"Long enough to see him bobbing up and down and waving crazily to flag down a cab. That was the best laugh I've had all week," he said, and let loose another laugh.

I scowled at him. "I was expecting you at noon. What happened?"

"Hah! Fucking cat."

"Your cat?"

"Sat on my clock."

"The cat sat on your clock?"

"Yeah, you know, hit the buttons and the alarm got changed."

"What time was it set for?"

"Noon. You said noon, right?"

"I said to be here by noon. Emphasis on 'be here.'" I glared at him in frustration. His eyes darted from mine to some young ladies walking our way. Three in a row, each about twenty or so. Their faces flush with the beauty only youth can provide. After they passed, I tapped his foot with my shoe. "The cat ate your homework? Really, is that it?"

He sat down next to me. "You think young girls like those, you think they know what they have? The power they have over men?"

I sighed and kicked my legs out to relax. "I don't know, Mill. What do you think?"

"Too young and naive, is my guess."

"They'd have to live a day with testosterone raging through their bodies to understand how crazy men are," I said.

"Experience is the sugar in your coffee," Mill said. "And man, I like my mine sweet."

"You only really attract acid and bitter."

"Sounds good though, don't it? Sugar and cream in my bitter dregs, baby, that's what they are to me!" He sat back as if in anticipation of a long afternoon of girl-watching.

I have to admit, it was a beautiful afternoon. The sun was out in all its Indian Summer glory. The sky, glimpsed through the trees and the buildings surrounding us, was azure blue and clear. A slight breeze cut through the warmth of the sun and made me want to spread a blanket under a nearby tree and whisper sweet nothings into Carla's ear. Shit, she kept popping into my head. I did my best to try not to think of her, but I kept seeing her lovely face. Mill and I sat quietly on the bench, each in our own thoughts.

After a while, Mill asked, "So, you want to tell me what happened with the professor?"

I squinted at him, as he sniffed that same sweat-stained, wrinkled cigarette butt. "What you saw was the end of a long and fruitful conversation with the old Prof," I said, "and I'm convinced he didn't kill Emma. Or have her killed."

"Because he told you all this? Was it in long story form, lots of metaphors and point for point? Sorry I missed it."

"Yes, you missed it. Thanks to your evil cat."

"Bellamy."

"You cat is named Bellamy?"

"Yes, Bellamy. What did you expect, Mittens? Pussy Galore?"

I laughed, then immediately sobered. "I saw it in his eyes, Mill. He loved Emma. Loved her and is still hurting from her loss."

"Shit! I wanted him to be an evil scumbag."

We watched two girls walk by. They wore pretty knee-length summer dresses and sandals. One of them, the shorter of the two, held an armload of books. They both had long brown hair that swayed back and forth in unison as they walked.

"I can only tell you, as sure as I saw Emma being killed, it wasn't him. I could feel it in my bones. No, the impression I got, Mill, is he's a fucked-up, lonely old dude who has status and money and things in his life, but none of it matters to him anymore. His world has been rocked to the core."

"Losing millions in a divorce will do that," he said.

"I just don't think he had anything to do with it."

"All that from a conversation with the back of his head."

I looked at him. "Are you going to trust me on this, or not?"

"I don't trust anything you say, Gus. Does that surprise you? I don't trust anything my mother says, either. She's been consistently wrong about every single thing in my life, up to this point."

"Up to this point?"

"Well, I mean, I haven't spoken to her today," he said, as if today was the day she might come through for him. "So that leaves Carrillo and who else?"

"Suspects are Carrillo, Colling and, as much as I hate to say it, what the cops thought…"

"Robbery gone wrong. Random act of violence," Mill finished my sentence.

"If it was a random act, which I am starting to suspect it could have been, then the chances of catching the perpetrator are slim to none," I said.

"That sucks."

"Yes, it does."

We sat in silence for a few minutes.

I stretched. The sun shone blindingly off the leaves of a nearby maple tree. I looked at Mill. His eyes were closed, his face toward the sun. The weathered butt hung from his lips.

"I need to trust you, Mill," I said. "I need to know, if I ask you to be my backup, no matter what, you'll be there."

"I'm there," he said, without opening an eye.

"That means no more cat problems."

He opened one eye. "Okay. I'll kill the cat."

"Don't kill it. Just wound it enough so it can't jump onto your damn alarm clock."

He smiled. "You're a mean one, Mr. Grinch, you know that?"

"I'm serious, Mill. I need your help."

"Me too." He squinted at me and smiled, then sunk back into his sunning posture. I stared at him, his face looking older, more used than I had ever noticed in the bar. I realized then that I couldn't really trust him, or anybody else for that matter. I was going to have to do this on my own.

"What's the next move?" he asked.

"Next move, we find Colling."

He glanced at me, then went back to lapping up the sun. "Shit, Motorcycle Jacket has a date with the man. What do we do when we find him?"

"All we need is a few minutes alone with him."

"And he'll talk?"

"No, but just talking to him, I'll know if he was the killer. I'm developing a knack for reading people. Like I'm connected to their thoughts and emotions. That's if your cat doesn't get in the way."

"Fuck it. Bellamy stays," he said, in feigned defiance.

"Okay," I said. "Fine. But the cat's on probation." I turned to him and put my hand on his shoulder. "I want you to do me a favor, Mill."

"What's that?"

"I want you to persuade your cousin the cop to get us a copy of Emma's case file."

"Can't do that."

"He must know someone in the Homicide Department."

"I can, however, my cat-loving friend, procure you a print out of some of the files."

"That could work."

"Maybe. I did hear him talking about another case where he'd gotten access to some files, so, it's not outside the realm of possibility. And he owes me," said Mill.

"Great. I just need to know who they interviewed. Have him send the files as soon as he can."

"You got it," Mill said, his attention now on three girls approaching from our left.

23

WITH A SIDE OF WHAT?

My stomach fluttered when she appeared at the doorway of Café Divine. I was standing at the bar and waved to her. She smiled when she saw me, the kind of smile that's involuntary. I could tell because she caught herself and pulled it back a little.

We sat at a nice table for two, near the window. The waiter took our drink order, a glass of red wine for her and a bottle of Pellegrino with lemon wedges for me. I wanted to keep my head clear, so I decided today was not the day to float away from lunch. Besides, I hadn't had anything to drink the past few days, and I wasn't about to start during a lunch with Carla.

"How are you?" I asked.

"Good," she said, smiling. "And you?"

"Good."

I looked down at her hand, which she had placed on the table. Her skin looked porcelain smooth and creamy soft. I wanted to take it in my hands and kiss it, maybe breathe in any lingering cologne. She noticed my attention and seemed fine with it.

"I want to show you something," I said. I held up my cell phone to show her a clearer picture of Colling. One that I'd taken the day he'd hung around outside my apartment. "Do you recognize him?"

She looked at it and said nothing. Then I zoomed in on his face. It was a little blurry, but recognizable.

"Oh, my God. Is that Crazy Gerry? He's changed his hair, but I think…Yes, that's him. I recognize that mole on the side of his nose, there. Why do you have a picture of him?"

"You know this man?"

She nodded. "Yes, but he doesn't have red hair, at least he didn't when I knew him."

"This is the same guy I showed you the pictures of before."

"Really?"

"Yes, you said you didn't know him."

"Look at him. His hair was blond, but that's red. He's dyed it or something. It didn't sink in before."

"So you're sure this is the guy?"

"Yes."

"How do you know him?"

"He dated Emma."

"This guy dated Emma?" I repeated, wanting her to be doubly sure. "What did you say his name is?"

"That's Gerry Cavanaugh."

"Gerry Cavanaugh. You're certain?"

"Yes."

I looked at the photo just to be sure I had the right one. "Tell me about him. Why *Crazy* Gerry?"

She took off her jacket, and growing more animated than I'd ever seen her, she said, "He's a stalker! Why do you have his picture?"

"He was hanging around outside my apartment, then followed me to a client's place. That was on the first day we met in Central Park. After that, he was on me like glue."

"He followed you?"

"I think you should tell me all about this guy."

"Emma met him through work."

"At the college, you mean?"

"Yes. He was a friend of Professor Phelps, I think. She was introduced to him at a reception at the college. He kept asking her out.

He finally wore her down and she agreed to go out with him."

"How'd that go?"

"It was a nightmare. The guy was just creepy. Not her type at all."

"When you say creepy…"

"Immature. Bad attitude towards people, folks he didn't even know. And always pushing himself on her." Anger and frustration was growing in her voice.

I gently nodded.

"He started to get aggressive and tried to force himself on her sexually. She just wanted out."

"This was on the first date?"

"The one and only. She literally ran into a cab. He wouldn't take the hint, though. Kept calling and showing up at places she'd go. Finally, she got nasty, yelled at him to fuck off."

"But he didn't?"

She pushed out nervous laughter. "He did, at first. Then the hang-ups started. She'd see him standing on the street outside her apartment or he'd do a drive-by on his motorcycle at odd hours. He had no reason to be on her street, yet she'd see him two, three times a week."

"A real sweetheart."

"An absolute creep."

"Did she call the cops?"

"Like that would do anything."

The desperation and hurt in her eyes made me want to hold her, tell her it would be okay, but what the hell did I know? Maybe it would never be okay. The pain of loss is personal. It has no home other than the grieving heart.

"Well, first of all," I said, "his name is not Cavanaugh, but Colling. Justin Colling. He worked security with our guy, Carrillo, at an energy trading company Emma's boss, Phelps, was involved with."

"Colling…" she said, her voice trailing off. "Why would he lie about his name?"

"Good question. My guess is he didn't want her to place him with Carrillo. His real job wasn't only security, but providing muscle. Carrillo was ex-CIA. I suspect Colling was trying to distance himself from that."

"Why would she care about that?"

"Exactly. Why would she?" I asked.

She sat back, suddenly looking a little older, a little smaller than when she first walked in. I glanced out the window onto Third Avenue. Bumper to bumper traffic inched by. *Like having a café next to a freeway*, I thought, scanning the area for anyone suspicious.

Carla took a sip of wine. "So you think it's significant he lied about his name?"

"I was trying to think of a reason for that. Like I said, the only thing I can come up with is he wanted to distance himself from his real job."

"Or he knew he would be stalking her right from the get-go and didn't want her to know his real name."

"Could be," I said, thinking about it. *Was he really that warped?* Probably. "Well, in any case, I'm pretty sure both Colling and Carrillo were questioned and cleared, with solid alibis."

"Professor Phelps," she said, pointedly. "That little jerk. He's the one that got her into the mess with Cavanaugh, Colling or whatever his name is."

"I had a little chat with the mighty Professor."

"Oh?"

"I think he had deep, genuine affection for your sister. Not that it matters. I just don't think he had anything to do with her death."

"To me, he'll always be guilty."

"I know how you feel," I said.

A glaze of hatred frosted her eyes. "Do you?"

I wanted to take up her hand and kiss it, look into her eyes and tell her it would all be okay. That soon, she wouldn't feel the wounds so acutely. That she was beautiful and young and vibrant, and that the here and now was all that mattered. But I didn't say any of that. Death is bitter. Trying to make peace with it is like trying to smell a flame.

I shook my head and said, "I understand."

She inhaled deeply, and sat back. For a moment I saw her as she truly was. Beautiful, scared, alone. Her sienna-colored eyes darted from her drink to me and back again.

The waiter came and I ordered the minestrone soup and a slice of pizza; she got a Caesar salad with chicken.

"If all three of these guys were cleared by the police, then who killed Emma?" she asked.

I shrugged. "Could have been random."

"No. I won't accept that. It was Colling. I know it was."

"Maybe. Alibis are easy to come by. Let me keep digging. I'll take an in-depth look at our stalker."

That put a slight grin on her face. "You're a good guy, Gus. I think I like that."

I smiled back. "I like it, too." I placed my hand on hers and gave a little squeeze. She looked into my eyes.

A sudden shift there told me to back off, and the room seemed to deflate a little.

"Here's to more info on Colling," I said, thinking it was a lame thing to say, but couldn't stop myself. We clinked glasses and sipped our drinks.

A few minutes of quiet passed between us. It felt comfortable and good, like we were safe together. She looked out the window. My eyes followed hers to a guy standing on the corner. He was partially obscured by a cab, so I couldn't see his face. I glanced at Carla; her eyes were glued to the guy. A look of fear colored her face. The cab finally moved and he crossed the street. It wasn't Colling. She turned back to me, her relief palpable. How many times a day would she do that, I wondered? So alone. On edge.

I placed my hand back on hers and looked directly into her eyes.

Dream State

She stared back at me, and this time she didn't move.

24

GRAY IS THE COLOR OF MY SOUL

When I got back to my apartment, the excitement of my connection with Carla, albeit only a small one, was still a jazzed-up flutter in my stomach. Despite my excitement, I was exhausted and horny and wanted to take a long, deep nap. I closed the curtains and crashed onto my bed. "Carla, Carla, Carla," I said out loud.

The light coming in from the hallway lit the room in muted tones. I closed my eyes. My thinking was directed only toward Carla, and dark pixels formed the shape of her beautiful face, her hand resting on the table, her eyes smiling at mine. My body tensed as I grew closer to her, our hands touching, caressing. I was in sex dream heaven.

My kisses, gentle and teasing, find her waiting lips. Her naked body is full and warm and soft as I slide on top of her. The gentle aromas of her cologne and skin intoxicate me, and release all tension from my body as I succumb to her. I look deep into her eyes, and they dance with excitement.

Then I sense something is wrong. We've lost our connection and a change has come over her. Her smile turns to a frown. She tenses convulsively and swings her hand across her body, slapping me hard on the face. A high-pitched squeal pulses in my ears. It stabs into my head like a sharp needle, digging into my brain. Robotically she pulls her hand back, ready to strike another blow.

"Stop!" I yelled, and sat up in bed. Awakened in my dark place, my chest heaved as I tried to catch my breath. My heart pounded. I tried to focus my eyes. Gray blotches solidified into my bedroom furniture, and I realized the ringing in my head was actually the telephone.

I took deep breaths until my pulse slowed, then I reached across my bed and picked up the nasty beast. "Yeah?"

"Let me clear things up," a squeaky male voice said.

"Who is this?"

A car alarm blared from the street below.

"I know we ended poorly the other day and I want to—"

"Frank?" I interrupted.

"I said a few things—"

"Why are you calling me?" I looked at the clock. It was four. "It's the middle of the day, Frank."

The question seemed to confuse him. I could hear slow breathing at the other end, and also a blaring car horn that strangely echoed the one blaring outside my own window.

"When should I call?" he asked.

How about a quarter to NEVER, I thought. "A quarter to midnight," I said, trying to make light of the rudeness in my own head.

"What?" He was stumped again.

Now I was beginning to feel bad. "Sorry, Frank. You woke me up."

I heard a relieved, "Oh," emanate from Frank's heavy breathing.

"What's up?" I asked.

The pulsing car horn was beginning to bother me. It was one of those deafening alarms that's supposed to shut off after a few minutes, but it didn't. It rudely ping-ponged in and out of the phone, making a reverb effect. It was strange, like he was calling me while standing right next to the car. I looked out the window but couldn't see anybody.

Frank cleared his throat, and I suddenly realized *that* sound came from two directions as well. I went to my apartment door and looked through the peephole. A hulking, backlit figure stood in the hallway. I slowly opened the door. Frank turned toward me, startled I'd figured out where he was. I lowered the phone and stood looking at him.

"Frank," I said, slightly befuddled. "What can I do for you?"

He held his phone in the air, as if to say, *Look, we were just talking.* I held up mine as well. Frank hurriedly stuffed his hands and the phone into his jacket pockets, then spread the coat open with his arms.

"Gus. Hello. I was hoping we could chat."

"Yeah, sure. You didn't have to come all the way up here though, Frank."

"Well, you're a difficult man to reach."

"Not, really," I said, thinking, *For you, yes.* "Can you give me a few minutes?" He gave a non-committal shrug.

I was dressed only in my boxers and beginning to feel a chill. "How about we meet across the street at Café Divine? Great Italian food. Pizza. We can talk there," I said. He pursed his lips and pulled his thick mustache with the fingers of his right hand. "I just need about five minutes." I smiled kindly at him.

His eyes searched the hall, like he'd find his words cowering in the darkened corners. Frank's posture reminded me of a kid I'd known in elementary school who was afraid to go into the bathroom alone. The teacher used to pull the kid's pants down for him as he stood in front of the urinal. This one time, his tighty-whities had holes in the back and exposed portions of his buttocks. Embarrassing as that was, so this situation would soon be if I didn't put a stop to it.

"You know what, why don't you just come on in and wait in

the kitchen. We can have some coffee." I could feel my soul leaving my body, even as the words escaped my mouth, as if in slow motion. "Come. On. In. Frank."

"Sure thing," he replied, a smile brightening his face.

Without missing a beat, he seemed to float in through the doorway. Yes, he was a happy puppy now, climbing into the family wagon. A spasm of horror jolted through me. Had I just invited the Fat Man into my apartment? I felt my throat tighten as he made his way in and express-tracked himself toward the kitchen.

I quickly pulled on my jeans and a shirt and walked into the bathroom to splash water on my face. "You seem a bit upset, Frank. Is everything all right?" I called out to him, over the sloshing and rinsing and drying.

He grunted something unintelligible, then I heard a kitchen chair squeal across the floor, and more grunting as his bulk came to rest.

Somehow, I got the feeling this was going to be a long meeting.

I returned to the kitchen. Frank was perched at the table, leaning forward, like he had a backache. His toad eyes followed me to the sink, as I ran water for coffee. I could feel his stare on the back of my head. His breathing was labored, as if winded by the short walk to the kitchen.

"What is horror, but examination of the fears of being...human? It's perfectly natural," he said.

"Seems about right," I answered brightly, not wanting to go deep just yet. I turned to him, leaning back against the sink. His arms were outstretched and his hands were resting on a black cane I'd never seen before, or noticed earlier in the hallway.

"Why horror, Frank?" I asked.

He breathed another heavy sigh, as if to weigh his answer. His eyes grew dark and he stared at the floor. "We all have our own version of hell, do we not?"

I nodded. "I suppose."

"What do most people know of suffering?" He looked up at me, a hint of shame in his eyes, then turned to look out the window. "I wanted to work with you to see how close you came to seeing the truth. You got very close, didn't you?" His eyes were penetrating now, as he turned his attention back on me.

"I saw what I saw, Frank. I'm generally pretty accurate."

"That's right. You saw something more than what was expected, though. You saw a truth that's haunted me my whole life. My personal horror."

"Well, I didn't mean to cause you any pain, Frank. I usually only see dead people." I laughed, then added, "Or rather, people who are about to die. Then I try to save them."

As absurd as that sounded, he seemed to take it as matter of fact. "Yes, I want to understand death. I want to see it, feel it. Be completed by it," he said.

I turned to get a cup of freshly brewed coffee, not sure if I should run out of the apartment screaming or hear him out. I took a long, deep breath and my nerves steeled. I turned, smiling, and offered him a cup.

We sat at the table. His back was to the windows and the backlight gave his round face a dark, spotty look, his beard and ears highlighted at the edges. He wore light-sensitive glasses that kept changing shades. His long, fat fingers delicately turned the spoon in his coffee cup, mixing in more sugar than I'd use in a week.

"I think we talked about this briefly before, Frank. I only see the people. I don't get inside their heads. I can't see what they see," I lied.

"I believe, with some practice, you may be able to…look inside their minds, see and feel what they are experiencing."

"Even if I could, and this is not saying I'm even interested in doing this, why would I want to? Death is…" I shrugged.

"Death is a new beginning."

"I was going to say, death is death. It's nothing. We are gone from the world and that's it."

"You don't believe there's more?"

"No, I don't."

"You've never had a glimpse? An inkling there's something behind that dark curtain waiting to be revealed?"

"No, Frank."

He took a delicate sip of the sugar-coffee and tapped his foot under the table. I followed his lead and drank from my cup. We stared at each other for a silent moment. I smiled at him, then looked past his shoulder to the bright window.

I knew what was coming and began to grow even uneasier. I could feel the words as they left his lips and flew into my ears, then flipped around in my stomach.

"I have money. I can pay you," he said, his eyes darting from the floor to mine, then back down again. "More than before."

"For what, Frank? I already saw the thing you asked about. I see nothing else there."

"Yes, but at the risk of sounding redundant, you saw more than I asked. From what you told me, you started to experience what it is to drown! From what you described, for a moment, you were her. A part of her. A split second inside her and you saw everything she saw, felt what she felt, what was happening to her."

"I wouldn't go that far."

"Couldn't you feel it? The water choking in your throat? The absolute panic? That horrible moment when she…succumbed?"

I slowly shook my head.

"Imagine if you had stayed with her a few seconds longer, when that fatal gulp of water caused her to blackout and she slipped into that last heartbeat of consciousness. Imagine if you could have gone with her?"

I stared at him now, sure my eyes were wide as apples.

"And you'd come back, of course," he added.

"That's not something I'd even think of doing, Frank."

"A near death experience would be nothing compared to this!" He tapped his cane on the floor with each of the following points for emphasis. "Why are we here? Why are we alive? The age-old questions…Are we a virus? What happens when we die? Do we change? Transmutation? Do we have a soul? A revolutionary breakthrough is what it would be. You have a power so remarkable, so unique, it's nothing anyone has ever seen before. Think of the science, the research, the books you could write."

I looked at his cane and he stopped pounding it. Science hadn't even crossed my mind. "I don't know what to say, Frank. You're exaggerating what happened. Perhaps I've misled you."

His expression froze, then crashed, as he considered this. A few seconds later, his mouth turned upside down and his eyes transformed from blue-gray to black. I thought he might cry.

"Come on, Frank. I don't do the things you're asking me to do. I merely dream."

"Merely. And Neil Armstrong merely walked on the moon," he said, seeming to rebound a bit.

It occurred to me that deep down, in some elementary way, this strange man was really just searching for some form of human contact. An affirmation that he didn't have to be solitary. This massive, bespectacled blob of a man, who stunk of putrefied cat urine, wanted to come out into the light, away from the dark maze in his apartment, and wanted me to help him do it. I smiled faintly and took a deep breath.

"What is it, exactly, you want me to do, Frank?"

"Why, I want you to go back into that dream and manipulate it, take her part. See what happens after the darkness comes."

"So literally, you want me to die?" A tinge of sarcasm colored my tone.

I didn't want to die, nor did I want find out what death was like. It was then that I decided I would be willing to pretend that I had died and come back to tell him that there is nothing beyond this life but dark emptiness, and that he didn't really want to be invested in that. Life was worth living and living well, every second used up in appreciation of the corporeal world. That all his senses were a miracle, and that it didn't matter what came after this life, only that he lived a good life now, as best he could under the circumstances, and that he strove to live a better life than he'd been allowing himself.

His expectant gaze told me he thought he'd won me over, and I accepted this as my cue.

"Okay, I'll do it. But only under one very strict condition."

"What's that?"

"That afterwards, after I come back, you never ask me to do this again. I have to move on."

He shook his head. "Yes, yes, I understand. That's fine."

"I'm in the middle of some delicate investigations, Frank. I'm concerned with the living. Exploring death and dying isn't on my list of things to do."

"Of course." There were a few seconds of awkward silence, then Frank stood up. "Come to my place tomorrow night. I'll have everything set up."

"What do you mean, like black lights, lava lamps? Incense?"

He gave me a pained look. I smiled innocently. "If this was 1970, I guess that would do," he said. "Around seven-thirty tomorrow night, does that sound okay?"

"Perfect," I said, feeling it was anything but.

"Good." Frank sauntered toward the door. When he reached the outer hallway, he turned and looked at me. "This means a lot to me, Gus. Thank you."

"You're welcome," I said. And closed the door.

"Oh, and one other thing," he said from the other side.

I opened the door slightly and fixed my eyes on him. "Yes?"

"When you...see my sister...After you see the other side, tell her to leave me alone." He had the look of an expectant child at the ice cream truck, waiting for his double scoop.

"Leave you alone. Yes, got it," I said, and nodded confidently.

He nodded back, smiling slightly, his fixed gaze trying to read me as I closed the door once more.

25

IF THE RED SHOE FITS

"You're not going to find anything on Bruno," he said.

Guy Jackson, the *Times* reporter, had a low, raspy quality to his voice that smokers get after years of abuse. He was speaking too close to the receiver and I could hear his mouth sounds. His words sprayed out like a guttural foghorn and grated in my ear. I pulled the receiver back from my head. "Why nothing on Bruno?" I asked.

"He's untouchable. Lost. Gone."

"Gone, how?"

"Had connections that allowed him to slip away from this story and any concrete links to it, and I honesty couldn't tell you where he is."

"Connections such as—"

"D.C. connections. I couldn't begin to tell you who, but I know he had them. You don't just walk away from being a person of interest in a federal case, then go MIA without some major support."

"I'd love to see your notes on this case," I said, perhaps a bit too patronizing in my tone.

"Yeah, you and everybody else. Listen, that shit's privileged. Why would I give you a look?"

"Because I'm gonna track down Bruno for you," I lied. I had no intention of doing any such thing. All I wanted was more insight into the Aileron Energy Trading fiasco.

He snorted, and it sounded like he took a long drag off a cigarette. "You said in your message you had something for me. What have you got?"

"I've got a connection between Carrillo and the death of a girl Professor Phelps was seeing, Emma Donati."

"Emma Donati," he repeated back, sounding like he was trying to place her. "How are they linked?"

"You knew her?"

"Her name sounds familiar. No, wait, Phelps was dating a *Carla* Donati, maybe." His mentioning Carla was like a cold slap in the face. I was momentarily stunned speechless. "Yes, a receptionist at AET, I think he said. Good-looking brunette."

"And her name was Carla Donati?"

"I think so. Donati, something like that. I didn't take notes on everything, for chrissakes. Tall chick, red shoes. I remember because her heels were so high they made her like, six feet tall. Hard to forget that face, too."

"And she was dating Phelps?"

"I don't know. She was introduced by him. I just assumed they were an item. Maybe not."

Words were trying to form in my mouth but were muted by the disappointment and sadness welling up inside me. My Carla was involved with Phelps? What else had she not told me? I took a deep breath and let it out slowly.

"Hello?" Another drag of his cigarette.

"Yeah. Sorry," I said. "Emma. She was Carla's sister. Emma was the one dating Phelps. Thirty-something, blonde, about five foot seven. She worked part time for the professor and as a chef in a local restaurant. Nothing fancy. Good eats place."

"Well, if I did meet her, it was quick because I don't have an image."

My throat was tight and my head was starting to ache. Visions of Carla dancing naked around Phelps, waggling herself in front of him, her smooth hips gyrating, tormented me.

"Anyway," I said, willing the visions into the swamp at the back of my head, "Carrillo was there when Emma was killed. Murdered on the street over on the West Side. And I don't think it's a coincidence. Carrillo's dead too, by the way."

"Yeah, I know. Horrible scene on the bridge."

"Yes." The whole slow motion event started to play in my mind, frame by frame. I was beginning to see it more vividly than ever before. The truck careening over the lane dividers into the car. Could the truck have swerved on purpose? But that would have been crazy. Suicide. It had to have been an accident.

Jackson's voice cut through the image. "Look, you haven't told me anything I didn't already know. Why don't you leave this to the pros downtown, huh?"

"What?" I crawled back from the vision.

"You're some sort of PI or something, right?"

"Yeah, hired by—" Carla's name stuck in my throat and I hesitated. "The family."

"Well, the DA has looked at AET Energy three ways to Sunday. You're not telling me anything new or relevant here."

"What I'm telling you is Carrillo, and by proxy, his boss, is involved in Emma's murder. You already knew this?"

There was a pause. I could hear him take another deep drag off his cigarette, could almost see the smoke billowing from his nostrils. "I don't see the angle," he said finally.

"You don't?"

"What evidence are you going on? You got a witness, fingerprints, video? What?"

"A witness," I lied. I couldn't tell him I saw it in a dream—that I was, in fact, the Dream Detective. An image of me throwing down a comic book, the first ever issue of *The Dream Detective*, subtitled *Death on the Bridge* and embossed with colorful cartoon colors, as my

169

calling card, flashed through my head.

"You've got somebody willing to swear they saw Carrillo kill Emma?"

"Ah, well, not exactly." I heard a long exhale on the phone. I sensed his attention waning. Was he on the internet, checking emails?

"You don't have video, a sworn witness, you got nothing. I got to go."

"Wait! Tell me more about this Carla. You saw her with Phelps?"

"She was a babe. Was introduced by Phelps. I thought she was with him, but who knows?"

"Anything else you notice about her?"

Now I could hear ice cubes clinking in a glass, and Jackson taking a sip and swallowing. "Nope. Good-looking girl, that's all."

"Did she leave with anybody?"

"Not sure."

"Did you leave with anybody?" A sharp exhale into the receiver. "Just kidding," I said. "You say you didn't notice a good-looking five foot seven blonde girl?"

"Not that I recall. I got to go. Call me if you get a witness, otherwise we can't go anywhere with this."

"I thought you were an investigative—"

He hung up.

I sat on my bed. The sting of him mentioning Carla started to gnaw at me, cloud my thinking. How could she have been there and not tell me? Did she know Phelps? Or worse, was she the one dating Phelps, not Emma? I thought back to my run-in with the professor outside the school. He'd quickly turned away when I mentioned Carla. His grief for Emma was apparent, but that was a strange reaction to my mentioning her sister. Was that because he was dating Carla, too? Was he seeing them both? A love triangle? I was sliding into bizarre territory here. I'd taken everything Carla told me at face value, never questioning any of it. How many lies had there been between us? What would she have to gain? Perhaps Phelps simply didn't like Carla. How much interaction did they have after Emma's death? Had she caused him to have feelings of guilt?

I wanted a drink. I glanced at my bedside clock. It was five in the evening. Time to find Mill and have a pow-wow over some ale. My phone rang and I picked it up.

"What's up, Gus?"

"Mill, I was just about to find you. How about getting a few pints and a burger?"

"I got something better than that."

"Okay…"

"How would you like to take a ride to Astoria?"

"Queens?"

"Is there any other Astoria?"

"Why?"

"How about I have Motorcycle Jacket's address?" There was a kernel of excitement in Mill's tone.

"Colling? You have his address?"

"Baby, I have his address, phone number, birthday, favorite color—"

"How?"

"How? Because The Mill knows how." He snickered into the phone.

"Okay," I said. "Let's go. Now."

"Now? No burger?"

"If we go now, we're more likely to catch him at home, don't you think?"

"During rush hour?"

"Oh, right. Okay, I'll pick you up at seven-thirty."

"One thing, though," Mill said.

"What's that?"

"I'm not taking the subway. We cab it or I don't go. I'd offer to drive, but my car is in the shop." Mill's phantom car had been in the shop, it seemed, since 1992. Every time he mentioned it, I just rolled my eyes.

"So, we split a cab. I don't have a problem with that."

"And what about some food?" Mill asked.

"You want a burger? Let's go to The Tavern," I said.

"No, I'm more in a chicken mood."

"Fine."

"Chinese sounds good. Or shepherd's pie."

"Okay, shepherd's pie isn't chicken, but whatever, The Tavern has that. See you there." I hung up before he could change his mind again. I knew from experience Mill could be a little quirky when it came to food. Even though he'd sit in The Tavern for hours at a time and order burgers and beer, sometimes he went on these food jags that could take us all over the city. Which was fine in concept, except the places he picked were generally long on character and short on quality. I wasn't in the mood for any culinary adventures. Tonight, I wanted to see where Colling lived. It suddenly struck me I had no idea what I would do or even say if I actually confronted him.

26
LITTLE BOY LOST

We got out of the cab at Twenty-Fifth Street and walked the few blocks to Colling's apartment building. It was dark outside, but well lit from streetlights and traffic. The apartments were row-type dwellings. A few industrial brick buildings were scattered in with some larger apartment buildings, many with cafés or bars underneath.

Typically for the area, some streets were nicer than others. Colling lived on one of the *other* streets. Below his apartment was a seedy-looking bar called Good Time—you could see the outline of the missing letter S on the faded paint—with wire cage windows and a large, shiny green door defaced with several long scratches that exposed red paint underneath. Good Time(s) indeed. Next to the bar, just a few doors down, was the entrance to Colling's apartment; just beyond that was a small, boarded-up storefront. I don't know what I was thinking going to his place, because there was no way we could get in without ringing random doorbells and hoping someone would buzz us in. Then there was the problem of what to do if we found him. Serious doubts filtered through me, not just about confronting Colling. The whole detective experience, up to this point, had turned into one uncomfortable situation after another. I was flying by the seat of my pants.

We stood across the street from his apartment. I felt sick to my stomach. My throat started to tighten and I felt dizzy. "I don't want to be here, Mill," I said, staring across the street at the blacked-out windows next to the bar, where I was sure torture and mayhem reigned supreme.

A man staggered out of Good Time and drifted around the corner.

"What's the matter?" Mill asked.

"Why do you believe me, Mill? You listen to all my stories, you track this guy down, come to Queens in the middle of the night—"

"It's only eight fifteen," he interrupted.

"Why? Why do you believe me?"

"We're buds." He gave me a lame puppy-dog look, the kind that said he didn't believe me at all, but was just humoring me.

"We're buds? That's it? You track down a dangerous creep, follow me out here, and that's your reason?"

"What do you want me to say?" Mill shrugged.

"Do you believe me when I say that I can see things? The Dream State?"

"Sure."

Again, his eyes betrayed him. He was just along for the ride. As I understood this, it came to me that he really was a true friend. His loyalty was without question. A feeling of pride and strength came to me and bolstered my confidence.

"Okay," I said, "Let's do this."

We crossed the street together and walked up to the apartment doorway. In the vestibule was a row of mailboxes and several labeled doorbells. I finally found the one with the name, *Colling*, scratched in black ink. It was for Apartment 3A. I turned to Mill, who was standing so close I could smell his bubble gum.

"Should I ring his, or someone else's?"

Mill pursed his lips and shrugged. "I don't know. Can you, like, go into a trance from touching his doorbell?"

"Can I go into a trance from the doorbell? No, I can't go into a...I need something personal that he touches all the time, and maybe then it will work. A doorbell is not personal."

The outer door opened and an old woman, who looked to be about eighty, pushed a small wire-framed shopping cart, loaded with groceries, into the vestibule. Mill and I crowded together in the corner. She stood staring at us.

"Who you want?" she asked in a strange accent. I think it was either German or Polish or something in between. A blue kerchief covered her short, white hair and was tied neatly under her chin. Her jowls bobbed up and down as she chewed on something.

"Ah, just checking to see if a friend lives here," I said, unsure of what to do.

"You have key?"

"No, no key," I said.

"Who your friend?"

I turned quickly to the mailboxes looking for a name other than Colling. She seemed to sense my distress and stomped a foot hard to the floor.

"You can' stay here. I call police."

"Of course," I said.

"Need room, need room!" She pushed her way past us, stood by the inner door, and turned her shopping cart to block us. "I call police."

We quickly exited the vestibule. Mill let out a guffaw and staggered into me, almost knocking me down.

"Shit," I said.

The old lady turned to face us, looking straight ahead through the glass paned, outer door. She fixed her eyes in a deadly stare, obviously telegraphing a final warning. Mill smiled and waved at her. I pulled his arm down and we walked a few feet toward the bar.

"What do you want to do now, Professor?" Mill asked.

"Shut up for a second, let me think." Trying to find Colling in his natural habitat seemed even more ridiculous now. "I guess we find the train back to Manhattan," I said. "I really don't think we can handle Colling after that old lady whipped our asses."

Mill chuckled and spat his wad of gum onto the sidewalk. I started to chastise him, but caught sight of a guy walking into the bar, carrying a motorcycle helmet.

"Did you see that?" I asked.

"I think so."

We walked slowly to Good Time. Mill peered in through one of the windows.

"Well?" I asked.

"Shit. I think it's him."

I looked around the corner. Down the street, just a few blocks away, a large black motorcycle was parked just behind a beat-up minivan. "I think that's his bike right there," I said.

Mill looked down the street then back to me. "Okay, so you want to get a drink?" he asked.

"He doesn't know you, Mill."

"What good does that do? You're the one who needs to touch his stuff."

"You can order while I hide in a booth."

"Are you serious?"

I wanted to run away. I had no plan. Then, what I was trying to piece together suddenly became clear. "He doesn't know you, so you—"

"Watch him while you search his apartment," Mill interrupted.

"Exactly. His apartment is on the ground floor. Text me if he leaves the bar."

"Why don't we just walk in there and confront him?"

"I told you, if I'm close to him, his things, I'm hoping to have a vision. A Dream State. If I do, it may show me whether or not he was involved in Emma's death. Or at least where he was when it happened. I don't want to go into a Dream State right in front of him, he's dangerous."

"And we're not?" he said with a smile. "Well shit, if that's what you want, I bet his seat is still warm."

We both looked toward the motorcycle.

I raised an eyebrow. "Mill, you've got a brain in there." I tried to tap his head but he pulled away. "You wait right here. Text me if he leaves the bar or walks this way. It shouldn't take long."

Mill nodded and lit a cigarette.

"Hey, what are you doing?" I asked.

He shrugged. "The spy biz is stressful, Gus. Got to do something."

"Horseshit," I said, and took the butt from his mouth. "Don't use me as an excuse to start smoking. Okay?"

He gave me a quick nod and turned toward the bar.

The motorcycle seat actually was still warm. I sat down and took hold of the handlebars, feeling like a kid in front of the grocery store. *Put a nickel in the slot and watch it go.* A few cars drove past and each time I expected someone to yell, "Get off that bike!"

The motorcycle was perched on a kickstand and was stable enough that I was able to swing both legs up onto the footrests. My inner child was shouting, *Vroom, vroom!*

Adjusting myself on the bike saddle, I looked down at the leaf-filled gutters and saw a trickle of water. I stared at the reflections of red neon light from a nearby deli, as my mind became less and less focused on the present. Soon, my eyes unfocused and a darkness began to envelop me. It was a darkness I'd never felt before. There was something there in that void, an emptiness I could tell wanted to be filled with the spirit of the living, something living, anything alive.

I see splashes of Colling's life, like pages of a picture book turning in front of me. A toothless toddler wandering around an empty house. Then a middle school boy dressed in shabby clothes, so needy for love I can feel it gnaw at me like hunger. He's older, his front teeth darkened by decay, a night spent in a homeless shelter. A feckless old man I know to be his father, staring down at me. A lack of love and self-esteem so palpable I want to cry. The darkness becomes blackness and envelops me. I feel it gripping my chest. I struggle to breathe. My head feels light. Black and white dots fill my vision. The blackness holds me there, squeezing me tight. Then I see Emma. She is running away from something. She turns to look at me. Terror grips her face. Is it him she sees? Is she running from Colling or me? Am I Colling now?

She turns to run, but falls forward. She's on her hands and knees now, desperate, crying. Then the blood splatters, her face on the ground, her eyes open, vacant. Blood pools and runs under her head. Carrillo is there. He looks at me, his mouth moves, but I can't understand what he is saying. I can feel the words, they hit me in the chest where the Black Hand grips me.

"What did you do that for?" Carrillo cries, fear, anguish and astonishment in his eyes. Those eyes turn and stare at me now. They are filled with hate. There's a sharp pain in my knee, and the darkness begins to slip away. I feel myself crawling, slithering free from a strangling vine.

When the darkness lifted, I found myself sitting on the street next to the bike. I rubbed my scuffed knee. My hands were numb from hitting the pavement. My jeans were ripped and my knee was bloody. Tears filled my eyes. I took a deep breath, then another. Oxygen filled my lungs and began to clear my head, but the words still rang in my ears, "What did you do that for?" The look on Carrillo's face was completely unsettling, and I shuddered to remember it.

"Are you all right?" A voice came to me from the shadows. A young man of about twenty stood on the sidewalk looking down at me. I smiled and nodded.

"Just tripped," I said. "Thanks."

He nodded and walked away. I heard footsteps running in my direction.

"He's out. Go, go!" Mill was running down the street toward me. "Did you have a dream?" I nodded and he helped me to my feet. "He's leaving the bar. We've got to get out of here."

He spun me in the opposite direction and we walked arm in arm for a few yards, then I pulled my arm away from his. As we rounded the corner of the first building, the grating boom of Colling's motorcycle rang out.

"Shit," Mill said. "He was right behind me."

"Did he see you?" I asked.

"If anything, he saw my back for a second."

I touched my finger under my nose. "No blood," I said.

"Lucky," Mill said.

"No, I mean my nose."

He looked at me and smirked. "Look a little lower."

I felt below my nose. Dried blood had crusted on my chin. "Shit," I said. "I thought I'd turned a corner." In the light from an appliance store window, I saw the dark droplets on my pant leg and the front of my shirt.

"What happened?" Mill asked. He held a cigarette to his nose and was huffing in the tobacco smell. "Did you see something about Colling?"

Yes, I thought to myself. *I did see something. Something dark.*

Mill turned to me. "Well?"

"I'm pretty sure Colling killed her."

"Seriously?"

"Carrillo was there, but I think Colling did the deed."

"Let's get out of here." Mill quickened his pace toward the train station. As I struggled to keep up, I wondered what the blackness meant. The blackness that had surrounded me, choked me, had wanted my life force. A part of me already knew the answer to that question, and I didn't want it to be true.

27
WHERE'S THE GROMMET?

I had a couple of choices. I could blow off work, thus burning some bridges and setting myself up for getting fired, or show up for work, complete the task at hand, and get out as quickly as I could. I chose to show up, and I hated every minute of it. It felt like going into an antique shop where every item in the store was broken. It was yesterday's news, junk. And of course, the two-hour estimate from my boss turned into almost a full day's work.

At mid-morning break, I called Carla for the third time. It went straight to voicemail, again. I figured it was because she was at work, even though I had a little voice telling me otherwise. The last time we'd met, at Café Divine, she was going off to work a night shift.

Now I began to wonder about her. Why had she not mentioned that not only did she know Professor Phelps, but he'd also introduced her to Guy Jackson as though he knew her intimately?

"Carla, I have vital information about the case. Call as soon as you hear this."

What else could I say?

Around two in the afternoon, I finally finished with work and decided to grab a bite to eat at a nearby café. I wasn't rich by any means, but Frank's money allowed me to eat out more than usual, and I was enjoying myself.

Café Dos was a little hole-in-the wall Mexican restaurant,

perfect for a quick lunch. It was friendly, had fast service and good food. I sat near the window looking out on to Columbus Avenue. My chicken taco plate arrived promptly. I was starving.

About halfway through the second taco, however, I could feel it coming on. A terrible ache in my temples, and my hands began to shake. My nose dripped blood onto my plate. "No," I said aloud, and tried to resist going into the Dream State, but it came on anyway. I covered my face with my hands and fought as much as I could, but suddenly I was there, downtown, near 5 Varick Street in Manhattan. I know it was there because I'd witnessed the same accident several times before.

It's a beautiful, late afternoon fall day. The low angle of the sun makes the narrow street a canyon of deep shadows.

Luke, the Skateboard Kid, skitches behind a water delivery truck. I see the tops of his black canvas sneakers on the skateboard, the closeness of the road as he cruises along. His earbuds are blaring skate punk music. Then the truck turns off to the left, Skateboard Kid lets go, but there is another truck directly in front of him, parked perpendicular to the street, and he's gone. Not under the truck, but lost under a city bus he doesn't see. It pulls out from a stop from behind the truck, and Skateboard Kid doesn't see or hear anything ever again.

"Everything okay?" A voice rang in my ears, bringing me back.

I looked up to see the waitress standing at my table. I was grateful for not having to see Skateboard Kid's head crushed in again.

"Yes," I said, trying to sound cheerful, but was unable to hide the tears in my eyes. "It's very good. Hot." I waved my hands over my mouth, wiped my eyes with my napkin and took a drink of water. That stupid kid.

I had to do something. If only I could make him listen. He was still alive, for now. Otherwise, the dreams wouldn't come. It had been maybe two weeks since I first saw his death. He was running out of time. I decided I had to do something about it right then. Right after I finished my taco, beans and rice.

Thirty minutes later, I caught a bus down to the skate park in Tribeca. Having some time to think about what I was going to do seemed of little use. Pleading with him was all I could come up with, and it felt very inadequate.

I jumped off the bus at the skate park and scanned the area for Luke, but nobody was there except a few hardcore skate dudes milling around on the street outside the park. I was thinking of going over to ask them a few questions, but thought better of it. The thing about skaters, generally speaking, is they're usually friendly, but world-class smart-asses and won't ever give a stranger a straight answer. And besides, I didn't want to get a skateboard in the gut again.

I sat on a bench near the skate park and, once more, dialed Carla. I hung up before it could ring. I didn't want her to think I was stalking her. Just as I disconnected the call, my phone rang. It was Mill.

"You tell Carla about Colling yet?" he asked.

"I haven't been able to reach her."

"That's a bummer."

Then I had an idea. "Hey, Mill. I want you to do a background check on her."

"What do you mean?"

"I want to know everything I can about Carla Donati. Her employment, marriages, schools, the whole enchilada."

"Why?"

"She's been a bit shady with me, I think. Just a hunch."

"You can't just dream it? Go into a trance and see all, know all?" His question sounded like a wiseass observation, but it actually made a little sense from his limited perspective. I decided to indulge him.

"It doesn't work that way, Mill."

"You took a seat on Colling's bike, and *bam*, you saw something."

"That's different. It was related to the dream I had about Emma. I can't just touch somebody and see things, unless it's related to a dream I've already had. Get it?"

"Not really," he said. "What about the Fat Man? You saw his stuff by touching a stuffed cat."

"It was a stuffed rabbit, and I have no idea why I was able to do that. I'm beginning to think it has something to do with the strong emotions associated with death. The Fat Man had a sister that drowned right in front of him. That emotion was one of the most powerful I've ever felt."

"Oh."

There was a slight pause. Mill made a sucking sound and I began to think he may be smoking again.

"So Carla, huh?" Mill asked.

"Let me know as soon as you can."

"Will do."

I was about to hang up, but could hear his strange breathing again. "You smoking?"

"No."

Another short pause.

"But, I want to."

"Don't."

"Yeah, yeah. I got it. So, you want to meet up later?"

"Only if you're not smoking."

"I'm not smoking!"

"Because I need a guy with backbone behind me, Mill. Not some wimp who can't beat cigarettes."

"Wimp? What are you, a tough guy, won't even walk into a bar with Colling? You calling me a wimp?"

"You calling me a name caller?" I asked.

He laughed. "I'll see you later, at The Tavern," he said, and hung up.

The wimp comment stung a bit. Mill knew going into that bar with Colling was not a smart idea. I started to wonder how much of what I did, and how much I cared, was even apparent to Mill. Then I took into account his quirky nature, and let it go.

A few more skaters were hanging around the entrance to the park, but Skateboard Kid was not among them. I called up a map of Manhattan on my cell, and located 5 Varick Street. It was just a few blocks from the park. I decided to walk there and see the accident scene for real. It had haunted me so much lately, I felt I knew every brick and crack on that street.

As I made my way down Monroe, I had a strong feeling the accident was imminent. If there was only some way I could warn Skateboard Kid, get him to actually listen for a change. From looking at the map, there was nothing special around the area of 5 Varick Street. It had a bus stop, the one near which he would be killed, and further down was an entrance to the subway, which I presumed was his destination. He probably took the train to Franklin Street station, got off and rode his board to the park.

A quick internet search revealed in 1996 Mayor Giuliani signed into law an ordinance against reckless skating. It provided that if you skated in a reckless fashion, so as to endanger others, you would be fined about a hundred bucks. Probably a lot of money to a kid like Luke. An earlier version of the law stated that if you were over the age of fourteen, you had to skate on the street. That law was later struck down. If you did skate on the sidewalk, however, you must move at the same speed as someone walking at a normal pace.

The slow speed of walkers would have given Luke, and most other skaters, incentive to get off the sidewalk and skate on a smooth street as often as possible.

As I turned right, off Monroe and onto Varick, I realized why Skateboard Kid would decide to skitch onto this street. There was about a hundred yards of freshly laid, smooth asphalt. The street was virtually irresistible to any skater.

I walked down to the bus stop and studied the area. I could see the reason for the accident. Skateboard Kid skitching behind a large truck would not be blind to the other delivery truck parked perpendicular to the street. If he let go of the truck, he'd swerve directly toward the parked delivery truck, then he'd immediately have to swerve left to avoid colliding with that, and back into the street he'd go, directly in front of the city bus. It made me nauseous to see it again in my mind's eye. At least I didn't go into a Dream State.

A feeling of helplessness fell upon me. I wanted to stop Skateboard Kid from being killed, but how to prevent it eluded me. I sat on a fire hydrant and searched the street for clues, an answer, some inspiration, and eventually I found it.

About twenty yards down the street, off the sidewalk to the right, was a sawhorse police barricade. I walked over to it. Several more barricades blocked an alleyway entrance. I presumed they were left over from the construction job and had not yet been picked up by the police. I looked again at the spot where Luke would get hit, then to the spot where the delivery truck would park.

"Shit," I said aloud. "Could it be that simple?"

I dragged one of the heavy police barricades to the spot where the truck would be parked the day of the accident and placed it parallel to the sidewalk with the large, white *Police Do Not Cross* lettering facing the street. I placed two more barricades perpendicular to those, so as to make a U-shape toward the street. When I was done, I stepped back and admired my handiwork. Immediately, relief washed over me and I was happy with the effort. It looked official, if not completely convincing. Short of tracking down Skateboard Kid and tying him up, I'd done the only thing I could to change the accident scene and, hopefully, stop the nightmare from occurring. If the police barricade remained in place, there was no way the delivery truck would park there. Luke wouldn't have to swerve toward the bus and get his head crushed. Thanks to me, and the New York City police, the spot would remain unoccupied, at least until they came to get the barricades. And even then, the workers retrieving them wouldn't know why mine were in place, and would probably leave them there. That's what I hoped, anyway.

Unfortunately, reality has a way of creeping along, unchanged by small glitches, and things that are supposed to happen generally find a way to come to fruition.

28

DREAM POOL

T *he pistol hand of the shooter rises slowly, finding its mark, and the gun fires. The blast of the weapon creates a violent turbulence propelled out in all directions, blowing out the windows and doors of the building, crushing the steel support girders, and melting broken glass in midair, turning the shards into molten drops of fire. The screams of the people are joined together into one single chorus of dread, their faces bubbling up in painful blisters, then shriveling away into gray ash, leaving bare skulls that slowly transform from scorched black to fragile white bone, until all the people in the vicinity are burned away, leaving only human powder falling quietly onto the scattered rubble.*

I woke up, sitting in the cool pool of light from my bedside lamp, my sheets sopping with moisture. I held a finger to my neck, but couldn't count the beats; my heart was racing so fast. I took long, deep breaths trying to calm myself.

Dreams of this magnitude don't come very often, but when they do...The last time I awoke in this state, it was just before a huge building fire killed twelve people.

I lay back, calming myself, trying to make sense of what I'd just seen. It was something to do with a handgun. I had a gun, or the man near me had a gun, or maybe we both had guns, and he was going to kill a whole lot of people.

The ridiculously huge report of the weapon is what took me out of the dream. I could still feel the blast on the right side of my face, the pressure bursting in my ears. I rubbed my face, holding in deep my breaths to slow my hurtling heart.

Breathe in while counting to four, hold it for seven seconds...

I couldn't place the location of the dream, or the shooter or how many people were there. I knew only the blast, and the sting of gunpowder residue hitting my face, and that he intended to kill every person there, including himself. Obviously, it was a grand nightmare, an exaggeration of reality, but I could feel in that grandness a pinch of stark reality. This dream was a warning of things to come.

I sprang from my bed, groped blindly through the darkened hallway and into the kitchen, flipped on the lights and took the pitcher of water from the fridge. I drank from the side of the pitcher, until my head ached from the cold, then held the cool wetness of the container to the side of my face. I leaned into the mirror over the sink and flipped on the light above. No sign of powder burns on my cheek, no bruising anywhere on my skin. I looked intently at the mirror and thought, *Hath sorrow struck so many blows upon this face of mine and made no deeper wounds?* Shakespeare had it right. Sorrow comes, but does not show outwardly until much later. I searched again for powder burns on my angled cheek and found none.

Returning to my warm bed, I flopped down onto my back. Restless and hot, I soon sat up again, resting my elbows on my knees. An image of all those burning faces lit in my mind. My throat tightened and my eyes welled with tears. All those people. Why me? I didn't ask for this power, and I couldn't handle another case, nor did I want to see another death.

When I discovered my precognitive ability after my first few Dream States, and had finally convinced myself that I was not crazy or madly ill, I went on a protracted binge, researching various paranormal experiences. I looked into every phenomenon, read dozens of books, watched many film clips and TV shows, and quickly rejected most of the claims of the paranormal.

I did discover, however, a remarkable cache of scientific research that confirmed my suspicions about the human mind and its power over matter. I read about the scientifically observed instant communication between atoms, and how they respond to human observation. How emotions can actually affect DNA.

One experiment observed how the human mind, concentrating on a leaf, affected the healing of that leaf from several miles away. Most interesting was an experiment involving a group of people who, just by thinking positively, reduced criminal activity, car accidents, and injuries in a particular area where they operated.

Now, I realize these were baby steps, but they gave me the confidence I needed to move forward. It was confirmation that some unseen force connects us all.

I became convinced this force was some sort of energy field surrounding all living creatures, and was capable of transmitting patterns, and those patterns could be seen, similar to a television broadcast. Somehow, I was able to tap into that energy and see those patterns. In essence, I was seeing future events through a specific wave pattern in time. Somehow, I believed, the future already exists, along with the past and the present. Everything that ever happened or will happen has already occurred: it is only our human form that requires it be in a specific order.

We may be as insignificant or as a grand as a momentary thought in God's mind.

Take Frank's dilemma, for example. Perhaps I could experience what a person sees and feels when they die. But I wasn't sure I was brave enough to experience his sister's horrendous drowning.

At any rate, I was the human conduit into which these recorded events could flow and be seen, usually created by some horrific event. I knew my theory didn't make perfect sense, but I was grasping at straws, and the explanation was only for my benefit, no one else's.

Carla's pretty face popped into my thoughts again. I checked my cell phone. There had been no calls or messages since I'd fallen asleep. The clock read 4:00 p.m. My nap had been forty-five minutes, just long enough for me to fall into that abysmal nightmare.

Feeling weak and run down, I forced myself up and into the shower. The hot water warmed and relaxed me and I began to feel human again. Still wet, I was about to call Carla, when my cell phone rang. It was Mill.

"Any word from Carla?" he asked.

"Nah. I'm starting to think she's blowing me off, Mill."

"That's interesting."

I took a deep breath. "Or something's happened to her. We should go down to the hospital and see if she's at work."

"Well, I was going to tell you later but…"

"But what?" I asked.

"I did some checking, like you suggested. She's not at Sloan Kettering."

"Oh?"

"Hasn't been working there since last week."

I paused, another twist in the gut. "Why would she lie about that?" I asked.

"Actually, she didn't even work there full time. It was a part-time thing. A fill-in situation."

"She told me she was a traveler."

"What's that?" Mill asked.

"A medical professional, travels from place to place, not staying anywhere for more than a few months."

"Well, that might explain the inconsistencies in her background. I don't see her having steady employment anywhere."

"It would be through an agency, I think. She is a nurse, right?"

"Seems to be."

"What do you mean, seems to be?"

"Well, I saw other types of employment, too."

"Such as?"

"Assistant Professor."

"You've got to be kidding me. Where?"

"Where do you think?"

"NYU?"

"Yes. But not in the Economics Department, like our friend, Phelps. She was in the School of Public Health."

"So, she was an Assistant Professor at the same college as Phelps."

"Yup."

"Did she think we wouldn't find that out?"

"It's public information."

I thought for a moment, trying to piece together any connections to Phelps that could help explain her behavior. I thought of her at that mixer, her nice red shoes being remembered by Guy Jackson.

"Gus?" Mill cut into my reverie.

"I'm blown away, Mill. Why didn't she just tell me these things?"

"Beats me."

"She works at the school," I said, "sees her sister getting involved with her boss, Professor Phelps, finds out she is sleeping with him, then her sister gets killed. She contacts me long after the fact and says nothing about the connection. She knows I was questioned in the case. She lies about herself. What's her angle?"

"Checking to see how safe she is?" Mill offered.

"What's that?"

"If Carla's involved, she hires you to see how safe she is."

"Involved? No, that doesn't seem right. That reminds me of the lady who poisoned her husband, got away with it, then called the cops to say she suspected he was poisoned."

"Exactly. But why would she report it?"

"Who?"

"The lady. She killed her husband and had gotten away with it. They thought it was a heart attack. But later on, she reports it may have been poison, because she wanted money from the ongoing litigation against the drug company. She'd put the poison in the drug company's caps of medicine," he said. "A copycat killing. Only they didn't catch it."

"Greed," I said. "You think Carla wants something from this investigation, besides wanting us to find the killer. That she has something else to gain."

"Exactly."

"Shit, Mill."

"I know." He sucked in a deep breath, and let out his words slowly. "You're going to have to take that goddess crown off her head, Gus."

"Maybe I don't want to."

"I have more," he said.

"Tell me."

"You sure?"

"Say it."

"My contact, the cop who shall remain nameless on the telephone, came up with a bunch of information on Emma's murder. It's an ongoing investigation, so I asked the questions and he read the answers from the file. But the file stays in house. It's too big to steal a photocopy, you know?"

"Of course. So what's the status of the investigation?"

"Well, it's starting to go cold. They interviewed several witnesses, came up with nothing. The witnesses said it was either too dark, or they only heard the screams and didn't see anything because, as you know, she was killed in an alley and who could bother finding out why a woman was screaming."

"Yeah, gotta love the city. I've seen that alley many times in person and in my dreams. Go on. What about Colling and Carrillo?"

"They were both interviewed and both had alibis."

"Fuckers. Who vouched for them?"

"Bruno."

"Bruno, the friendly disappearing spook?"

"Got that right. It's the only mention of Bruno in the files. He's listed as a Government Contractor."

"Yeah, I bet he is."

"And you're named several times, Gus. Were you stalking her?"

An involuntary laugh blurted out of me. "Yeah, I guess you could say that. But trying to warn her. I had that dream for weeks before…" I paused and took a deep breath. Flashes of her murder filled my head. The deathblow descended. Blood spattered. I blinked, trying to make it stop.

"You want to meet up?" Mill asked.

"Wait." My throat tightened, making my voice crack with emotion. Holding the phone away, I took a few deep breaths. When my throat relaxed, I asked, "Is Carla…Has she ever been married?"

"No record of a marriage."

"Is she dating anyone now?"

"I don't know that, Gus."

"Is there a lawsuit against anyone involved in Emma's murder?"

"What do you mean?"

"A civil suit related to the case?"

"I don't think so. My source didn't say anything about that. Like I said, the case is still open, but growing cold."

I paced my bedroom, craving a drink to calm my nerves. "Meet me at The Tavern in fifteen minutes, Mill. And bring all your notes."

"Oh, I got notes. I got—"

I hung up. I didn't mean to cut him off, but I was jumpy.

My vision of Carla as the protective and loving sister had blackened. Like the poor souls in my dream, her beautiful face rippled and scorched in front of my eyes. Every curve of her was now suspect. I'd craved to get to know her, and now it looked like I was going to get my wish, only not in the way I'd hoped. It was time to put a tail on Carla to find out exactly what she was doing.

29
WHEN FIRST WE PRACTICE

Mill took a deep drag on his unlit cigarette and gave me a sly glance. "Carla lives in a corner apartment in Greenwood Heights, Brooklyn," he said.

"Good," I said, and sat down next to him at the bar. I still hadn't heard from Carla, and I was beginning to worry. "I want to go there."

Allen stood under the glow of the fuzzy TV screen and watched an old rugby match from twenty-odd years ago. He turned from the screen and raised his chin at Mill, whose cigarette dangled from his lips, as if to say, "What's that?"

"Fucking Nazi," Mill said under his breath, and held up the butt to show it to Allen, then pretended to smash out the burning embers in the palm of his hand. Mill grimaced in faux pain, then flicked his hand open and held it up ceremoniously. Allen gave a perverse smile, nodded and winked, as if getting the joke. Mill gave a sneering nod, then looked back at me.

"Always a partier, that Allen. I love it when he dances, all the way to the bathroom."

"When are you two kids gonna kiss and make up?" I asked.

"I can't answer that, Gus," Mill said, with false gravitas. He smiled menacingly at Allen, who was now busying himself with a rag on the bar top.

"The animosity keeps us young…"

"Brooklyn," I said, trying to get Mill back on track. I didn't relish the idea of going all that way, but infatuation, longing and mystery have a way of driving a person to do stupid things. "Can you get a car?"

"Guess what, man? Mine's ready," he said.

"I was hoping you'd say that," I replied, knowing full well it had been in the shop for years.

"But it'll cost you."

"Me? Well, I'll pay for gas, obviously."

"And the beer."

"Okay, beer."

Mill sucked on his unlit cigarette, then took a few swallows of stout. "What are we hoping to see? Besides her changing near the bedroom window, I mean." He snickered.

"Look, Carla came to me looking for answers. We dug a bit and uncovered a whole lot. The energy company, Bruno, Carrillo—"

"And don't forget our favorite asshole, Colling," Mill interjected.

"And now," I continued, "I have questions about her motives. She lied to me by omission."

"My wife did that on our wedding day."

"I realize she may have legitimate reasons, but damn it, she's not answering her phone."

"So really, you're just checking up on her."

I thought about that and realized he was right. As much as I hated to admit it, I was more worried for her safety than upset about the lies. It brought me back to my problem with idealizing women in general. "Well, shit, Mill," I said.

"Hey, that word! I'm *drinking* here," he said, in faux disgust.

"I think it's the right move. I haven't heard from her in a few days. I've left several messages."

"Oh, wow. A woman who won't call back?" He rolled his eyes.

196

"And now that I know she could be mixed up with the professor—"

"Say no more, my good man, say no more. But buy me one for the road. And a hot dog, too."

We left the bar around seven, a little too indulged for my taste. We walked a few blocks from The Tavern to the garage where Mill kept his car. At his insistence, I stood at the exit to the garage and waited for him to retrieve it. Tires screeched, an engine roared, and a horn tooted as he came barreling around the corner in his fully restored 1967 Chevrolet Camaro SS in metallic black. The car skidded to a halt in front of me. Mill leaned over and smiled from the driver's seat. "Get in," he said.

"You've spent your money wisely, my good man," I said, as I climbed into the front passenger seat.

"The wife won't be able to touch this little baby. I put it in my brother's name." He laughed and the tires squealed as we wove our way past a parked car and zoomed out onto the street.

The traffic was light and we arrived at Greenwood Heights in about an hour. It was getting dark and it must have been fifty degrees. A few raindrops pelted the windshield. Mill parked the car on the street near Carla's apartment and switched off the ignition. I noticed a dark area at the end of Thirty-Second Street, which I assumed was a park. Mill turned to me and took a long pull on his unlit butt.

"I'll wait here, Chief," he said.

I pulled my collar up against the cold rain and climbed out. The building was a five-story brick job that looked newly renovated. I wondered if it was a little too pricey on a nurse's salary, even if she had a roommate.

A small vestibule held the usual inner door. Mailboxes flanked the walls on both sides. I quickly found the one marked *Donati*. The box was stuffed full with mail. Unless she was extremely popular or got fan mail, it seemed likely that it hadn't been emptied in a few days. I pushed the doorbell, but didn't expect an answer.

As I stood in the entrance, the chill dampness seeping in through my jacket, a steady rain started outside. I could see Mill sitting in the car with the window part way down, puffing on his unlit cigarette. I gave him a wave, but he didn't see me. After a few minutes of pushing the bell, I turned to leave.

Lights flashed directly in front of the doorway and a motorcycle pulled to the curb. I opened the door and about ten feet to my right, Colling got off his bike. He was dressed in black leather from head to boot. We both froze as we sized each other up, before he jumped back on his bike and roared off.

Mill's engine was already running. "That's Colling!" I cried, running back to the car. "Follow him."

Mill put it in gear and fishtailed into the street, skidding on the wet pavement as we turned the corner at the end of the street. I caught a glimpse of Colling as he made the turn toward the dark, tree lined area to our right.

"Into the park," I said.

Mill slammed on the brakes. We skidded again and slid into the turn, driving in through the gate. Immediately, I realized it wasn't a park, but a cemetery. Up ahead, the bike's brake light betrayed Colling's location.

"He's in there," I said, pointing. "Take a right."

Mill slowed, but still fishtailed around the corner. I saw the back of Colling's motorcycle as he disappeared around another corner.

"Step on it."

"What do we do if we catch him?" Mill asked, his eyes glued on the darkened road.

I didn't answer. I had no idea. He'd probably have a gun, but his instinct had been to run, and mine was to give chase. "He's heading to the nearest exit up ahead," I said.

"I'm on him."

We slid into a hairpin turn. Up ahead, a light flipped in the air, and we stopped dead in front of Colling as he stood over his dumped bike. He had indeed tried to exit, only that particular gate was closed. The bike had skidded on the wet pavement and came to a stop against the metal gate. Colling stood hunched over his bike, sopping wet, leaves and debris clinging to his black leathers. Mill turned the car directly on him, illuminating the scene. I quickly got out and stood by the car.

"What do you want?" Colling shouted.

"How about we have a little chat?"

Colling looked beyond my right shoulder. I glanced back and saw Mill standing by the car, a tire iron in his hands. "Fuck you," Colling said, and started to lift his bike.

I sprinted over and put my foot on the seat. The bike slipped from his grasp, and he let out a yelp as it landed on his foot. Mill raced to my side.

"You're fucking crazy," said Colling.

"Where's Carla Donati?"

"How should I know?"

"You stopped in front of her apartment."

"I saw an open spot."

"Where's Carla," I repeated. "Did you kill her, too?"

Colling's demeanor changed. Removing his black helmet, he wiped some rain-slicked hair from his face before pulling out a switchblade.

"I thought you preferred a pistol or a brick," I said, getting ready to run. Mill raised the tire iron.

"Back off," Colling warned, carving the air in front of him. I stepped back. Mill followed my lead.

Snippets of the Dream State from Colling's bike raced through my mind. The sad, neglected kid with rotten teeth was standing right in front of me.

"Little Justin Colling," I said. "Last kid in the milk line. Never anybody home to give you that nickel, huh, Justin? Mommy always gone, and Daddy, well, he didn't really care much about anything, did he?"

Colling narrowed his eyes, then took a step toward me, thrusting the knife. Mill raised the tire iron.

"What the fuck do you know about anything?" Colling said.

"I know you killed Emma Donati. I saw you there."

"You're crazy," he said, and looked around uneasily.

"That's right, I saw the whole thing. Emma running. Carrillo and you chasing after. Only Carrillo didn't want to kill her. You did that on your own, didn't you? In the heat of the moment."

"I don't know what you're talking about."

"But why were you chasing her? What threat was she to you? Or was it Bruno, did he send you after her?" Colling stiffened visibly at the mention of Bruno. "So, Bruno was the boss, huh? What did Emma discover that made her such a threat? Was she blackmailing Bruno? Or maybe the professor?"

Colling flipped the knife into his other hand and glanced down at the prone bike. Multicolored gasoline seepage ran onto the wet pavement and snaked slowly toward his boots.

"What about dear old Professor Phelps?" I asked. "Where does he fit into all of this?"

Colling leaped toward me, grazing my arm with the blade. Mill took a swing at Colling but missed. I took a step back. Colling swiftly righted the motorcycle. I ran toward him, but he mounted the bike and kicked out, connecting with my stomach. I slipped on some wet leaves and fell back, hitting my head on the pavement hard enough to see stars. The bike roared to life and disappeared in a cloud of exhaust.

Mill stood over me. "You okay?"

For a split second, I didn't know where I was, then I saw Mill and it came back. "He got away?"

"You're lucky he didn't kill you. What the hell were you thinking?"

"I don't know."

"Are you bleeding?"

I sat up and felt the back of my head. An open cut seeped blood. "Shit," I said, and tried to stand, but suddenly felt nauseous and sat back down.

"Let me see." Mill checked my head. "You're gonna need stitches. How do you feel?"

I shook my head. "He's a dangerous man, Mill. We've got to get him."

"I think he got you," Mill said, and helped me to my feet.

"He killed Emma. I'm sure of it. Did you see his face when I mentioned Bruno? White as a sheet."

"We should get that cut looked at. Did he get your arm?"

I checked my sleeve. The blade went no further than the outer layer of my jacket. The nausea lessened, but was still there. "Thanks, Mill," I said.

"For what?"

"For backing me up. It gave me the courage to face him."

"Shit, if I'd have known that, I'd have dropped the tire iron."

30
ARE YOU GOING TO EAT THAT SANDWICH?

I was feeling a bit woozy when we got back in the car. I turned to Mill and said, "Hey Bud, how far are we going?"

He gave me a quizzical glance. "What do you mean?" he asked.

My brain began to feel like a fish in a barrel on a roller coaster. I was more nauseous than before and thought I might throw up. I leaned back in the seat.

Mill looked concerned. "You all right?"

"I don't feel good," I said.

"Hang in there, buddy. It's just a short hop to the hospital."

I closed my eyes. My sloshing brain felt like it was in the deep end of a lake, in a dark place, surrounded by choppy waves. Trees, leaves and frogs appeared, dancing about on the bank. I had a strange, unsettled feeling as they danced. Tiny round frog eyes stared at me expectantly, waiting for my reaction to the entertainment.

Then, I was standing on a dark city street. Skateboard Kid was flying around, doing zigzags in the air. He flew up the sides of buildings and turned his board in mid-air, heading back toward me as I stood on the side of the street, watching. An invisible crowd reacted with cheers and whoops at each of his tricks. Motorcycle Jacket was there, sitting on his bike at the end of the street, ripping the motor to full throttle, waiting to come forward.

Skateboard Kid crossed the street, and Motorcycle Jacket took off, heading in my direction. The bike vibrated me to the bone as it approached and smashed into me. I shattered like glass, into infinitesimal pieces, almost vaporizing into a mist, lost in the turbulence of the motorcycle's wake. Motorcycle Jacket rode up the side of a tall brick building, completed a 360-degree turn in mid-air, miraculously clinging to the side of the building, and came zipping back around again.

Suddenly Frank was there. The Fat Man waddled across the street like a stuffed goose but he didn't make it to the other side of the street before being struck by Motorcycle Jacket. Frank exploded into a puff of white doves that dispersed in all directions.

Mill was touching my shoulder. I turned and smiled. "Are we there?" I asked, not knowing where *there* was, only that I needed to get somewhere.

"Had to park in the back," Mill said.

As I got out of the car and followed Mill toward the hospital entrance, my head began to clear a bit and I realized where I was. The faint blue hallway, illuminated by cool lighting, contrasted with the dark red blood splatter on one of the emergency room walls. The hallway looked like a war zone. Dabs of discolored gauze and medical tape lay scattered across the floor.

I looked into a room full of disaffected people. Some sat and talked quietly, others milled about aimlessly or stood because there were no more chairs. Most were hunched over their cell phones, staring at tiny illuminated screens.

I turned to Mill. "Let's get out of here."

"Got to get you sewn up. Stay here." Mill walked over to a window at the other end of the room and stood in a short line.

I turned toward a row of chairs. A woman dressed in pajamas, who had been lying down, sat up and motioned for me to sit. Reluctantly, I took the chair and nodded to her. She gave me a weary smile and closed her eyes, her head dipping forward onto her chest. The man sitting on the other side of me held his wrist in his hand like a makeshift cast and moaned softly. Sitting directly across from me was a man in a wheelchair: a diabetic foot covered in open sores, raised on a leg brace, protruded out for all to see. Three of his toes were missing.

I got up and stood behind Mill in line. "Let's go somewhere else," I whispered.

"Where?" he asked.

"Next," a loud voice emanated from the induction station. Each person in line took a step toward the window in unison. My senses were starting to come back, but a dull headache was beginning behind my eyes. The sharp light of the room caused me to look down as I talked to Mill.

"I don't care, as long as it's not here." I felt a trickle run down the back of my neck. I swiped at it and saw blood on my fingers.

Mill looked at my hand and said, "Go back and sit down. This shouldn't take long."

He retrieved a few tissues from a box sitting on the induction station window. The two other people in line, a middle-aged man and a young woman, followed his hand to mine, obviously curious about my ailment. I gave a wry smile and said, "Cut my head."

I handed Mill my insurance card, then walked back to my previous spot and sat in the chair. The cut on the back of my head was beginning to sting as I held the tissue firmly in place.

After a while, they called me to the window to fill out a form. Later, I'm not sure how long, I was escorted to a small room draped by curtains, and was told to sit on the bed. The doctor came in and flashed a light into my eyes and asked me what happened. I told him I slipped and hit my head. He gave me a very painful shot of lidocaine directly into the cut and sutured my wound, then left me alone.

I began to drift off again. Just as another bizarre dream began to take me, the curtains opened with a loud *swish*, and I popped my eyes open. An angel, radiantly backlit from the hall light stood before me. I was speechless. She stepped into the room and closed the curtains.

"I heard you had a nasty fall," she said.

She was wearing blue scrubs. I looked her up and down in disbelief. "Carla? How...how did you know I was here?"

"I saw your chart."

I must have looked as confused as I felt, because she smiled and said, "I work here."

"Oh," I said, still trying to grasp that it was really her and not another dream. "When did that happen?" I asked. "I thought you were at Sloan?"

"I started here a few days ago. It's been non-stop. Getting the lay of the land."

"You work in this emergency room?"

"Yes. I needed a break from oncology, and I had experience in the ER."

"I've been trying to reach you."

"Strange way to do it."

I smiled and touched my head. "Yeah. You didn't answer my calls. I thought you—"

"What?" she said, defensively then added, "Sorry, Gus, I'm a bit bogged down right now."

I looked down at my sore hands. The knuckles were bloody and scraped.

"You're going to get a tetanus shot," she said. "I have to go, but I'll be back soon." She shut the curtains, then opened them again. "You might need a CT scan for your head."

"Wait, I need to tell you something."

Carla stood in the opening and looked expectantly at me.

"I know it was Colling," I said.

"Colling. You know that for sure?"

"Yes."

"You have proof?"

"Not exactly." She frowned. "I know it was him and it's only a matter of time before we get him."

"He was questioned. The police let him go," she said.

"I know, but we've got him. You wait. He'll get what he deserves."

An expression of grief passed over her face, before she nodded in affirmation.

"I promise, Carla. We're going to get this guy."

She checked her watch. "I have to go. We'll talk later."

I went to her before she could walk away. "Wait."

She turned to me. "You should sit down," she said.

"I almost have this sewn up. You should be happy."

"I know. And I thank you. But I've been living with this nightmare for months now and the police—"

"The police aren't me. I swear to you, we're gonna get this guy." I wanted to take her in my arms and pull her close. Whisper in her ear. Kiss her.

"Because you saw it in a dream?" Her sarcastic tone froze my warm feelings for her instantly.

"Well, no. I—"

"I'm on until eleven-thirty," she interrupted. "I'll be back." She smiled. A conciliatory gesture, I assumed. "We'll talk more then."

Carla disappeared into another curtained room down the hall. Somewhat crestfallen, I returned to the bed and sat down again.

A while later, I was awakened when Mill poked his head into the room and cleared his throat. "I brought you a midnight snack."

"What time is it?" I asked, clearing the sleep from my eyes.

"Not quite eleven," he said. "The cafeteria's pretty good. I had some chicken. Brought you this."

I looked at the wrapped package he held out. The label read *Chicken Salad* in a generically happy font I presumed was intended to entice the reader into devouring the plain, white bread sandwich. My stomach was still turning small circles. Food was the last thing on my mind. "I saw Carla," I said.

He placed the sandwich on a tray near the exam table. "What

do you mean?"

"She works here."

"No shit. She's here now?" He poked his head out between the curtains, then looked back at me. "She works here?"

I nodded and immediately regretted stirring up my scrambled brain. The nausea returned. "She gets off at eleven-thirty. We're gonna talk then."

"You didn't know?"

"She just started. I guess she forgot to tell me."

"Wow, that's a fucking fluke. Hmm." He rolled his eyes.

"What?"

"Come on, man. You have to get knocked on the head to find out where she is? That's fucked up."

"Strange coincidence," I said.

"That's what I'm saying. I don't know, man. This chick is a flake. Here you are, getting your head busted, and she's nowhere to be found."

"I'm not so sure, Mill." I closed my eyes for a few seconds. The dizziness was pretty much gone now, as long as I didn't shake my head. "She's just a bit overwhelmed. Demanding new job..."

Mill shoved his hands deep in his front pockets and gave me a doubtful look.

"I'd believe she was a flake if I was a cynical prick like you, but I'm not, and she's not, so..." I said.

"Okay," he said, dismissively.

"For cripes sake, she's a charge nurse at this hospital. She just started here and didn't have time to get caught up. She's probably working twelve-hour shifts, and has been sleeping in a break room here."

"Well, she's good-looking anyway. You know what I think about that: they'll getcha every time. And don't forget, she didn't tell you she worked at the school."

I inhaled deeply and let out a sigh. "You're right, Mill. She is…"

He gave me a look that said, *Really?*

"Beautiful, that is."

"Beauty is deceptive, Gus. Skin deep. Something to think about. Where there's beauty, there's danger." Mill leaned on the counter near the sink and turned on the faucet, checking to see if it worked, I presumed. After a few good on-off-on-off turns, he stepped back and nodded toward the food. "You going to eat that sandwich?"

"You worried about the sandwich?" I asked.

"No, I just…I got it for you, is all…"

"And I appreciate the thought. Seriously, thanks for sticking around." Mill half-smiled and gave me a nod. I could tell he was happy I'd mentioned his loyalty. "You're a good man, Mill. The best, in my book."

He smiled again, then sat in the chair next to my bed. "So, you saw Carla, and she works here now?"

I nodded. Mill stared at the sandwich on the tray.

"How long ago did you eat?" I asked.

"Oh, I had the chicken, but that was a few hours ago."

"You have it." I said, gesturing toward the sandwich.

"No. I couldn't."

"Well, it's going to go bad. I'm not gonna eat it. Three hours and you have to throw it out."

"Who said three hours? That a rule or something?"

"Yes," I said. "It's a rule."

"Well, shit." He looked at the clock on the wall. It read five minutes to eleven. "Can't have it go to waste."

The curtain opened and a man in black scrubs came in. "Mr. Chase?"

"That's me," I said.

"I'm here to take you for a CT scan."

Mill threw the sandwich back onto the tray and gave me a startled look.

"Can he stay here while I'm gone?" I nodded toward Mill.

"Sure," the man said. He pulled the side railings up and unplugged the bed from the wall outlet.

"Can he eat in here?" I asked.

"No problem."

The technician wheeled my bed out into the hallway with practiced efficiency. Mill stood at the open curtains as I was wheeled down the hallway, the chicken sandwich in his hands. He waved and took a bite, his jaws engulfing almost the whole sandwich. Then his eyes bulged and he grabbed his throat. I laughed as he pretended to choke.

31
WHAT'S THAT BUZZ?

I had no idea where Mill parked his car, but it seemed impossible that it could have been so near the hospital. That part of lower Manhattan is very busy and the streets were jammed with EMS vehicles, pedestrians, and construction equipment most of the time.

My guess is he just got lucky and found a spot somewhere near the back of the building.

I sat on a large concrete planter outside the ER entrance and waited for Carla while Mill went off to retrieve his car. Three ambulances were lined up at the receiving doors to my right, about twenty yards away. A few people in scrubs stood nearby, smoking cigarettes and talking quietly.

"How's your head?"

I turned to see Carla standing behind me. She wore a dark, waist-length jacket over her navy blue scrubs. The red and blue lights of the *EMERGENCY* sign above our heads gave her an ethereal quality.

"It feels tight on the outside and slushy on the inside, like I shook something loose," I said. We both laughed.

"Well, at least you don't have any internal bleeding, so that's a plus."

"That's true. I suppose it could have been much worse."

We stood looking at each other for a few seconds. Her hair blew into her face and she pulled it back. I wanted to reach out and run my fingers through it, touch her cheek.

"I have to admit," I said, "I'm a little confused by your lack of communication. I left several messages." She looked away, then turned back to the hospital entrance. "Is there something you're not telling me?"

She sat on the planter. "I've been crazy busy, like I said."

"So have I." I rubbed the back of my head.

"I'm so sorry you got hurt."

"Come on now, Carla. I need to know if something's changed. You want me to get this guy, right?"

"Of course I do, it's just…" She stood up and looked around, like she was trying to find someone. I scanned the area, but nothing caught my eye. I stood next to her, almost boxing her in behind the planter.

"I want you to explain something."

She looked expectantly at me, moisture glistening in her eyes, like she thought the hammer was about to drop. But I couldn't drop a hammer. I wanted to kiss her.

"Why didn't you tell me you knew Professor Phelps?"

"Who says I knew him?"

"Really, you're going to go there?" She seemed surprised by my reaction. "I have a witness who saw the professor introduce you to a newspaper reporter at a college party." Carla gave me a look of both horror and fury. Before she could respond, I added, "Just tell me the story and I'll believe you. I'm not here to judge. Only to help." I sat down on the planter, letting her see I was backing off. That seemed to calm her down. Slowly, as if carefully measuring her response, she cleared her throat.

"I was ashamed to admit it. Yes, I dated Phelps for a few months."

Even though I anticipated this answer, it still felt like a slap on the face. "But wasn't he dating Emma?" I tried to remain as neutral as I could, under the circumstances, and purposely gave no hint of being judgmental, but my heart was sinking.

"Maybe. After we broke it off."

"And how did he meet her?" I asked.

"I introduced them," she said, then added quickly, "I knew he needed an assistant and she was perfect for the job. Highly qualified, as a matter of fact."

"I don't doubt that," I said.

She scanned the area again, then turned back to me. "I didn't think it relevant to the case. I mean, so what if I dated him?"

"And you dumped him?"

"Well, sort of. I tried to dump him. He wouldn't take no for an answer, started calling at odd hours, sending me text messages every day. He said he wanted to know what he could do to make things right."

"Old Professor had it bad." She gave me a blank stare. I cleared my throat and said, "So, *could* he fix it?"

"Nah. He was…boring." I snickered a bit and she smiled at me. "It was nothing serious. I just wanted to have some fun. I liked the parties and he came on kind of strong. I decided to give it a chance."

"His energy trading company had money to burn back then," I said.

"I never really thought it would go anywhere with him. Ever."

"He took it hard?"

"Well, I guess. But the hard feelings didn't last long. And I found out why. He'd started dating Emma."

The knock on my head and the sour feelings seemed to have released some of the restraint I normally have, and to my horror I found myself saying out loud, "Sisters. Boo-yah!"

She shook her head at me, "Don't be disgusting."

"No, no, of course," I said, trying to regroup. "What I mean is, you carry similar traits. Share DNA. The professor probably found that instantly gratifying, those similarities."

"Creepy." She covered her mouth with a hand and tucked her knees up under her chin. "I don't even want to go there."

"No, no, I don't either."

I felt completely drained, like I'd taken a few downers and was fighting to stay awake. We sat silently for a few minutes. The persistent background buzz of the city seemed louder than even a few minutes before, and the lights looked brighter. I dared a glance and caught her eye. She gave me a perfunctory smile and looked down at her feet. Somehow, in the colored lights she seemed a lot younger, a teenager perhaps, outside the school dance, waiting for the boy to kiss her. Or was that just another movie playing in my head?

She looked up and furtively scanned the area again.

"Who are you looking for?" I asked.

"No one. I just…" She took a deep breath and looked at me. "After Emma broke up with Phelps, that asshole Colling started following her around. Stalking her."

"So, Colling dated her before Phelps?"

"Yes, just before Phelps, but only very briefly. I told you about this."

"Emma liked them nutty?"

"What?"

"Nothing, just…" Again, I almost had to bite my tongue. The way my head ached, I really had no idea what I was thinking.

"No, she didn't like them nutty. She liked exciting guys, fun to be with. And Justin Colling, as you call him, seemed that way at first, but quickly turned into a mega-creep."

"The guy I showed you a picture of, right? The guy who's been following me? And now, you think he's following you." She looked up at me in surprise, as if I'd just pulled another rabbit out of my hat. "Isn't that who you're looking for out there?"

We both glanced out at the street.

"I thought I was going crazy, at first," she said. "I kept seeing the motorcycle, then a guy in black leathers, always taking pictures, following me to the store. I think it's him, yes."

"You recognized him?"

"He never shows his face, at least I haven't seen it. But it looks like his bike."

"Look, I don't want to frighten you, but you can stay at my place." She shot me a hesitant look. "Or we can get you a room somewhere."

"Why would I need a room?"

"Colling was outside your apartment tonight. I saw him there."

She stood up, a frightened look on her face. "When?"

"Just before I came here. That's how I got this." I tapped my head, and explained to her what happened outside her apartment and at the graveyard.

"What does he want from me?" The fear in her voice was palpable. I put my arm around her and she slouched into me.

"I don't know what he wants, but he's dangerous, and he's not going to stop. I can almost guarantee that."

She moved in tight and put her arms around me. Holding her this close was like slipping into warm PJs after a long day out in a cold rain. I closed my eyes and immediately drifted off, unconscious of anything but her warmth. After what could have been a few minutes, I opened my eyes and said, "We'll get a restraining order."

She pulled back and wiped her wet cheeks. "Why is this happening to me?"

"I don't know. You're welcome to stay at my place for a few days until we get this settled. I have a living room sofa," I said.

"Okay," she said. "If you think I should."

"I riled Colling up pretty good. You're safer staying with me."

"Okay, then. Besides, somebody has to make sure you don't fall asleep," she said, sounding relieved.

"Oh, yeah. Concussion protocol." I shook my head in affirmation and looked at my written instructions from the doctor. "See, I need you there anyway," I said, half-jokingly.

She put a hand on my chest. Her warmth spread throughout my body. The thought of her in my apartment immediately energized me, and I turned toward the street.

"Where the hell is Mill?"

His car was about twenty yards away, under a streetlight. I wondered how long he'd been there, watching us. It was nearly midnight. I'd been up since five-thirty that morning, and felt like I'd run the gauntlet, but looking at Carla's beautiful face in the blue neon light, the pain didn't seem to matter.

32

CUDDLES

By the time we reached my apartment, Carla was sleeping in the back seat and I was asleep in front. Mill and I spoke maybe two words before I crashed.

I live in a railroad-style apartment, meaning it has one room after another like a box car, starting with the kitchen in the back, then an extra bedroom with no bed in it, the bathroom, my bedroom and then finally, a small living room. The space between my bedroom and the living room is separated by just a few feet of open space.

Carla stood by my bed watching me as I made up the sofa. "What can I do?"

"There's some clean sheets in the bathroom pantry." I pointed in that general direction.

"Screw that," she said, and flopped down on my bed. I turned to see her lying spread-eagled on her back. I had to laugh.

"You look about as tired as I feel," I said.

"I feel about as tired as I look." She sat up, kicked off her sneakers, grabbed some sheets and lay back down.

"If you want to wash up or anything..."

"I did that at work." She was rolled up in a ball of sheets with just her face poking out. Her eyes were closed, a slight smile softening her face.

"Night," I said, and turned off the lamp. I sat quietly on the hastily made-up sofa, and looked in her direction.

Shit. There was an angel not five feet from me. The woman who pushed all my buttons was lying on my bed. Only now she was real, with real tears and real sweat. She somehow seemed smaller. A child-sized woman with real issues. I wondered if she had any scars on her body, from some childhood accident perhaps, or a surgery. Had she been a happy child? I didn't even know if I liked her. I mean, I adored her, but did I *like* her? I hadn't a clue. Not to mention the breach of trust. I was her detective, her protector; how would she react if she knew how I felt? Then, the sting of her omissions nudged me.

I pulled off my clothes, and curled up on the lumpy sofa. I tried to get comfortable, but felt a chill and decided to turn up the heat. As I walked past my bed to the kitchen, she said, "Are you coming?"

I stood looking at her, not sure if she was talking in her sleep. Finally, I said, "What do you mean?"

"You can sleep with me, but we can't do anything. Understand? Only cuddle."

"You want me to cuddle you?"

She was silent for a moment. I could barely see her in the dark. I thought maybe she was sitting up, but wasn't quite sure. "Is that something you're okay with?" she asked.

I remembered the last time I was asked to *just cuddle*. A six-month nightmare relationship had resulted, followed by a messy and embarrassing public break-up in my favorite restaurant. And it had all started with a premature, unwarranted and unwise cuddle.

"Sure, sure," I said. "Love to cuddle."

I sat down on the bed with my back to her, then slid over to get cozy. She moved close and wrapped an arm around me from behind.

No need to turn up the heat now, I thought.

She smelled of soap and sweat, and lightly of shampoo. I could feel her breath on my neck. The distraction was too much and I turned toward her.

Feeling her close, but not able to see her face, I said, "Is this okay, or do you want me to lie on my back? Or cuddle with your back?"

"No, this is good."

I turned away again. A few seconds later she asked, "Why, is this okay for you?"

"Sure," I said. Truthfully, I couldn't stand her breathing on my neck. It just made me so horny.

"Because I can do this any way you want," she said.

"No, I just want to go to sleep," I lied, and twisted around to face her.

My eyes had adjusted just enough to see her eyes were open and she was trying to see me as well. I leaned in and kissed her cheek. She didn't say anything, so I kissed her nose, then her mouth. She received my kisses and suddenly we were kissing like crazy. Short pecks and hugs and deep, sensual kisses.

I climbed on top of her and kissed her, grinding my erection into her crotch. She grabbed my butt and squeezed me like she was kneading dough. I slid off her and was about to rip off my shorts when she turned onto her side, facing the wall.

I stared at her for a few seconds, not sure what to do or say. It was all so new.

"Remember, you can't sleep for another few hours," she said.

"You're kidding, right?"

"Actually, I think it's probably okay. You're certainly not showing any symptoms that warrant you staying awake. It was only a slight concussion."

"Thank you," I said.

"Now, go to sleep." I slid down next to her, my jockeys halfway down my thighs. "And remember, we're just cuddling."

"Cuddling," I repeated, for clarification.

"Yes. Just," she said.

"Okay," I sighed, realizing she was actually serious.

I pulled up my briefs, lying on my left side now, facing her, and slid my left arm under her neck. I scooted my body in close and wrapped my other arm over her. She slid closer to me and we spooned.

I was wondering what to do with my still erect penis—if I should push it against her or leave it alone and hope it would soon go away—when I realized she was asleep. I decided to just let it fall where it may, and dozed off.

33
IT'S GREEN FOR A REASON

Morning light snuck in through the living room curtains and illuminated the bed. I turned over and saw I was alone. I lay there for a while, pondering what had happened the night before, wondering how things would be between us from now on, hoping it wouldn't be too awkward, until the warm aroma of toast and coffee roused me from bed.

"Carla?" I got dressed and walked into the kitchen.

She stood over the old gas stove, frying a couple of eggs in a grease pan. A nearby plate held perfectly browned and buttered toast. She dished the eggs onto the toast and handed me the plate. "Good morning," she said.

"Now that's service. You do this for all your boys?" I immediately regretted the line. It smelled of familiarity and desperation. But she said nothing, just smiled a charming half-smile, and poured herself some coffee.

"Are you gonna eat?" I asked.

"I have already."

"Thanks for thinking of me."

"How could I not? It's your house."

I smiled again and dug in. The eggs were over easy and perfectly cooked.

She sat near me and looked out the window at the overgrown

courtyard below. The cats were out, no doubt running in all directions, playing whatever games feral cats play. Some mewed for food, others screamed and hissed. I was surprised they were so active this early. I sipped the coffee. It was hot and slightly bitter, just the way I liked it.

"You're an amazing cook," I said.

"It's just eggs."

"Yeah, but you have the touch. I can tell."

"My mother was a good cook. I learned by watching her." She was just as beautiful in the morning light. Her hair was unkempt and wild. A fresh rose blush tinted her cheeks.

"What are you doing today?" I asked.

Before she could answer, my cell phone rang. I pulled it from my pants pocket as quickly as I could, but missed the call. It was Frank. *Shit*. I'd forgotten to meet him last night.

"Crap," I said.

"Anything important?"

"Well, that depends on who you are. To me, no. To him, well, probably."

"Sounds ominous."

"Does it?"

"You shouldn't disappoint people. Client or a girlfriend?" she asked.

"Why would you want to know that?"

"Because I'm a client."

"And a girl," I said. "No, I take that back. A beautiful woman." She smiled and walked into the bathroom.

"There's a new toothbrush in there if you want to use it."

"Is that a hint?" she asked. She stood at the bathroom door and smiled.

"He's actually a client," I said. "He wants me to do things I can't really do. I don't know…"

"You don't know what?" she asked.

"I don't know why I keep talking to him. I guess I feel sorry for him."

She looked at me while brushing her hair. "Do you feel sorry for all your clients?"

"Only the ones I can't help."

She stopped brushing, as if to let that register. I smiled at her, and she went back into the bathroom. "I hope I haven't misled you," she said.

Shit. Okay, here it comes, I thought. The big brush off. The *Oh, I think we made a mistake last night* moment, when it all turns to awkward shittiness. "No," I said, taking a shot in the dark. "You didn't mislead me at all."

"I mean, I never meant to. I was just so ashamed I'd ever dated him."

"Right," I said, realizing she was referring to Phelps. "We all make mistakes. Some bigger than others. I'd say dating Phelps was pretty insignificant. Just chalk it up to a learning experience."

"Experience," she said, almost at the same exact time as I. We shared a laugh, then she went back into the bathroom. I took out my phone and played Frank's message. He didn't speak. There was, however, lots of slow, heavy breathing, then cat purring, then throat clearing. "Frank, come on, you're killing me," I said.

"What's that?" she asked.

"Nothing. This phone message." More cat purring, then a *click*. The message, which turned out to be two-and-a-half minutes of assorted breathing, was over. I stuffed the phone back into my right hip pocket.

"How long do you think Colling has been following you?" I asked.

She came out of the bathroom and stood in the hallway, holding a towel in her hands. "I started noticing him…Wait. Now that I think of it, I noticed him at Emma's service. But I didn't talk to him. Then, I kept seeing that bike. But I never thought about it, because I didn't know it was him at first, not until you showed me that photo, and put the motorcycle and Colling together. Then, as I thought about it, I realized he'd practically been stalking me." She returned to the kitchen and stood by the stove. Her hair was neatly combed and her face shiny clean. "It's so creepy," she said. "I mean, I never noticed this guy following me? I'm supposed to be a New Yorker."

"That's okay. You weren't looking for him. What reason would he have for following you? And going to your apartment?"

"Besides him being a pervert," she said, "I have no idea."

"Did Professor Phelps go to Emma's service?"

"Yes, he was there."

"Did you talk to him?"

"No. I was too upset to talk to anybody who wasn't family."

"Did he try to contact you afterward?"

"He tried calling me a few times, then left a short message of condolence. I never called him back."

I took a sip of coffee and watched her as she walked to the window and stared down at the cats. "Do you think there's any possibility Emma found out about the illegal nature of the energy company?" I asked.

She turned to look at me, studying my face for a moment before she answered. "AET? I don't think so."

"What about you, what did you know?"

"I thought it was great. His company was killing it. I didn't question if it was legal. I never had any doubts. Why would I?"

"Well, the company was legal. What he did with it wasn't. What about his wife? Didn't she get in the way?"

"He told me his marriage was in name only. They hadn't been together, really, in years. I only dated him a few times, Gus."

"What did you think when the story of AET's illegal trading broke?"

"I was horrified."

"Did you sleep with him?" She gave me a startled look. "Sorry," I said, and shrugged it off.

She took a deep breath and let it out slowly. "It sounds so gross now, but yes, I slept with him."

A screw turned in my stomach. The picture that played in my head was revolting and I immediately tossed it aside. "But first he dated Emma. Slept with Emma. Is that right?"

"I guess. What are you saying?"

"I don't know. Seems kind of strange. You both slept with him." I wanted to reach out and take back those words as they came out of my mouth, but I watched them roll out and slap her in the face.

"I don't like your tone, Gus."

"I'm just trying to understand the situation."

"Are you going to ask if we had a threesome?"

"Did you?"

She marched to the bedroom, each step punishing the hardwood floor. I sat looking at my coffee. Part of me wanted to hurt her for sleeping with the creep and part of me wanted to run after her and try to fix it. I had no claim on her, yet I was filled with a strange jealousy. An inappropriate feeling, I knew. I thought it best to wait a few minutes and let it pass, but it wasn't going to pass. I had been incredibly crude, and I didn't know why. I was afraid she'd walk out the door, and I'd never talk to her or see her again, so I followed her.

"I didn't mean to say that, Carla. I'm not judging you." From the hallway, I could see her collecting her things.

"Who the hell do you think you are? You have no right!"

"I'm your damn protector, that's who I am!" She stopped and looked in my direction. "I have to find out the facts of the case. It's not personal." She scrambled to put on her socks. "Look, I don't want you leaving just yet. It's not safe."

"I'll take my chances."

"Please." I touched her hand as she tied her sneaker. She swatted me away, like a fly. "I'm only doing my job."

"Is that what you call it? Was last night your job?"

"No."

My phone buzzed in my pocket. I pulled it out and saw it was Frank, again. "Last night was awesome," I said. I put the phone down on my bedside table. She picked up her coat. I pulled it away from her. "Look, I just want to protect you. This is serious stuff. Colling was at your apartment." She walked to the door. "I don't care that you slept with Phelps. I don't care. I want to help you, and I like you so much. Please. It was none of my business and I'm sorry." She turned to look at me, a pained expression on her face. "I really liked spending time with you last night, Carla. I really did. I hope you did, too." She leaned back against the wall. "I was stupid," I continued. "It was a stupid thing for me to say. I was just trying to establish this thing with Phelps."

Carla shook her head. "I told you I was ashamed of what I'd done, and you threw it in my face. Haven't you ever done anything stupid?"

An involuntary smiled crossed my face that I immediately stifled. "Of course I have, all the time. I'm a dope. Are you kidding me? I wake up remorseful every day for something I did, maybe years ago. I'm the biggest doer of no good doings ever, in the history of everness!"

She smiled. I could feel the ice beginning to melt. "Well, then, you just can't talk about it anymore." She looked into my eyes. "Understand? Don't say another word about the professor."

"I understand," I said. "Yes." I nodded in affirmation.

"Not a word, a look, a snigger, nothing..."

"I promise," I said, wanting her to finish that thought. "Or, you'll what?"

She gave me an incredulous stare.

"Oh," I said, "It's started already?"

She zipped her mouth with her fingers. I nodded again and sat down on the sofa, holding her coat on my lap.

The charged atmosphere began to deflate. I wanted to tell her I was just being stupid, that I was jealous and that I cared deeply for her. That a part of me worshiped her. But of course, that would be too much. And a huge mistake. After a few minutes of quiet reflection, I said, "We have to talk about tonight."

She gave me a tight-lipped stare, then relaxed her lips. "What?" she asked.

"Okay, look," I said, "Here's what I think we should do. We get you a room at a nearby hotel. Mill and I go to Colling's place and see what we can find."

"What do you mean, break into Colling's apartment?"

"I'm not saying that, but yes. I want to see what this creep is hiding in his little nest. I have a strong feeling we may find something connecting him to Emma's death." She gave me another tight-lipped stare. "When are you working again?" I asked.

"I'm scheduled for tomorrow night. Swing shift, three to eleven-thirty."

"Good. Can you lie low today and tonight?"

"I guess. But, I'm not staying in any fleabag hotel. I want something decent."

"Of course."

"It's a huge inconvenience."

"It could escalate into a lot more than that," I said.

"Why don't we just go to the police?" she asked.

"I want to get you an Order of Protection."

"A what?"

"A restraining order. From the criminal court."

"A lot of good that would do." Then she added in a sarcastic tone, "Well detective, she's dead, but at least she had a restraining order."

"It's not going to come to that. I'm going to protect you." She gave me a doubtful look. "Look, if Colling has a criminal record, which I think he does, with a restraining order, he'll be doubly screwed next time he steps foot near you. My friend Mill has a lawyer. We'll take care of it today. If Colling's on probation, he'll get locked up right away. If not, he'll be under more scrutiny. And we have ways of getting him off the street. Trust me. I have connections." I was thinking of Mill's cousin, the cop, and my willingness to use him for everything he was worth.

She nodded. "Okay."

"Also, my friend has police connections. We can have Colling brought in for questioning."

"You can do that?"

"Yes," I said, in truth completely unsure of anything at this point. I just wanted to make her feel safe. She had a look on her face I couldn't quite read. Incredulity, I guess would be the right word. "I'm here to help you, Carla. Remember, I don't judge you, I protect you."

"Okay," she said, and sat on the sofa and started checking emails on her phone.

I felt like a liar. That green devil, jealousy, still slithered around in my gut, and like it or not, I still felt judgmental toward her for sleeping with the creep. But, I also knew I had no right to feel that way.

"I haven't even paid you for any of this," she said.

"I haven't given you a bill, yet."

She shook her head in amazement. "It better not be huge."

I thought of a wiseass innuendo, but pushed it out of my mind. "Not even close," I said.

As much as I had wanted to, I still couldn't trust that she was telling me everything. There had to be a reason Colling was so interested in Carla.

I gave her a shy smile, which she returned, then resumed scanning her cell phone. From that instant on it was going to be strictly business. Carla was just another client. I had no claim on her whatsoever. And it broke my little green heart.

34

WHEN THE DUST MITES SETTLE

I found a good, fairly inexpensive midtown hotel online for Carla. Mill and I dropped her off mid-morning. She wasn't happy about hanging around a hotel by herself, so I promised we'd be back to take her out for a great dinner.

We were on the FDR, headed to Colling's place, when my phone rang. It was Frank. I let it go to voicemail. When the message alert chimed, I dialed Frank's number. He picked up right away.

"Frank? Hello, Frank. Can you hear me?" I said.

"Yes, yes, I hear you." The desperation in his voice was revolting. I hung up and immediately hit redial. The call went straight through to his voicemail.

"Frank, can't seem to reach you," I said into the phone. "Bad connection. So sorry I missed you last night." Mill looked at me over his sunglasses. "I had to go to the ER," I continued, "Got hurt. I'll explain it later. We'll meet up tomorrow." I hung up and smiled at Mill.

"Gus, you're such a chicken-shit. Call him back and tell him you love him."

"He told me he loves *you*, Mill. Can't get over your baby-smooth ass."

"Whatever, man," Mill said, his eyes glued to the road. "Besides, he told me he likes your *hairy* ass." And so it went.

Mill had already talked with his lawyer and gotten us an appointment for that afternoon, so we had to get this done in a hurry. He'd also spoken to his cousin about getting Colling picked up and taken in for a heated once-over by the boys in blue. His cousin had said he'd see what he could do and would get back to us later that day. Things were looking pretty good in the cop department—pun intended—and I was feeling fine.

It took less than an hour to reach Colling's apartment. His bike was sitting in the same spot as last time, on the side street opposite the Good Time bar. We decided to park the car a few blocks away, so Colling wouldn't see it if he came outside.

We walked across the street from the bar into a berm area, where we could get a good bead on both the bike and the apartment entrance. The berm was filled with weeds and assorted trash, and covered in the kind of dark, filthy grime you only find in large cities. Dozens of beer cans lay scattered under an anemic little tree. I hated to do it, but I sat down under it, trying not to get myself dirty. Mill crouched nearby.

"Good thing you didn't wear your white pants, Mill," I said.

"Shit, and I was gonna, too. Maybe a white belt to go with it."

"And your white go-go boots."

"Nah, that'd be too much." Mill took a few tugs on his unlit cigarette. "So, how we gonna do this?"

"Well, shit, he's got to leave sometime. I mean, he does work, doesn't he? If you call stalking work," I said.

"Think maybe we should check the back side of his apartment building?" Mill asked. That was something I wanted to do the first time we'd surveilled Colling, but we'd never gotten around to it. The apartment was on the ground floor so it was ideal for a little breaking and entering.

"Good idea. I'll check it out," I said, "You stay here and call me if you see him leave."

"Got it," Mill said, as he sat in the spot I vacated.

As I crossed the street, I noticed a narrow grass-covered alley to the right of the building. I took a last look in both directions, then walked down the alley.

A few small fences and a rickety tool shed later, I was standing at what I assumed was Colling's back door. It was a gunmetal gray slab that appeared to be impenetrable. Next to that was a barred window. I leaned forward and cautiously peered inside the apartment. My stomach turned over when I glimpsed Colling walking down his hallway toward me. I turned away, crouching with my back against the building. An old lady hung clothes on a back patio clothesline about fifty feet to my right. I kept in the shadows and prayed she didn't see me. After a few minutes my phone buzzed in my hip pocket, and I nearly jumped.

"Yeah?"

"The boogeyman has left the building," Mill said.

"He's out?" I turned to see the apartment was now dark.

"Yes."

"Mill, go to your car and get the tire iron. We're gonna pry this sucker open like a tin can."

"Will do."

"And Mill?"

"Yeah?"

"Move your ass. I want this to be quick and easy."

"How about a crowbar?"

"You got one?"

"Of course."

"Well, shit, yeah. Get that."

"Yes, Kemosabe."

He hung up. I looked at my phone. *Did he just call me Kemosabe?*

I peered to my right and saw the old lady hanging bed sheets. She was taking her sweet time. I was grateful for the wind and cloud cover. Not as much chance of an audience of sun worshipers from the neat row of back patios that ran opposite the alley. It dawned on me that as crappy as Colling's building seemed, it was one of a handful of buildings untouched by Williamsburg's never-ending urban renewal.

My phone buzzed again and I almost dropped it. "Yeah?"

"Can I come, now?"

I glanced at the old lady, who was taking her sweet time. "She's fucking killing me, Mill."

"Who?"

"The old lady." I snuck another peek. She seemed lost in her methodical work. "Fuck it. Come on back anyway. She won't do anything."

"Yes, Kemo—"

"Hey Geronimo, don't start calling me that."

Mill laughed, then stifled himself. "Gotcha. Just a bit of nerves."

"Come on back."

"Right."

The phone clicked dead. I tried to see into the apartment but the bars on the window prevented me from getting close. I started to pull at the bars where the attachment to the window appeared weakest. The lower-right corner window jam appeared weakened by the beginnings of dry rot.

Mill rounded the building like he owned the place. The old lady didn't even look up from her work. Mill knelt down next to me, and pulled the crowbar out from inside his sleeve.

"Did you see Colling get on his bike?" I asked.

"Yeah. He took off right away."

Some of the wood was rotten and weak where one of the screws attached to the house. I jammed the crowbar behind the bars and wedged it free. The partially rotted wood released the screws one by one on the right side. Soon the bars sung far enough away from the window for a person to gain access to the apartment.

"I brought this." Mill said, and handed me a roll of blue painter's tape. "In case we want to break the glass."

"You carry burglary equipment in your car?"

Mill shrugged. "I was gonna paint my apartment, but never took the bag out of the trunk. I forgot I had it."

I peered out from behind the bushes and saw the old lady was gone. The clothesline was completely full, the sheets lightly swaying in the cool autumn breeze. "Good," I said.

We plastered tape onto a window. I stood up and poked the glass with the crowbar, but it didn't do anything.

"Here. You do it, maniac," I said, and handed the crowbar to Mill.

A gleam lit his eye as he slammed the bar into the glass. A muted pop exclaimed as the window broke. I turned and checked the area. As far as I could tell, we were safe.

Mill reached in, unlatched the lock and pulled up, but the window wouldn't budge. He lifted the crowbar toward the glass for another smack.

"Stop," I said, taking the bar. "Pry it open. Use the bar to lift it."

He nodded and began prying under the sill, but the window was painted shut.

"Now what do we do, genius?" Mill asked.

I pulled out a small pocketknife and began to dig at the paint. Fortunately, it was painted shut on the outside only. It took a few precious minutes to pierce enough of the paint to loosen the window, but when we tried again, it popped open.

"I'll go in. You stay here and keep an eye out for anyone outside," I said.

"No, I want in. Nobody's coming around here," he protested.

I gave him a look that said *shut up*. He sat down near the sill and pouted. I ignored him, throwing one leg over the sill after the other, and soon knelt in Colling's kitchen. I turned to Mill.

"How's it look out there?" I asked.

"Clear," he said, in a bored tone.

"Okay, fine then. Come in. But be careful."

Mill scraped his way up and over the sill and landed hard in the kitchen, his heavy boots clomping on the floor.

"Shhh," I said, and held a finger up to my mouth. I noticed a small green satchel he'd brought with him. "What's in the bag?" I whispered.

"Tools of the trade. I may be able to hack his computer."

"Good," I said, and slowly moved forward.

The kitchen decor was vintage crappy and badly needed updating. The floors were covered in red paint that was chipping up and left flakes everywhere. The cabinets were painted white, but were horribly stained with greasy fingerprints and grime. The sink was filled with cockroach-laden dirty dishes. Filthy plates lay scattered on the counters and table.

I made my way into the next room. Unnerved by the squeaky floor, I turned to Mill and said, "Stay here. Look for anything we can use. Notes, phone books, anything."

"Find his computer," Mill said.

The next room was a small living room-bedroom combo. The place was a mess. Dirty laundry, sheets, and blankets were scattered everywhere. On a tiny wooden desk in the corner lay a charger cord for a laptop. The desk drawers held a few small black notebooks, the kind I'd seen cops on TV use for taking notes. I prayed he'd used them.

I sat on the bed and looked in the first notebook, which was empty except for a few scribblings, like he was trying to get a pen to work. On the next few pages there were drawings of what I supposed were human heads. He had no talent. The drawings were crude at best. Something equivalent to an elementary school level effort: large round heads with wobbly eyes, too high on the face, pointed demon-like teeth with horns growing out from the crown.

I grabbed the next notebook. It was worn, older, the cover weathered. Inside were phone numbers and names. I didn't recognize any of them. Again, the writing was sloppy and childlike in execution.

Footsteps echoed in the outer hallway. A key rattled in the door.

Colling's voice rang out in conversation. From the kitchen, I heard heavy footsteps and banging against the wall, and prayed Mill could get out in time. There was nothing for me to do but dive under the bed, notebooks in hand. I got a face full of dust and choked back a sneeze as the front door swung open, then slammed shut. Colling clomped into the room, talking loudly on his cell phone.

"I don't know what the fuck is wrong with it. Yeah, I tried cleaning the fuel line, and I checked the plugs. I'm a fucking mess. How long will you be?"

I closed my eyes from the dust, my hand covering my nose and mouth as my throat began to close. Tears streamed from my eyes.

"Okay. I'll be here."

He plopped his backpack onto the bed and sat down hard. His bulk almost jammed into my face as I turned to get away from the sag. He unlaced his black riding boots and let out a ripping fart, challenging my breathing yet further.

In a few minutes, Colling's clothes lay on the floor in front of me. His lumbering bare feet stomped into the hallway and then the kitchen. Bottles clanked, and I presumed he'd opened the fridge. He cracked open a beer can, then stomped into the bathroom.

Sweat poured down my face and mixed with dust as it trickled down the back of my neck. As the blood rushed to my face, I stifled a moan. My face felt like it was on fire, and my head was about to explode.

I heard water running in the bath. It was time to get out of my hellhole. I no longer cared if I was caught: I couldn't breathe under that bed. I slid out and slowly got to my feet. In front of me, on the bed, was Colling's backpack. I pulled open the flap. His laptop was stuffed in the front compartment. Then I noticed his cell phone on the bed. I grabbed the laptop and the cell and crept back into the kitchen, while trying to see out of my partially swollen eyes. My face felt scratched, like I'd walked face first into a pricker bush. Every pore of my body screamed in itchy, prickly pain.

Mill was looking in through the kitchen window. I handed him the cell and laptop and took slow, deep breaths as I alternately choked back a coughing fit and gasped for air through my swollen throat. Turning to the sink, I ran the water over my face and hands, then lathered them with soap. I coughed and gagged while splashing cool water into my eyes.

Colling's voice boomed from the shower. "Whoa! Shit! Fucking shit!"

I didn't care if I was using all the cold water as I washed my itching face and eyes. After rinsing my mouth and gargling, I lathered again and literally put soap in my eyes to try to clean them out. At last I began to breathe more easily. Next to me on the counter, I found a nasty little towel that smelled of beer and stale fried food, but I didn't care, and used it to dry my hands and arms. I moved to the window and saw Mill pounding away on Colling's laptop keyboard.

"Let's go, just take them," I whispered, and started to climb out the window.

Mill held up a hand to stop me. "No, it's almost complete," he said.

"What is?"

"I've set up a RAT. We're good."

"What's that?"

"Remote Access Trojan. I'll explain it later. Just put the phone and laptop back exactly where you found them. We don't want him to know we've been here," Mill said, handing me Colling's belongings. "We've got him!"

I crept back into Colling's bedroom, the floor creaking with every step. As I crossed in front of the shower, I could hear him mumbling to himself over the din of the shower, but couldn't make out any words.

The knapsack lay open on the bed. I slipped the computer back into the backpack and placed the cell phone exactly where it had been positioned on the bed. I stood admiring my work when the shower shut off and incoherent babbling emanated from the bathroom. I tiptoed as quietly as I could back into the kitchen. Each creaking step shot spikes into my ears. Colling had to have heard me, but I kept going, half expecting an arm to grab me by the hair and yank me as I passed the bathroom door.

When I reached the kitchen, amazed to be still alive, I realized he'd soon discover we'd been there because of the broken window. He'd know his place had been vandalized, but not necessarily that he'd been hacked. "We have to fix this," I said, pointing to the tape on the window.

Mill reached through the broken glass and handed me a golf ball. Part of the ball had turned black from the decaying foliage that had been its cradle. "This was out here in the weeds. Put it on the floor, like it crashed through the window."

"He won't buy that," I said.

"Better than nothing."

Suddenly the bathroom door swung open and Colling, toweling off his hair, walked naked down the hall and into the bedroom. I carefully released the golf ball onto the floor and it rolled to the middle of the kitchen. Mill plucked shards of glass off the painter's tape and spread them around outside as if shattered by the errant missile.

I slipped out the window. Mill grabbed me as I fell onto my back.

"Why are you crying?" he asked.

"Dust mites," I said, my voice scratchy and barely audible. "I'm allergic."

The TV boomed from the bedroom. We replaced the window bars, trying to align them as best we could. I jammed some rotted wood in the screw hole and reintroduced the screws using my trusty pocketknife. It was a flimsy repair, but seemed to hold.

I turned away from the apartment, tears and sweat dripping into my eyes. Taking a deep breath and filling my lungs with sweet autumn air, I ripped opened my shirt and exposed my skin to the cool breeze, which instantly felt like an angelic salve. "You think we got away with it?" I asked Mill.

"Shit. We'll know soon enough."

As we turned the corner of the building and crossed the street, I looked at Mill striding confidently next to me. "So, what did you do to his computer back there? Is it a tracker, a program or what?"

"His phone and his computer. All in good time, my man. All in good time…" He threw the tools and satchel into the back seat and we got into his car.

"Mill…" I gave him a peeved look.

"You look like shit," he said.

I rolled my sore eyes and sat back, knowing he was holding all the aces.

35

I SMELL A RAT

Sitting in the front passenger seat of Mill's car, my heart finally started to slow down and I could breathe more easily. Mill and I didn't speak until he put his blinker on and we crossed toward a midtown exit on the FDR.

"Where are we going?" I asked.

"Don't you want to see Carla?"

"Not now. Let's head to my place and look at what we've got."

"Well, what we've got, my friend, is a direct link to anything Colling sends or receives from his computer or phone. I can access all his files, emails, photos, everything."

"Okay. How'd you do that?"

"It's all technical wizardry, my friend, too complex for your tiny brain. Let's just say it's a Remote Access Trojan, or RAT. I installed a little program that makes his laptop my slave."

"Sweet."

"No need to take his electronics and let him know we've broken in."

"If he buys the golf ball bit," I said.

"Doesn't matter. He won't suspect a thing. Plus we can track all his movements using his phone."

"Is any of this legal?" I asked, already knowing the answer. Mill tightened his grip on the steering wheel and laughed. "Great," I said. "Just great. I mean, none of this can be used in court, then."

"We don't even know if there's any evidence. Besides, has the legal system done anything to find Emma's killer?" Mill asked.

"They questioned her killer and let him walk. Does that count?"

Mill smiled. "All we do is collect the data, photos and emails, and track him, see what he's up to. Bring everything we've found to my cousin, the friendly neighborhood cop, and the police can find a legal way to nail him. They can't ignore the obvious, no matter how it comes to them. They will find an angle that'll be admissible in court, believe me."

"I like it," I said.

"Most criminals, confronted with the evidence against them, fold like a deck of cards." Mill took his eyes off the road to give me a wink.

"I'm starting to think you might actually be worth what I'm paying you, Mill."

Mill rolled his eyes. "Better watch out, I'll cash that rubber check you wrote me."

"The fuck you will," I said, laughing.

First thing I did when we arrived at my place was take a few Benadryl. Mill set up his laptop on my kitchen table, and without any difficulty, he was able to hack into Colling's computer.

There were hundreds of emails, but more importantly, numerous photo files. I remembered Colling had previously used a handheld digital camera for surveillance instead of his phone, so I knew he'd probably have downloaded them to his laptop.

The photo files held several folders, all with a different female name.

My heart froze when I saw the file marked *Carla*. I nodded to Mill and he opened it. Digital photos. Lots of them. Several were outdoor shots: Carla walking down the street, Carla going into a grocery store, picking up her dry cleaning, etc. There were a few shots of Carla and me talking outside Café Divine, and one of her getting into a cab. There was another folder entitled *Carla Night*.

Mill clicked on that file and voyeur shots of Carla inside her apartment popped up on the screen. There were shots of her naked in the bathroom, on her bed, sitting on the toilet. I suddenly realized these were not photos, but digital captures from hidden cameras.

"Holy shit, Gus." Mill closed the file and turned to me. "Sick fucker's inside her place."

"Those were from video, right?" I asked.

"Oh, yeah. He's got hidden video cams all over her apartment. In her kitchen, bedroom, and bathroom. Two in her bathroom from what I saw. We have to show these to my cousin."

"There's no way we show these to Carla," I said.

Mill nodded in agreement. "Man, she'll be freaked out. It may scar her, permanently."

"And the cops, they'll want to show them to her, maybe even show them in court. Big blowups of Carla naked for all the world to see? No way, Mill."

"They'd put black bars across her private bits, don't you think?" Mill clicked on a photo file named *Julia*. A hi-res photo opened of a brunette girl, about twenty years old, standing naked in what appeared to be a bedroom. "This guy's a disgusting pig."

"How many different photo files has he got?" I asked.

"I see five file names. All female."

"And there's Emma." My stomach did a little flip when I saw her own file, separate from the others. Mill clicked it open and Emma's smiling face popped up in an outdoor shot. Her blonde hair and sparkling blue eyes made my heart sink. "That's enough, Mill. I don't want to see anymore."

"Well, it's proof Colling stalked her."

"Yeah, but I don't need the memories right now."

Mill closed her file and looked at me. "So, he's probably stalking five different woman. Plus the *Emma* file. Where does he find the time?"

"Or the money. Full video in each apartment? The equipment is not cheap," Mill added.

"Check his emails, Mill. I want to see if he's sending these to anyone."

"Right."

Mill switched over to Colling's emails. In the Sent folder he found several emails addressed to Fluffy5@gackmail.net. Virtually all of the emails had attachments.

Mill clicked on one of the attachments marked *Phone Carla*. It was an audio recording of Carla talking on her cell phone. It was garbled and unclear with whom she was talking, but clearly, it had nothing to do with Colling or Phelps or myself. The snippet was just a few seconds long.

"So let me get this straight," I said. "Colling is sending these files to the same person. He has audio files from phone calls, and videos and still shots, too. Is that right?"

"Seems that way."

He played the audio again and near as I could make out, Carla was talking to someone from work. Then something dawned on me. "Play it again, Mill."

Carla's voice: "Yes…I wanted…for reaching out. I start…downtown…a week."

Carla had been talking about her new job in Lower Manhattan. Colling knew she was changing jobs. I'd noticed Colling watching me the day I met Carla for the first time. It seemed obvious now he'd recorded our conversation and had come to check me out before she'd even met with me.

"He's in every corner of her life," I said.

"And he's got video of Carla naked," Mill added.

"When did he make the *Carla* files? What's the earliest one?"

"Looks like just over three months ago." He visually scanned the files. "Yeah, July 2 is the first file date."

"Why then?" I wondered out loud.

"I don't know. Did something happen about that time?"

I couldn't think of anything. Carla had contacted me several weeks after the surveillance of her had already begun.

"So, what kind of sicko are we dealing with?"

Mill looked at me and shrugged. "A voyeur, I guess. Maybe he's posting these on a website. I ran a search and the receiving email is a dead end. I wouldn't be surprised if this Fluffy5@gackmail.net character is a webmaster. Or the government."

"Government? Why would they care about Carla?"

"They wouldn't, but Bruno and Carrillo have that connection. But my bet is it's a webmaster," he added.

"Shit. All Carla needs right now is to find out she's all over the web."

"Well, not all over the web. One porn site. Or maybe a lot of them," Mill said. "Voyeur porn is very popular now." He gave me a sheepish look, then added, "I hear."

Mill opened another email addressed to Fluffy5@gackmail.net and read out loud: "'Here's the latest. Let me know if this works for you.' He doesn't mention any names, doesn't even sign off."

"When was that sent?" I asked.

"About a week ago."

"His message says, 'Let me know if this works.' What do you think that means?"

"It may be referring to technical issues."

"Which implies somebody is doing something with them upon receipt. They're not just going into a dead file."

"Yeah, but it could be anything. Personal viewing, uploading to a site. We just don't know."

Mill opened the video file. It was Carla, standing naked in her bathroom, drying herself with a towel. The video was poor quality, but it exposed her bottom and top.

"Shut it off, Mill."

He closed the file and looked at me. "I don't know what laws they have against this kind of stalking. But I think this qualifies as illegal."

"Yeah, but it was illegally obtained by us," I said.

Mill held up his cell phone. "Well, our boy Colling hasn't left his apartment. We can find my cousin and see what he thinks about all this."

"Maybe," I said. "But we have to come up with a plan. I want to take this jerk off the street ASAP."

Mill looked at me and smiled. "You want to hurt him, don't you?"

"Well, I don't want to kiss his hairy ass." I jumped up from my chair and paced the kitchen. "If he killed Emma, he'll kill again. I *know* he killed Emma. This is a dangerous man, Mill. He may be a serial killer for all we know. He may have killed other women out there. I'll do whatever it takes to takes to get to him."

"Within reason," Mill said.

I looked at him. "Whatever that means."

"Well, it means—"

"Look, I've done a search of the stalking laws here," I started, not wanting to get into what I would and wouldn't do to protect Carla. "If he's found guilty of putting cameras in her place, he may get a Class A misdemeanor or something. The pictures we've got will help with the restraining order, and that's a good thing. But I want to nail his ass for Emma's murder."

"And how are we gonna do that?" Mill asked.

"We're gonna get him to confess. On camera." Mill gave me a satisfied look. "Now, let's check the rest of these files," I said, and sat down next to him. "These poor girls are never gonna know about this, I swear to God."

36
IT COST HOW MUCH?

Carla sat on the queen-sized bed with the soft white duvet in the midtown hotel and gave me a puzzled look. "So you have the evidence to get him for stalking, but not for Emma's murder?"

My throat was dry. I sat on the desk next to the free Wi-Fi display. Glancing at the water bottle conveniently placed on the desk, I turned to her and said, "I'm going to drink this, if that's okay."

"Fine," she said.

I opened the bottle and drank about five dollars' worth, I thought. She stared at me in silence. A serious stare. One that had seen violent death, live birth, and everything in between.

"You know I want to nail him for murder, Carla, but let's get him off the streets before he can do any more harm. I think this is the best way. If you pursue a restraining order, we immediately get him for stalking. They'll have to arrest him."

She wore a fluffy white hotel bathrobe pulled tight around her waist, and a towel wrapped around her head. The way she sat, with one of her legs protruding toward me, reflected light from the windows, and her skin appeared smooth and freshly shaved. Her toes were a healthy pink. *This little piggy...*

Stretching out on the bed, she propped herself up on one elbow, head in hand. She looked very cozy. "Oh, man. I haven't felt this pampered in weeks. The double shifts are killing me." A picked-over room service tray and an empty bottle of Pellegrino sat on a small table.

I smiled and said, "I bet."

"You know, it was surreal seeing your chart at the hospital. I was almost sure I was dreaming, I was so frazzled. Then, when I saw you'd really been hurt...How are you feeling now?"

"Much better. But my arm is black and blue from that tetanus shot. What the hell do you guys put in that thing, anyway?"

"Oh. You got the Tdap," she said joyfully, apparently finding humor in my pain. "Tetanus-diphtheria-whooping cough combo. You feel okay otherwise, though, right?"

"Sure. I guess." I exaggerated the stiffness, moving my arm up and down and grimacing.

"Come here. Let me see." She waved me over to the bed and I gladly plopped down at her feet. "Show me."

I pulled off my shirt and flexed my bicep. "I know it looks swollen. But I can't help that, just built that way."

She squinted. "Where, exactly? I see a tiny bump." She squeezed my muscle and laughed. The injection site was still various shades of green. "Wow, look at those colors."

"I told you. They mangled it pretty good." I flexed again, for good measure.

"Well, that's not unusual. I deal with crybabies all the time."

We both laughed. I touched her face with the back of my fingers. Her mood became more serious, and she looked into my eyes. Unwrapping the towel from her head, she started brushing her damp hair. "What exactly did you find in his apartment?"

"Well, Mill managed to steal a few digital photos from his computer."

Carla stopped brushing her hair and gave me a worried look. "Photos of me?"

"Just a few jpegs. Just enough to show he's been stalking you," I lied. "But we have to catch him in the act, otherwise he can claim no knowledge of those photos. If we apprehend him with evidence on his phone, a photo of you, it may go a long way toward putting him away."

"How much danger am I in, Gus?"

The screen capture of her standing naked in her bathroom flashed into my head. I couldn't un-see that, but I tried to block it out. She deserved better. I shrugged. "He's not going to harm you. I think he's just infatuated, likes what he sees."

"Ugh." She made a sour face. "That is so gross."

"Well, I can't blame him, really." She gave me an incredulous look. "I mean, you are pretty stunning."

"Is this a joke to you?" she asked.

"Of course not."

"He's got pictures of me. I bet he took them through the windows, right? Was he watching me all night? I want that son of a bitch to pay for what he did to my sister. And to me."

I sat up, startled by her tone, and put my shirt on. She walked to the window and looked out onto Madison Avenue. "That's a tough thing to say," I said.

"I'm a tough girl. Remember?" Her tone was remote, impersonal. I saw a coldness in her I'd never seen before.

"I know that. I'm doing everything I can. We'll make him pay."

"Well, maybe it's time for the police to do their job. You have the evidence, you said. The cops could arrest him. What else is there for you to do?"

"I think we need to see what the lawyer says first. What time is your appointment?"

"Maybe we should stop pretending a restraining order will do any good."

"Hey, Carla, I said I'm gonna take care of this."

"What's a restraining order going to do? If he wants to hurt me—"

"He would have done so by now…Listen to me." Her face was expressionless, cold as the windowpane beside her. "I have a plan.

We're going to get him to talk. We'll record it and play it for the cops."

"How are you going to do that?"

"I can't divulge that right now."

Actually, I was still devising my plan as we spoke. Colling would run the minute he saw me, or turn on me with that handy knife of his. I was poison as far as he was concerned. The only thing that might work was using Mill's cousin. Use him in a trap against Colling. Any other way would be too easy for Colling to slip away from. There was no proof he set up the cameras, no proof he put them on his own hard drive, and no real proof he was stalking her. It was still a case of he said, she said.

I looked at the beautiful woman standing by the window and a fierceness grew in me that I hadn't felt before. A higher power rose up within me and a bold new personality started to emerge. *Just do it*, it said. *Seize the moment!*

Reaching out, I turned her to me and said, "We'll get him, Carla. I promise you." Then I kissed her hard on the mouth. I wrapped my arms around her and held her close. She didn't resist. We hugged tenderly, and her sweet, hot breath caressed my neck, encouraging me further. Pushing her gently toward the bed, I continued to kiss her deeply. We fell onto the bed as one. I could feel the heat of her body through the robe. I gently slid my hand under the terrycloth and touched the tender flesh of her breast. She recoiled.

"No, stop," she whispered.

"Carla, it's okay," I said, but I was starting to lose steam already.

"I don't think we should be doing this," she said, suddenly stiff as a rock under me.

"Of course," I said, getting to my feet and moving back to stand by the door. She stared at me, holding her robe closed, her hands clenched tightly on the terrycloth like I was an unwelcome guest. "You're right, Carla. I don't know what I was thinking. It was stupid."

"It's just not the right—"

"No. You're right," I said. "You're a client. You hired me. I can't—"

"It's just confusing. I don't know what's real. My sister, a new job, Colling. I can't separate one feeling from the next. My stomach is in knots."

I grabbed my coat off the desk chair. "Of course. You're in a bad place, I'm in a bad place. It's just bad."

"Well, it's not that bad," she said with a slight smile. "I mean, it's not a horrible idea."

"No, no, it's a good idea. I mean, if you weren't my client..." I stood awkwardly by the door as we stared at each other. After a few seconds I said, "Well, I've got to get going." I turned to leave.

"Here, take this."

She grabbed the half bottle of water from the desk. "You're paying for it, anyway."

I nodded. "Right."

She handed the bottle to me and I held it up to the light and shook what was left. *About three bucks worth.*

"So, you're working tomorrow, yes?" I asked. She nodded. "Mind if I come by and see if you're all right, say, at the end of your shift?"

"If you like. That would be great." She gave me another slight smile.

"Great. And I promise..." I put my hands up in surrender. "None of this...Awkward..." I grabbed the door handle. "After you see the lawyer, take a cab to work. Mill and I will give you a ride home."

"Okay. That sounds good."

"Right," I said. "We've got you covered. This thing will blow over soon. The creep will be gone, and you'll start to feel better in no time. I promise."

"That would be great, Gus."

She walked to me and gave me a peck on the nose. I smiled and backed out of the room, letting the door gently close behind me.

37

SOUP TO NUTS

I hadn't expected it, but across the street from the hotel, Mill was sitting in his souped-up Chevy SS and waving at me. I walked over and tapped on the driver's side window. He rolled it down and said, "You do her?" I shook my head. "You did," he laughed. "She's fine, too."

Ignoring the jibe, I said, "I'm surprised to see you here."

"I got my cousin, the cop, coming over in a little while. He's gonna indulge in some burgers and beer. Hop in." Mill stepped on the brakes and gunned the engine while leaving it in drive. The beast under the hood roared as the car strained to cut loose. A few kids turned and stared at us. Mill was sitting like a cowboy on a bull about to be let loose from the stall.

"You're a freaking exhibitionist," I said as I got in.

"Oh, yeah, baby. We got the mojo." He goosed it, and the car rocked again. People walking nearby darted past us or stopped to admire the car. Mill beamed with pride. He finally popped the clutch and laid about thirty feet of rubber before he let off the gas and we sped away.

The ride was a short one, made even shorter by Mill's manic driving. He darted into a parking spot a block from The Tavern, and we sat for a minute. "I'm surprised you park this beast on the street," I said.

"It's only the second time. But I take measures." He reached across me, opened the glove box and dug deep, hitting me with his elbow in the process.

"What're you doing?"

"Kill switch. You didn't see me do that, or else I'd have to kill you, too."

When we walked into The Tavern, Mill's cousin was already a few beers deep at the bar. Mill slapped him on the back and he turned sharply, with a wild look in his eyes and a menacing grimace on his face. "Gus, this is my cousin, Randall."

Randall stood up, looked me in the eyes and shook my hand, the way real men of character do. "Pleased to meet you." His grip shot a jolt of pain through my hand that made me cringe inwardly, but I managed a smile and thanked him for meeting us. He turned and started to walk away. When we didn't follow, he stopped and motioned for us. We joined him in a dark booth in the back corner of the dining room, as far away from anyone as possible. Randall sat with his back against the wall, facing the room.

"So," Mill started gravely. "Randall has seen the evidence. We went over it last night."

Randall looked around the near empty room, then gave me a knowing glance. A small red scar under his left eye caught the light, accentuating his high cheekbone. His short dark hair reminded me of a military man. In fact everything about him looked military. His eyes darted around the room, as if taking constant inventory. He leaned in and said in a soft but firm voice, "Mill explained the situation, showed me the captures and the photo evidence. We've got one sick fuck working some foul magic." *We?* I thought. "From the blurred quality of the video grabs, I'd say he's capturing it remotely," Randall continued. "I'd say he's an amateur. Probably sitting in a car on the street, outside her apartment."

"He rides a bike. Custom Harley knock-off," I said.

"Then he borrows a car, or he hides in the bushes. Either way, he's got to be near her place because of the weak signal."

"Okay, well, we're hoping that with a restraining order and the accumulated evidence, we can get this guy off the street. Carla is starting to get pretty freaked out, having recently changed jobs, being stalked—"

"Why did she change jobs?" Randall's eyes sparked excitement as he stared at me.

"I don't know. I think she said something about needing a break, a change of pace," I said.

"We'll have to look into that."

"Oh?" I said.

Randall squinted, then seemingly reconciled with the fact that he was dealing with an amateur PI. He leaned in and spoke softly. Mill and I strained forward to hear him. "Often people who are being stalked have strange things come into their lives without them even knowing it. Someone starts telling stories at work, character assassination, maybe. A rumor gets started, usually by the stalker himself, then things slide downhill from there. Friends leave, neighbors are afraid, and the victim may not know why these things are happening. She may have been a victim of something like that."

I looked at Mill. "She never mentioned those things."

A glow of satisfaction lit Randall's face, and he said in a louder voice, "Well, she probably hasn't put two and two together, yet."

Mill gave me a *what a shame for her* frown and took a swig of beer.

"You mean to tell me, he could be messing in all aspects of her life?" I asked.

"Control," Mill said, obviously speaking out of turn.

Randall shut him down with a glance. Mill shrank in his seat. "Yeah, that's what he wants," Randall said. "Complete dominance. Ultimate control over her. It's only a matter of time until it gets worse. He could be breaking into her apartment on a regular basis, watching her sleep. Masturbating at the foot of her bed. Sniffing her panties."

"Shit," I said.

Randall leaned in and whispered, "It's only a matter of time until he does something to her...physically. He might be putting his hands around her throat as she sleeps."

"You think he'd kill her?" asked Mill.

"Placing his hands..." Randall held his hands out, as if on a neck. "Just letting them rest there, waiting to tighten his grip...Squeezing." His face turned red, and his eyes bulged out as he held his breath and choked the air. After a few seconds, he said, "But he won't kill her right away." He let loose the imaginary throat and sucked in a mouthful of air. "No. He'll play with her first, like a cat after catching a mouse—slap her around, save the kill for later. When the time is right, he'll choke her out. But only when the time is right." Mill and I stared at him in disbelief. Randall leaned back, a look of satisfaction on his face. "He may have a ritual. One he sticks to at all costs. "

"I'm not gonna let any of that happen," I said.

Randall stared at me, his eyes too large for any sane man. "How are you gonna stop it? Huh? Do you know where she is every second of the day? You know where she is right now?"

I sat back and blinked. "She's on her way to the lawyers, I think."

Randall scoffed. "No. No lawyers."

I looked at Mill. "What's going on?"

"Listen to him, Gus," Mill said. "He's been in the trenches."

I looked at Randall and thought, *Trenches? PTSD maybe.*

Mill said, "She's getting a restraining order and we're going to nail this guy with the stalking charges."

"It won't work," Randall said, as he lifted his glass and he took a long swig of beer.

I smiled politely and said, "Look, I know we need your help, but you can't just go changing the plan."

"What plan?" Randall gave me a large-eyed stare and folded

his rough hands on the table.

"Look, Randy—"

"Fuck!" Randall said, slapping his hands on the table. "Who walked in? Somebody walk in?"

I looked around the empty room in confusion. Mill appeared to be sinking lower in the booth, as if the weight of Randall's personality was bearing down on him. Mill mouthed the name, "Randall." I sat back, eyeing Randall, who was staring straight ahead now. "It's Randall," Mill said out loud, in a high-pitched squeak, after shrinking further into his seat. I was expecting him to disappear under the table any minute. "He hates being called Randy."

"Okay, sorry. Randall. The thing is—"

"The thing is, you want to get this creep?" He leaned in so the only thing I could see was his intense face. I was feeling completely disarmed. I shot Mill a *Who the fuck is this guy* look.

"Listen to what he says, Gus. He knows what he's doing."

"You're with the police now, right?" I asked Randall. "I mean, you're a detective or something? You're on duty?" His clothes screamed soldier on vacation in Hawaii.

"I'm a detective. Vice. Currently on administrative leave, with pay."

I sat back and let out a grunt. "On leave. What does that mean?"

Randall linked his hands up over his head and sat back. "I did something to someone's head. It's a long story." He smiled and took a sip of beer.

Mill piped up, his voice fading between squeak and grunt, "He was in the middle of an investigation and got accused of something. It'll all be cleared up," he said. "Just be grateful we got him. He's here to help."

"You getting sick?" I asked. "Your voice is..."

Mill shrugged defensively and said, "What?" Then cleared his throat.

This meeting was starting to irk me. I wasn't prepared to let my plan go, or to go a few rounds with this thug on police procedure, so I sat back and let him talk. "Go ahead," I said. "Please continue."

"Call off the lawyer. You don't want to get mixed up with the courts right now. A creep like this, the evidence you got, it's all gonna get thrown out. You were breaking and entering, so you can't prove where you got the photos. You can't prove he's menacing her. Has he called her, talked to her, or threatened her in any way?"

"No," I said. "Not that I'm aware of."

"That's right. Because he's smart. My guess is he's a worshiper. Started out that way, anyway. Worships the ground she walks on. Wants photos, private phone calls, pieces of clothing. He wants to hear her, smell her, taste—"

"I get the picture," I interrupted.

Once again, I got the stink eye. After a few uneasy seconds, he resumed, "He adores her, but really, deep down, he hates women. Then, one day something's going to happen to knock her off that pedestal, set him off, and…" He paused for effect. "He tightens his grip…"

"What about the other girls? He's got five files, all with the same kind of stuff in them."

"He's a serial stalker," Randall shrugged. "I checked and none of those girls match any murders in the past year. My guess, he got tired of them and moved on to Carla."

"My God, you really think he'd kill them?" asked Mill.

"I said he hasn't. Yet."

"I think he killed Emma," I said.

"I know. Mill told me. He was questioned and released. Had an alibi."

"But I know he did it."

Randall paused, a smirk growing on his face. "Yeah, Mill told me about your gift." He took a long pull on his beer, then snapped, "Emma. That's an example of what I'm talking about. She may have done something wrong in his eyes. He couldn't take it. So he took her out." He slashed his finger across his throat.

"Okay," I said. "If we're going about this the wrong way, tell us what to do."

The waitress decided to finally make an appearance. She apologized for ignoring us. Randall barked out his order for a burger and fries better than any drill sergeant. Mill smiled and politely gave his order, then winked at her. She blushed and walked into the kitchen.

"She's new," Mill said, his voice back in a normal register. I rolled my eyes, then looked at Randall and said, "I'll do what you think is best. Tell me how to get this guy."

"You want to catch a rat," he said, with a crooked smile, "you got to bait the trap."

38
DING-DONG, RANDALL COLLING

We split up. Randall and I were on our way to Colling's apartment, while Mill was supposed to hang out near Carla's place. I'd called Carla and told her the meeting with the lawyer was postponed and that it was safe to go home. I felt terrible doing it, but Randall convinced me it was the best thing to do, for now.

If Colling showed up at her place, Mill was to call immediately and begin digitally recording him with his cell phone. Since we were able to track Colling with his own cell phone, we were almost certain he was still at home, but we didn't want to take a chance that he'd switched phones since the break in.

Randall's beat-up 1995 Chevy Cavalier was a far cry from Mill's SS. The pale blue interior was filthy. The windshield was so yellowed with cigarette smoke, I was sure he couldn't see out of it, until I noticed the round clean spot in front of his face. The ceiling upholstery was falling down and dangled on my left shoulder. I brushed it away but it kept landing back on me.

Randall was a slow driver, his eyes constantly scanning the road. He seemed fidgety, nervous at best, and I started to wonder if he was on something.

"You ex-military," I said, breaking the ice.

"Marine Corp. Two tours in Iraq, one in Afghanistan."

"What did you do there?"

"What didn't I do?"

We swung onto FDR Drive and he turned on the radio. A country tune started to twang from the huge custom speakers in back. Tanya Tucker singing 'San Antonio Stroll' pounded through my head. Suddenly, I was in a strange movie with characters only central casting could find. The soundtrack pounded on. I'm not a country fan. The music began to grate on me.

"Hey, can we talk a minute?" I asked. He turned the radio down and glanced in my direction. "Tell me again what the plan is?"

He popped a Marlboro into his mouth and pushed down the lighter. When the lighter popped, he lit the cigarette and took a deep drag, all while staring thoughtfully at the road. "You want to get this guy?" he asked, finally.

"Yeah, sure."

"Then don't worry about the plan. Just do what I tell you. Everything will be fine." He took another deep drag on the cigarette, closing one eye, as if to ensure the exact draw he wanted. I watched and waited, but saw no smoke exit him.

"You ever kill anyone?" I asked.

"Not intentionally," he said.

"How'd that make you feel?"

"What? Fucking up or killing?"

"Killing, I guess."

"Made me feel like I fucked up." Smoke finally emerged from his nose and mouth as he spoke.

"How did you fuck up, exactly?"

"By killing him." And so it went with Randall, the ex-military, on administrative leave, cop.

We pulled up in front of Colling's apartment. I texted Mill to let him know we'd arrived. He responded quickly, verifying Colling's phone hadn't moved.

Randall stepped out of the car, zipped up his green nylon military flight jacket and put his sunglasses in the side arm pocket. I got out and started to walk across the street.

"Stay with the car," Randall said, without looking back.

"Hell no."

"Who's running this show?"

"You are," I said, keeping in step. "But I'm coming with you."

"Then stay back. Follow my lead. Do what I say."

I wasn't sure if I should salute or say *Oorah!* I fell back a few feet and watched him approach the apartment. Randall stood in the vestibule and rang every doorbell until the door buzzed open. He pushed through to the inner hallway and stopped in front of Colling's door. I stood off to the side and nodded. Randall let loose a barrage of fists upon the door.

Colling appeared in the doorway dressed only in a terrycloth bathrobe. "What the fuck is going?" he yelled.

"Justin Colling?"

"Who wants to know?"

"I have a warrant to search your apartment." Randall flashed a balled up piece of paper in front of Colling.

"What for?" Colling asked, his voice raised in alarm.

"For being a dickhead." Randall grabbed Colling by the robe and pushed his way inside, slamming the door shut. Thumping sounds emanated from the apartment, followed by a loud crash. I turned the door handle and peered in.

Colling was spread-eagled on the floor with Randall's knee stuck in the small of his back. The terry robe was up over Colling's head and his tighty-whities barely covered his large ass.

"Get off!" Colling shouted.

"Shut the fuck up, Justin, or my knee is gonna make its way into your mouth." They tussled a bit as Randall cuffed him and turned him over.

Colling sat on the floor against his bed, blood trickling from his nose, looking ridiculous with his open robe and bulging private parts, his alabaster legs stuck in black, unlaced, riding boots.

"Get a chair," Randall commanded. I ran to the kitchen and grabbed one of the metal-framed vinyl numbers and dragged it into the living room. Randall sat Colling in the chair and tied the cuffs to the back brace with a zip tie.

"You," Colling said, when he noticed me.

"Now, Justin," Randall said, "we're going to play a little game. It's called show and tell. You remember that, from when you were looking up little girl's skirts in kindergarten, don't you?"

Colling stared sullenly at the floor, as if looking anywhere else might get him hurt. "You can't do this. I've got rights."

"That's right, and if I violate any of your rights, you let me know." Randall swiped a piece of paper from the floor. "Here, write it down on this." He rubbed the paper in Colling's face.

"Stop it!" Colling yelled.

"Wow. Did you hear that? Our friend Justin wants to help us." Randall turned to an imaginary announcer. "What have we got for Little Justin, Jim?" Randall held his hand to his ear. "A what? *A brand new car*?" he crooned in a second-rate announcer voice.

Randall jumped and spun in the air, his knee coming down hard on Colling's thigh. Colling moaned in pain. Staring at Colling, their faces almost touching, Randall pursed his lips and blew on Colling, making him flinch. A giggle escaped me. I couldn't help myself. This was crazy. Absolutely bonkers.

"Now, Justin, *we*, meaning the people of the civilized world—not the royal we, but we the people—want to know, who, what, why and when. You got that? Who, what, why, when, and...Go!" Randall held an imaginary microphone in front of Colling's scratched-up face. Colling turned back to the floor, his eyes dead to the whirlwind above him.

Randall threw me an exasperated look. "I don't think he's getting it. Perhaps you should try?" Randall bowed and opened his arms toward Colling, encouraging me forward.

Walking through the debris and clothing scattered on the floor,

I stood somberly in front of him. Colling looked up at me, his face cut, scraped, and red with rage. "I'm going to kill you!" he seethed.

Randall made an annoying loud buzzer sound and cracked Colling across the face with the back of his hand. Then he grabbed Colling's hair and pulled his head back, whispering into his ear. "We, the civilized people of the world, do not want to hear that kind of talk. Please refrain." He gave Colling a gentle slap on the face and stepped aside. "Ask him a question."

I gave Randall a non-committal nod, then stepped closer to Colling. "How long have you had digital cameras in Carla's house?"

"I don't have to talk to you!" Colling raged.

Randall made the buzzer sound again. "Wrong answer!" He slapped Colling in the face, harder this time, then started poking him on the cheek with his index finger. "We can do this all night."

After the tenth poke, Colling shouted, "Okay, okay. Stop!"

Randall smiled and stepped back.

"Only for a couple of weeks," Colling said, answering my question.

"I hate perverts!" Randall yelled, walking around in circles, looking for a place to vent his rage. He finally decided on a wall and kicked a hole through the wallboard.

"What are you doing with those images?" I asked. "Why are you collecting them?"

"They go with the rest of them. To the study."

"What are you talking about?"

"What the fuck are *you* talking about?" Colling yelled.

Randall grabbed Colling by the hair and drew back as if to strike, but I placed my hand on his arm, and he stopped.

"You said, a study," I said to Colling. "What study?"

"The study I'm collecting data for, assholes."

"Wrong response!" Randall slapped Colling on the head.

"What study?" I asked again.

"The study at the college."

"Whose study? For who?" I asked, dumbfounded.

"The professor."

"Phelps? This is a study for Professor Phelps?"

"Phelps, that's right. Been collecting data for a while now."

"There is no study, you pervert!" Randall said. "You get your tiny nuts off looking at frilly panties, don't you?"

"Tell me about the study," I said, ignoring Randall.

"I email it to him. He sends me checks."

"You email the photos and he pays you?"

"That's right."

"Oh, my God," I said. Out of anger, I stalked down the hall toward the kitchen, then doubled back into the living room. Colling had an evil grin on his face. "For how long?" I asked.

"Almost a year."

"You said a couple of weeks," I said.

"Her a couple of weeks. The study, a year."

I played back my visit with Phelps. Why hadn't I seen it? Were there clues? An image of the smiling, beautiful Emma lit up in my mind's eye. "What about Emma? You killed her!" I yelled.

"I know you're not cops."

I grabbed Colling's hair and pulled his head back. "Why did you kill Emma?"

"Nobody killed Emma. She fell down and hit her head."

"Bullshit. She was bludgeoned to death and I want to know why."

"I swear to you, she fell down and I got the hell out of there. What happened after that, I don't know."

I looked at Randall. He took that as his cue and smacked Colling in the face. Colling's nose started to bleed again.

"You trying to tell me someone else killed her?" I asked.

"I didn't do it. She was hurt. Maybe she got mugged."

My mind was reeling. Could he be telling the truth? I walked into the kitchen and tried to get Emma's murder to play back in my head, but drew a blank. Was it possible I'd been wrong? Had my expectations been influencing what I'd seen? And if that was the case, could I trust *any* of my Dream States? I returned to the bedroom and stood over Colling. "Was she conscious when you left her?" I asked.

"I don't know," he said, his surliness returning.

"Ding-dong, goes your bell, scumbag." Randall slapped Colling hard on the face.

"Stop it!" Colling shouted. Randall backed off. Colling took a deep breath and said, "She was groggy after she hit her head. I got the hell away."

"Why were you there in the first place?" I asked.

"I was collecting data for the study, and she saw me. She was following me after that. I ran into an alley hoping she wouldn't come in, and she tripped and hit her head."

"You fucking liar!" Randall yelled, raising a foot and launching it at Colling's head, but stopping short of hitting him.

"She was following you?" I asked. Colling nodded. "Was Carrillo there?"

"Carrillo? Dumb, lazy fuck. No, he wasn't anywhere near there."

"You're a liar," I said. Randall hauled back, his fist ready to strike. "No!" I yelled and he stopped short of making contact.

"Carrillo never did field work. He helped set up surveillance and that's it. I did the collecting," Colling offered.

"Let's see if I get this straight," Randall said. "Emma tripped and hit her head. And instead of helping her, you left her there to bleed to death?"

"I had to. I wasn't supposed to make contact."

"Why not?" I asked.

"It could taint the study."

"Did Phelps say what kind of study this was?"

"No." Randall made the buzzer sound again and wound up for another blow. "All right, all right," Colling said. Randall relaxed his arm. "I remember he said something about a socio-economic impact study, or something. I don't know."

"Carla has endured nothing but hardship for the past several months," I said. Leaning forward, I grabbed Colling's face and said, "Is he doing that to her now, sabotaging her life?"

Colling shrugged. "I don't know." He ducked Randall's blow, and slipped to the floor. "Probably," he yelled, to ward off the assault. "I've seen a lot of the problems these girls face. It starts to go bad for them after we begin observing."

I looked at Randall. "I can't fucking believe this," I said.

"Who else is involved?" Randall asked.

"I don't know," Colling said. "I just do the collection."

"Who set up the surveillance cameras?" I asked.

"Carrillo and me."

I whispered to Randall, "There's no way this is a sanctioned study. This is too far out there."

"Maybe the real perv is the old professor. I think we need to pay him a visit."

"Okay," I said. "What about him?" I indicated Colling, who looked pathetic sprawled on the floor.

Colling looked up at me with his puffy face and swollen eyelids and said in a small voice, "Untie me, please."

"Let's bring him with us," I said, answering my own question.

"Get dressed, Justin." Randall tapped Colling on the side of the head. "You're going for a ride on the choo-choo train to see the professor. Are you ready? Choo-choo!"

Colling looked to me for rescue from the madman leaning into his face, but I had other things on my mind.

39
WE ALL HAVE HANGUPS

With the practiced finesse of a real cop, Randall dressed Colling then threw a shirt over his handcuffs and walked him to the Chevy. Once his charge was seated in the back, he zip-tied the cuffs to the door handle. I got in on the passenger side, the drooping upholstery immediately assaulting me. "How can you drive this shitbox?" I asked.

Randall laughed and said, "Look under your seat."

I pulled out the tail end of a roll of duct tape. I stuck a few pieces on the upholstery to keep it in place.

"What you're doing ain't right," Colling spoke up. "Assault, kidnapping...You're in a world of shit when I get my lawyer. I'll sue you so bad—"

Randall grabbed the roll of duct tape and waved it at Colling, who got the hint and immediately shut up.

"The professor's place is on the corner of Spring and Sullivan," I said. Randall nodded. I held up Colling's cell phone. "This is your phone. You have two numbers listed for Prof. I'm going to dial one and you're going to ask for him. When he answers, you're going to tell him that something is wrong and you have to see him immediately."

"Why should I do that?"

The car swerved to the side of the road and Randall was leaning into the back seat before I knew what was happening. "Do you really want me to answer that?" he said. Colling shook his head vigorously. Randall let go of him and returned to the driver's side, adjusting the rear view mirror so he could see Colling. "I'm through playing games with you," Randall said. Colling slumped down in his seat, a deep scowl on his face.

I pressed the speakerphone function on the cell phone and dialed the first number. A recording made by Phelps played and I hung up before it finished. I dialed the second number and a meek male voice came on the line.

"Hello?"

Reaching back, I put the phone in Colling's face and mouthed for him to speak.

"Ah, hello Professor? This is Justin." Silence on the other end of the line. I waved for Colling to continue. "I have to see you." I mouthed, "*Something has happened,*" and he said in a monotone voice, "Oh. Something has happened, and I have to see you."

"No. Don't come here. I forbid it," the professor responded.

I gesticulated at Colling for him to continue. "It's a really big emergency, Professor. I need to come right now."

"What emergency? What's happened?"

"I have to come now. We'll talk then."

"Listen to me. If you come here, I'll call the police."

I put the phone on mute. "Tell him it's about Carla, and you can only tell him in person."

Colling gave me cockeyed sneer. I unmuted the phone and held it out toward him. "It's about Carla," he said.

"Carla? What about her?"

"I can't talk. I mean, I can't tell you on the phone. I need to see you."

"Are you alone?"

I ran my finger across my throat for him to end the call.

"Uh, she's hurt, I think."

"Hurt? How? What happened?"

I waved frantically and reached for the *End Call* button. "I'm coming now," he said. I disconnected the call.

"What the fuck are you doing?"

"What? You made like her throat got slit."

"Fucking dumbass," Randall muttered. We drove in silence for a few minutes, then Randall said, "Well, that was awkward as shit. He knows something's up, now."

"You got that right," Colling offered. "That's 'cause I didn't use the code word."

We both looked at him. "What code word?" I asked.

"I give him a code word that says everything's all right and it's okay to talk. You blew it." Colling laughed. "He's probably packing his suitcases right now."

We sat in silence for a few seconds, then I said, "If you were doing a legal study for the school, why did you need a code word?"

Colling snorted. "I don't know. Ask the professor. That's what he told me to do."

"You fucking scumbag. I ought to beat the shit out of you right now," Randall said, and reached into the back. Colling kicked at the seat, rocking Randall, and screamed bloody murder as the car swerved back and forth between lanes. I yelled at Randall to stop. Colling continued screaming like a little boy. Finally, the car settled into a lane and Randall mouthed obscenities as he gradually gained composure.

"There's nothing else we can do except go down there and talk to him," I said.

After few seconds of silence, Randall turned to me. "We have enough evidence to put him out of business, but it ain't legal. How far do you want to push this thing?"

I looked at Colling in the visor mirror. His insolent face made me want to hit him. "Look," I said. "We go down there and show the professor the evidence, make sure he stops what he's doing. I don't care if we go to court or not. I doubt he'll press charges. He's got nothing to complain about."

"I'm pressing charges," Colling said.

"You, my friend, are an insignificant turd, and you're going to jail," Randall said. "You admitted to leaving an injured party who later died from those injuries."

Colling blinked, as if thinking this over. "You're crazy," he said, at last.

"That's a crime, dummy. You can be tried and sent to jail," Randall said, egging him on.

"Bullshit."

"You never heard of the Good Samaritan law? You're fucked, buddy. I have it all right here." Randall took his hand off the wheel and pulled out a handheld digital recorder, waving it at Colling. "I got it on the recorder. You left Emma after she was hurt and she died."

"I didn't touch her!"

"Not to mention the fact that you had a witness testify you were elsewhere at the time. That's perjury."

"And, Justin," I added, "just as a reminder, you did have a restraining order against you at the time, so you're double-fucked, buddy."

"But if you testify against the professor," Randall continued, "we can probably cut you a deal, get you immunity. It's your choice." He regarded Colling in the rear view mirror. "Not much of a choice, huh, Justin?"

Justin was quiet and didn't say anything for the rest of the trip.

*** *** ***

Arriving at the professor's place, we found parking on Sullivan Street, right around the corner from the apartment. The main entrance to the building had the usual line of mailboxes and doorbells.

"I'm gonna ring the bell, Justin," Randall said, as he pulled on Colling's handcuffs, handling him as expertly as a seasoned dog walker would a naughty poodle. "You tell him you have to come up."

Randall rang the bell, and waited a few minutes, but nobody answered. Behind us, the outer door swung open and a hipster-looking guy in his mid-twenties stepped into the vestibule. Randall flashed his badge and said in a grim tone, "Do you live here?" The young man nodded vigorously, as if he'd been caught huffing paint.

Randall said, "We're gonna walk in behind you. Go straight to your apartment and lock the door and don't come out." The hipster nodded and did as he was told, disappearing up the stairs two at a time.

"What's the secret word, Justin?" Randall asked.

Colling stared at the floor, shirt untucked and partially open, his white belly dangling out over his undershorts. Randall pushed him against the wall.

"It's 'citation'," Colling yelled, cowering away from the coming blow.

"Citation?" Randall responded.

"Yes. I have to use it in my greeting or he knows something's wrong."

"Such as...Give me an example."

"I have that citation, Professor. Then we start the conversation. If I don't say it, he knows it's not, you know—"

"You're gonna give him a speeding ticket?" Randall asked, sarcastically.

"No, he means a different citation. I don't know. It's just what he said to say."

"Okay, step back." Randall pushed Colling over to the stairs and zip-tied the cuffs to the handrail.

"Why'd you bring me if you're just gonna cuff me here?"

"Shut up, Justin. I don't want to hear you."

"Fuck off," Colling said. Randall hauled back to hit him. Colling whined, "No, no. I'll be quiet." He leaned heavily on the railing, then slid down onto his ass, his arms stretched upward in an awkward position. "I'm not very comfortable, you know."

Randall eyed him suspiciously. "Okay, Justin. I'll tell you what

I'll do. Only one hand, how's that?" Randall secured one wrist to the rail and released the other.

"Thanks, I feel so much better," Colling cracked.

"Would you like a piece of mint gum?"

"Sure."

Randall pulled the last piece of duct tape off the end of the roll and put it over Colling's mouth. "You only get gum if you're good." Randall laughed. Colling murmured under the tape.

Randall walked over to me and whispered. "Okay, I'll knock and say the word. You stand back in case he's armed." Randall knocked on the door.

"Yes?" A voice came from within.

"I have the citation right here, Professor."

The chain on the door rattled and the dead bolt scraped. The person inside was speaking before the door was all the way open. "Yes?"

Randall kicked the door open and rushed in. A shocked and frightened middle-aged woman wearing a housekeeping apron backed into the corner. She held up a broom, ready to strike, while shrieking in Spanish. She swung the broom and managed to hit Randall a few times before he could get his badge out.

"*Policia! Policia!*" he yelled. He flashed his badge, holding it up to her face as the broom came down again on his arm.

She backed into the corner and held her chest. "You scare me, you scare me."

"I'm sorry, madam," Randall said. "I'm looking for the professor."

She pointed with the broom and said, "His room," then held her free hand over her mouth.

"You see this guy?" Randall pointed to Colling out in the hallway.

She nodded. "I see him," she said from behind her hand.

"He's a bad man, you understand?" Again she nodded. "If he

tries to run, you call us, okay? Yell, and I'll come running. *Comprende?*"

"*Sí, sí,*" she said.

"Good. *Bueno. Gracias,*" Randall said.

I stood in the doorway, smiling like an idiot. When she looked at me I nodded politely, in affirmation of nothing in particular. Randall took off toward the other rooms, and I followed.

The hallway led to a set of double doors. Randall stood with his back to the door, and raised his pistol in front of his chest with both hands.

I shook my head at him. "No guns," I whispered.

He gave me a look of incredulity, then shook his head, no. I shrugged. Stepping away from the sightline of the doors, Randall turned and kicked them open.

I stood in the doorway in amazement. The walls of the room, which I assumed was a study, were covered in photos and screen captures of women, all candid shots. Some of the women were naked; others were simply walking down the street. In the middle of the wall, among all the photos, were charts and graphs. To my right, I saw a bare elbow moving. I pointed and Randall slowly made his way around the door, aiming his gun.

"Don't move!" he yelled.

I ran into the room and froze in my tracks. A rush of adrenaline shot through me. I was having another out of body experience, only this time it was the real deal.

The professor, a noose around his neck, stood precariously on an old wooden chair. The rope ran from a nail secured in the wooden sash above the window to a beam directly above him. The old man wore boxer shorts, a wife-beater tee and black socks. His spindly white legs shook in his knee-highs. Tears streamed down his face. He held a small revolver to his head.

"You can't shoot me," he said.

"I'm not going to shoot you," Randall replied.

"You have to put the gun down," Phelps said.

"I'll put it down as soon as you lower yours."

"Then you'll shoot me."

"I'm not gonna shoot you."

The professor glanced in my direction. A look of recognition washed over him. "I know you," he said.

"No, I don't think so," I said, suddenly aware I was in the line of fire.

"You...You chased me. You asked me about Emma."

"What happened to Emma, Professor?" I asked.

"She was a good girl. So much tragedy." He looked at Randall. "Colling, that little pig, he killed Emma after I told him to leave her alone. But he couldn't. He was obsessed with her, you see? Couldn't leave her alone."

"Colling killed Emma?" I asked.

"Smashed her brains in, is that enough for you? Poor girl. I realized it had to be fixed or else I'd be implicated. Because of my study, you see. She was my first subject. Bruno vouched for Colling. Gave him that alibi."

"Colling told us she hit her head and that she was alive when he left."

The professor smiled sadly. "Poor girl. I loved her, too, you know. In my way. Everybody did. How could you not? Such a smart girl. She knew about the...*trouble* with the trading company. How would it look if that had come out?"

"You covered for Colling because of the energy company?"

"I was losing everything!" he yelled. "All gone. My wife. She left me. I lost millions. Now they want me to move out. Take everything. Where will I go?"

"We can figure this out, Professor," I said.

"We can? You'll do that, figure it out? My IQ is a hundred and fifty seven, and you're going to figure it out?"

"What he means is, there are better solutions than this,"

Randall said.

"Oh, another genius." A little laugh escaped his lips, then he cleared his throat. "I undertook this study because I saw the devastating effects of my own economic collapse. How it impacted me. I wondered what would happen to an ordinary person under such circumstances. Certainly, they don't have the same mental capacity for reason. What other mechanisms come into play? What approaches would they take to circumvent disaster?"

"I don't know, Professor," Randall said.

"Of course you don't know," Phelps scoffed, as he looked Randall up and down. "You're probably a moron."

The professor's feet squirmed on the chair, the fingers of his free hand running up and down the rope between the noose and the flesh of his neck. "I'm in this particular situation," he gestured to the noose and then the gun, "because I wanted to see how the police would handle it. Statistically, there are predominant outcomes, but how many variables lie within the training and execution of the police?"

"We usually do pretty good."

"Oh, do you? Do pretty *good?*" the professor mocked.

"Got to figure, you'd have already killed yourself if you really meant to do it."

"Determination always has to fit into the equation."

"I mean, statistically speaking, it's usually just a cry for help."

"And what about this, statistically, is it a cry?"

Phelps pointed his gun at Randall and it exploded in his hand. The chair overturned and he fell into the noose. Randall fell back onto the floor, his arm gushing blood, a stunned look on his face.

I grabbed Phelps as he squirmed and twisted in the stranglehold. He was turning crimson, kicking and gurgling, hitting me in the chin with his sweat-soaked feet. I fell back onto the desk. Phelps' eyes rolled back in his head. I grabbed his thrashing legs and managed to lift his weight off the noose. The professor gasped in some air. Randall yelled to me and pointed. I saw Phelps had pulled a knife from his waistband. I wrestled it from his hands and between kicks and spittle coming from the flailing professor, I managed to cut the rope. Phelps fell hard to the floor.

Screams erupted from the hallway.

"He's loose! The bad man's loose!" The housekeeper came running into the room. She saw the professor sprawled on the floor, then Randall siting in a pool of blood, and screamed some more.

While Randall tried to get up off the floor, he yelled to me, "Go! Go get Colling." I hesitated, then turned to go. "Wait, take this," he said, and held his revolver out for me to take.

"I won't use it," I said.

"Hide it. I can't have it when they find me."

I reluctantly took the gun and ran to the door. Colling was already clambering down the stairs.

"Fascist pigs!" a voice echoed through the hallway. The Hipster Dude, from earlier, stood defiantly a few steps down from the first landing. He turned and started to run ahead of me, trying to block me as I pushed my way down the stairs. When I got the front door, Colling was high-tailing it out to the street, and Hipster Dude stood blocking my exit.

"Fucking pigs! You can't do that to people!"

"Get out the way!" I yelled.

"Fuck you, man. Tie a dude up? You think you can—"

I showed him the pistol. Instantly, he turned pale and moved sideways away from the door. I pushed past him and out onto the street.

40

ACCIDENTS

I sprinted outside and looked right, then left, and caught a glimpse of Colling turning onto Sixth Avenue. I ran as fast as I could to catch up, but he was a speedy guy. He dodged and weaved through a small group of tourists, who were evidently delighted their rough vision of The Big Apple was coming true. The crowd, in unison, turned their cell phones at us and chatted noisily as I gave chase down the busy sidewalk.

I soon lost sight of Colling, but kept running, scanning from side to side in case he'd crossed the street. My lungs ached and my legs felt weak, but I pushed myself to keep going. Just a few yards ahead, I saw a crowd of people part and Colling emerge, like a Pamplona bull on the run. He was probably in worse shape than I, because he had a slight limp and was breathing heavily. He looked like he was about to keel over. Beach Street was just ahead.

Colling ducked under some construction scaffolding on the right, and into its dark under hang. I thought I might lose him, but he immediately ran back out into the street. He appeared to be running out of gas with each labored step.

I wasn't sure why he'd reemerged into the light so quickly, until I saw him grab a guy on a ten-speed bike. He and the rider held each other by the arms in a strange dance, until the rider was thrown to the ground. Colling mounted the bike and sped off, turning left onto

Varick Street.

As I rounded the corner of Varick, an unmistakable feeling of déjà vu possessed me. Visions of Luke, the Skateboard Kid, shot into my head. That terrible crash. The sounds of the skateboard scraping into the pavement. The screech of truck tires. Luke getting sucked under the bus, the monster devouring his young body. Then it became all clear: this was the spot. This was the street. This was the moment. I'd seen it all in my vision. Luke dodges a parked truck and gets mangled under a bus. The irony crashed down on me like a ten-ton press. Colling was leading us right into that very moment.

"Stop!" I yelled.

A heavy dump truck rumbled past and turned the corner onto Varick. Behind the truck was someone who looked a lot like Luke. It *was* Luke, skitching behind the roaring dump truck, squatting down on his skateboard and holding on for dear life. He looked like a bug about to be squashed.

As the truck approached the middle of the block, it swerved to avoid another equally large truck parked perpendicular to the curb. At the same moment, a bus pulled out in front of the moving truck. Luke was flying out from around that truck and would land under the bus.

"Luke!" I yelled at the top of my lungs. "Stop!"

I raised Randall's pistol and fired into the air. The gunshot cut through the noise of the truck and Luke turned toward me. I lowered the gun and waved to him.

Luke jumped off his skateboard and flipped it up into his hands at a full run. A nifty trick. Colling was close behind Luke, his legs a blur on the ten speed. He swung out into the street to pass the dump truck. The screeching sound of truck brakes rattled through the air. The truck skidded and shook violently, laying a patch of thick black rubber onto the street. The bus shrieked to a stop. I could see the passengers inside fall forward from the momentum.

The kill moment had come, as I had known it would. Only now, somebody else lay under that bus.

"Luke," I yelled. "Are you all right?"

Skateboard Kid gave me a puzzled look, and hopped back onto his skateboard.

Tucking the gun back into my waistband, I stood in the middle of the street, trying to catch my breath. I was sure Colling was lying dead under that bus. But I wasn't ready to see it. I was just so happy Luke was alive.

Then something even more unexpected happened. Instead of the drivers rushing out to the death scene and following a trail of blood and viscera beneath the wheels, the truck burped free of its brakes and rolled on down the street. Then the bus released its own brakes with a loud *whoosh* and moved forward. I prepared myself for the bloody scene: Colling's mangled corpse crushed into the frame of the bike.

I kept waiting for the bus to stop, but it just kept rolling. I watched it go all the way to the end of the street and turn left onto West Broadway. I turned my head sideways, trying to see if Colling was being dragged under the bus, but it was too low to the ground to tell. How could they have just rolled on down the street like that? Didn't they realize what they'd done? I was afraid to look at the spot. The gristly corpse lying in a pool of bloody guts. Finally realizing I had to look, I turned and focused on where I'd see the red streaks, but the street was empty. Colling was gone. There was no bloody body, no mangled bike, and no crushed-in head. Somehow, he'd managed to scoot out from under a moving bus and disappear, cheating death. Cheating me.

Luke was standing on his board, giving me a disgusted look. I turned to him and an involuntary smile crossed my face. Eyes watering, I choked back tears and my throat tightened.

"Fucking perv," he muttered, and rolled away.

A giggle rose from within me. Luke wasn't dead. Skateboard Kid was alive. The incongruity of what had just happened jolted through me in waves of happiness. Had I just changed a predetermined outcome? Did I rearrange a reality that was destined, and as a consequence, that filthy-mouthed little kid was still alive? I sat down on the curb and took deep breaths, trying to gather myself.

In front of the alley stood the two police barricades, right where I'd left them. It occurred to me that an accident, no matter what I did to prevent one, was going to happen. Only this time, Colling had changed the outcome. He was the new denominator that had changed the equation.

Hope rose within me. It was clear to me now: the future could be changed. Nothing was *destined* to happen. If Colling had altered the outcome, or if I had, it didn't matter. My Dream State was only a *suggestion* of one possible, however probable, outcome.

I pulled Randall's pistol from my waistband and dropped it into the sewer drain at my feet, then started walking back to Phelps' apartment. When I arrived, two police cruisers and an EMT vehicle were parked out front. I made my way past a few spectators and ascended the stairs. A cop stood at the doorway to the apartment.

"I live upstairs," I said, pointing up the stairway.

"Then keep going," he said, and waved me past.

I stole a peek into the apartment, and saw Randall sitting in a chair, being tended to by an EMT. Behind him was a stretcher; the bald head sticking out from the blanket was unmistakably that of the professor. A couple of cops were talking to the housekeeper. One stood over Randall, and was making notes in a small notepad.

"Keep going," said the cop at the door.

"Anybody killed?" I asked.

"Nobody killed, nothing to see, keep it going."

I walked up a flight of stairs and sat down on the top step of the third floor landing, where I pulled out my cell and speed dialed Mill. He answered on the first ring.

"What's going on?" he asked.

"Your cousin is a crazy son of a bitch, you know that?"

Mill laughed and said, "Tell me something I don't know." After a short pause he asked, "What did he do?"

"I'll tell you later."

"Where's Colling? You find him?"

"We got him, then he got away. Your cousin took a bullet in the arm. But he's okay."

"Holy crap! You have a shootout?"

"Not exactly. I'll tell you about it later. How's Carla?"

"She's okay, getting ready for work."

"I need you to stay there. Colling's on the run and I have a feeling he isn't done with her yet."

"You think he's headed here?

"I don't know. Just keep an eye out."

"Yeah, sure. But does he have a gun?"

"Not when I saw him, but that doesn't mean anything. I'll be there soon. We're gonna escort Carla to work."

"Yeah, right," Mill said. I heard him sigh before disconnecting the call.

41

CHARGE OF THE WHITE RHINO

We dropped Carla off at work without any problems. I told her nothing of the morning's drama, though I was tempted to spill my guts more than once. I just didn't want her to be hurt or worried any more than necessary, especially since she was just starting her second week at a new job. I did warn her, however, that Colling was still on the loose and that she should be vigilant even while doing everyday tasks, and that for the foreseeable future, I was to be her eager chaperone. She did not protest.

Cruising up the FDR in Mill's SS on the way to my place, the impact of what had happened began to gnaw at me. The image of Randall, bleeding from a gunshot, and handing me his gun was not a pleasant one. "Your maniac cousin almost got us killed," I said.

"What do you mean?"

"Well, after he broke the law by slapping Colling around, he thought he could talk down the suicidal-crazy professor who'd just lost everything he'd ever had. After the professor shot Randall, and hung himself, I managed to save him, but my reward was for him to pull a knife out of his underwear and try to stab me."

"What a shitstorm. At least Randall's gonna be okay," he said.

"Lunatic."

"Yeah. That's my cousin. Always has been crazy." He laughed, and stepped on the gas.

"None of the evidence obtained with his bullshit is admissible in court. I don't want him anywhere near this case."

"Yeah, sure. Ingrate." Mill booted the gas and we lurched into the passing lane.

"No, I'm grateful...To be alive," I said, and grabbed hold of the passenger door strap.

Mill changed lanes to avoid some exhaust-spewing delivery trucks. He gunned the engine and the car lurched past a snarl of traffic, pushing me back into my seat. We zipped back into the same lane a few cars ahead of where we were. My stomach finally caught up, and I turned to Mill and said, "Randall's as crazy at policing as you are driving."

"But he got results, didn't he?" Mill sucked on the dilapidated cigarette hanging from his mouth. A few grains of tobacco fell onto his lap.

"He got results. Just nothing admissible in court. At least Professor Phelps will probably be locked up in a loony bin after the stunt he pulled. Plus, he did confirm something very useful."

"That Colling killed Emma," Mill said.

"Yes. Colling killed Emma." A sadness flowed through me when I said those words. I felt like I could reach out and touch Emma's sweet, smiling face. "Unless the professor is completely delusional, which he could be, but I choose to believe him."

"So he testifies and Colling goes down," said Mill.

"Something along those lines. But they have to find Colling first."

Mill's cell rang and he put it on speaker. Randall's unmistakable baritone rang out.

"I'm giving the collected evidence to the detectives investigating Emma's murder," he said.

"Randall! You're my freaking hero, man. How's the arm?" Mill said.

"It sucks. Is Gus with you?"

"Hey, Randall," I said.

"Gus. Job well done."

"Not until Colling is behind bars," I said.

"Colling is screwed, any way you look at it," said Randall. "Police detectives are good at their jobs, Gus. We'll get him."

"You just get some rest. We'll talk later."

"Right." The phone clicked dead.

Mill took another toke on the unlit butt and changed lanes. This time I held onto the dashboard, waiting for the goose, but it never came. He was stuck behind a Prius. I relaxed my grip and looked at Mill.

"He's still out there, Mill. And I'm afraid for Carla."

Mill stepped on the gas. The car jerked left and we flew into the passing lane, then we zipped back into the middle lane, squeezing in front of the Prius. "Fucking cars!" Mill yelled.

"Take it easy, Champ," I said. "We're not in any rush."

"Fuck that," Mill said, and goosed it past a cluster of slow cars, weaving in and out of the passing lane. I was resigned to holding onto the door handle, hoping the contents of my stomach would stay down. We didn't speak for the rest of the trip.

I was relieved when we pulled up in front of my apartment, and quickly got out of the car.

Mill rolled down his window. "See you tonight?" he asked.

I bent down to see him. "Tonight? What's tonight?"

"Steak and a beer. I'm buying."

"Shit, Mill. If I'm awake. I feel like I've run a marathon, then been beaten by Randall."

"So take a nap. Don't be such a baby. See you at eight."

As I straightened up, a jolt went through my lower back. Something had pulled or let go, and I was momentarily paralyzed with the pain. Mill drove off in a happy cloud of dust. I was left hunched over in front of my fourth-floor walkup, unable to move. I could feel the color draining from my face as I stood there. After several moments frozen in place, watching an old lady lumber up the street with a grocery basket in tow, and after the mailman made his rounds and winked at me as he passed—apparently, it was normal for people to stand frozen in place, gawking with their mouths open, as he did his route—I took a tiny step forward, then another, and another.

After inching my way into the building and climbing the stairs sideways—the least painful approach—I finally made it to my apartment and managed to open the door. Even little things, like turning the key in the deadbolt, caused agony. Sharp pains shot through my lower back and down my right ass cheek. I took tiny steps to the fridge, got out a bag of frozen peas and hobbled to my bedroom.

I took a couple tabs of ibuprofen and lay down on my bed, gently sliding the bag of frozen veggies under me. Gradually, as the room grew darker and the pain began to fade, I slipped into a dreamless sleep.

I awoke to a loud banging in the hallway, then shouts. The couple next door were arguing again. Suddenly realizing there was a wet spot under me, I reached around and found the thawed bag of now inedible peas. The dampness under the bag went through the bedding to my mattress.

I stood gingerly, hunched over and waiting for the burning pain to subside. After a minute, I tottered to the bathroom and flicked on the light switch. Nothing happened. I didn't have the mobility or the energy to replace the bulb, so I hoped for the best and tried to see by the faint light coming in from the bedroom. After I finished making a mess around the toilet, I backed out of the bathroom and turned slowly, like an ancient automaton, toward my bedroom.

In the darkness of the hallway, the outline of a figure stood in the bedroom, facing me. I froze in place, which was actually a relief, and waited for the mirage to fade away. But it didn't. It stood firm.

"Who's that?" I asked. The intruder said nothing. My eyes adjusted and I could just make out his face.

Justin Colling stood holding what appeared to be a small pistol in his left hand and a large hunting knife in his right. I reached into my pocket for my cell phone and remembered I'd placed it on my bedside table. My heart began to quickstep in my chest.

"How did you get in here?" I asked, fighting to keep a tremor out of my voice.

"You forgot to slide the deadbolt."

"I locked it." I tried to recall locking the door, but failed. "What do you want?"

"I said I was going to kill you, remember?"

I put my hand on the wall to steady myself. "Why do you want to kill me? You'll only go to jail for it."

"You hurt?" he asked, a bemused smirk on his face.

"Do you want to spend the rest of your life in jail?"

Colling lunged forward, thrusting the knife toward me. I jerked back and a jolt of pain shot through my lower spine muscles. Colling seemed puzzled for a moment and stood pondering my reaction. "I never touched you," he said.

"I hurt my back."

Colling laughed, then walked toward me. I crept backwards into the kitchen. Each movement felt like flesh being ripped from my spine. Light shone in through the kitchen window and illuminated Colling just enough so I could see the crazed stare of his eyes. His face was still flushed and bruised.

"You cheated death today," I said. "How did you get away from that bus?"

His head turned like he was examining a Picasso painting. "I've got nothing to lose now," he said.

"Why? Why have you nothing to lose?"

"Your buddy beat me and you watched."

"I want to know how you got away from that bus. You should have been killed."

The neighbors banged into the wall again and he looked in that general direction. I shot a glance toward the knife block on the kitchen counter, designing a move toward it in my head. Colling turned and followed my gaze to the potentially deadly blades. I wanted to make a move, but was frozen in place by the pain in my back.

"Go for it," he said, nodding toward the knives.

"I can't," I said, hoping my honesty would raise in him some sense of pity.

He took a step toward me and I scuttled back a few inches, painfully aware I was running out of room. His eyes locked onto mine and, like a snake about to strike, he recoiled, his knife hand at the ready.

A faint buzzing sound emanated from the bedroom. It was my cell phone. "My cell. That's my friend. I need to get that."

"The one who beat me?"

"Yes," I lied, knowing it was probably Mill.

"Get it." He strode back into the bedroom and grabbed the buzzing phone, then handed it to me.

"Hello?" I said.

"Where are you?" Mill asked. I could hear classic rock music playing the background.

"Tell him to meet you tonight," Colling whispered.

"Hey, Randall. How are you?"

"No, this is Mill. Where the fuck are you? Aren't you coming? Steaks on—"

"Yeah, I'm coming right now. Not like I have a knife to my throat."

Mill paused. I could hear the gears grinding in his head, and I prayed he wasn't too buzzed to get what I was saying.

"Tell him to come here," Colling whispered.

"Why don't you come here, Randall?" I asked.

"I'm about to order the food, Gus. Get your ass over here," Mill said, and hung up.

I held the phone out to Colling. He listened for a second, realized it was disconnected and put it in his pocket.

"He wants to meet me," I said.

"*Not like I have a knife to my throat,*" he mimicked. "Try something like that again and I'll stick you. Where does he want to meet?"

"At The Tavern. It's just a few blocks away."

Colling grabbed my jacket from the sofa and threw it at me. There was no way I was going to try to catch it. The coat hit my face and slid down my body. Colling chuckled with glee at my immobility. "You're gonna get him to come outside, you understand?" he asked. "Then I'm gonna push this knife into his eyeball." He found Randall's name in my contacts and pressed to dial. He waited for an answer then handed me the phone. "Outside. Tell him."

"Hey, can you meet me outside The Tavern?" I asked. "I'll be there in a few minutes."

"Gus! Have you ever seen a more determined case of suicide? I mean, the guy pulls a knife from his undies while he's hanging from a rope!" Randall laughed. "That takes some balls!"

"Okay, great, Randall," I said. "See you in a few."

I disconnected the call. Colling grabbed the phone from my hands. "Let's go, shithead," he said, and reached out to grab my arm. I managed to turn away and his hand slid off me. That pissed him off, and he slapped me on the face. I fell back onto the bed, the shock of getting hit and the subsequent fall unexpectedly loosening up my back. I slowly got to my feet. With one hand on my shoulder and the other holding the hunting knife, Colling marched me toward the door.

Gingerly, I took one step after the other, Colling snorting with impatience behind me. I felt the sharp sting of the blade resting on my back. When we finally got down the stairs, I was in so much pain, I had to stop and bend over. Colling pushed me out the door, and I almost fell into the plastic trash bins to the left of the doorway. The abruptness of stopping my fall sent shockwaves up my back and through my brain, like a jolt of lightening. I think I started to go into shock.

"Feel that? he asked, pushing the knife into the small of my back again. "Make a move and I'll take out a kidney." I craned my neck to see the glint of his blade. "And don't forget this." He shoved the gun between my shoulder blades and pushed me forward.

"I can't move," I said. "My back is locked up."

"I really don't give a shit."

My only real play now was to get Colling to come inside The Tavern. There would be a roomful of people very happy to tear him apart. I hoped I'd given Mill enough clues, and that he was sober enough to realize something was wrong.

The image of Colling handcuffed and beaten into submission by Randall inspired me, and I retorted, "Randall thinks you're a pussy."

"Randall is gonna regret hitting me," he said.

We inched our way down Second Avenue toward an inevitability I'd never dreamed. Dust blew in our faces, making it difficult to keep a steady gaze on what lay ahead. My pace slowed and Colling poked me with the blade.

"Quit it!" I yelled.

"You're a lousy faker," he said, and shoved me forward. Pain shot through my back and I stumbled, but somehow managed to stay on my feet.

We were a few blocks away from The Tavern. I could see the heavy wooden sign swinging in the wind. My phone began to ring in Colling's pocket. He looked at the caller ID and said, "Mill. That your little faggot buddy I seen you with?"

"He's just a friend," I said.

We stood in place until the voicemail alert sounded, then Colling pressed play. "Hey, Gus," Mill's voice rang out over the noise of The Tavern. "I got some people here waiting for you. You're taking your sweet time."

"Faggot," Colling mumbled under his breath. He shoved the phone back into his coat and we continued walking.

A few yards from The Tavern, Colling grabbed my shoulder and turned me around. Pain radiated down my back in waves, but I did my best to ignore it. "This Mill asshole I don't care about. Where's Randall?"

"Randall's in there, don't worry."

"Get him out here. Now."

He handed me the phone. I speed dialed Mill. "What?" Mill answered. "Don't tell me you're not coming because—"

"Randall, I'm outside. You should get your good buddy, Allen, and come join me."

Before Mill could respond, Colling grabbed the phone and threw it against the building.

Moments later, Mill appeared in the open doorway of The Tavern. "Gus, what's going on?" he said, looking at Colling. Allen emerged behind Mill, looking concerned and holding a baseball bat at the ready.

My relief at seeing friends instantly vaporized when out the corner of my eye, I saw a dark mass moving rapidly up the sidewalk toward us. Colling stood securely behind me, his knife point still touching my back. He looped his arm under my own, the pistol aimed squarely at Mill.

"Tell him to get Randall out here or I start shooting," he whispered in my ear.

"Where's Randall?" I asked.

"Why?" Mill responded.

A guttural scream cut through the air. The heavy clomping of feet hitting cement punctuated by the barking tones of a raging animal. The dark mass was moving faster now, headed straight for us. "I won't be treated this way!" the mass screamed. "I paid good money, I deserve respect!"

The Fat Man came barreling at me like a great white rhino. He sideswiped Mill, and crashed into me, knocking Colling back against the storefront. Colling let go of me, confused by the onslaught of the beast.

Randall ran out of the bar and, using Frank as a shield, made an end around, plowing hard into Colling, who fell back against the brick building. The knife flipped out of Colling's hand and onto the sidewalk. Randall picked it up. Colling seemed stunned, then lunged forward, aiming his pistol at Randall. Ignoring my back pain, I leaped onto Colling, landing on his arm and hitting my head against the brick building. I saw stars and moaned in pain. A gunshot rang out. Randall clocked Colling with a roundhouse to the face, and Colling collapsed in a heap on the sidewalk. Randall kicked the gun away.

"Are you shot?" Mill asked me.

"I don't think so," I said, but my head hurt and my stomach churned. I lay crumpled on the ground next to Colling.

"Is everyone all right?" Mill yelled.

"Where's Frank?" I asked. The crowd that had formed outside the bar parted, and I saw Frank sitting on the curb, his head bowed down between his legs.

"Frank! Are you all right?" I got to my feet and staggered over to him. Frank held his gargantuan left thigh in both hands.

"I think I've been shot," he said. Blood trickled down his fingers and dripped onto the sidewalk.

"Shit!" I said, and sat down next him, pressing firmly on the wound. Frank screamed in pain. The warmth of his blood sickened me. My stomach turned and seemed to swirl up into my brain, then everything faded to black.

42

COOKIES AND DREAMS

I swam in a warm, soothing place of darkness, comforted by its corporal familiarity, melting into that comfort, like a chocolate morsel in a freshly baked cookie. I opened my eyes just briefly enough to ascertain an object a few feet from my bed. It was dark and round and moved ever so slightly toward me.

"How are you feeling?" came an angelic voice.

The angel floated above my bed. Radiant light pulsated out from her golden halo. I smiled. At least, I think I smiled. That's what I told my body to do. Then I drifted back into that soft, doughy darkness.

Later I awoke feeling like miners were excavating something from the back of my head. My eyes ached the instant I opened them. Fuzzy colors coalesced into forms, and I realized I was at home in my own bed. The angel had gone. Now Carla, a fair substitute, sat at my bedside. She held her warm hand out and I took it.

"Two concussions in as many weeks. You're not gonna get any more playing time if you keep this up," she said.

"Not sure I like the game anyway."

"Do you remember the hospital?"

I reached into my inventory of memories and tried to find one, but there was nothing. Then I started to recall the jostling ambulance ride, being strapped to a gurney in the ER, and having a strange conversation with the doctor while he shined a bright light in my eyes.

"Sure. You danced in your sexy nurse outfit and I did the flamenco." Just as I realized that was the dumbest thing I'd ever said, she smiled.

"You danced your head right into a brick wall," she said.

"We got Colling at least. Right?"

"You got Colling."

The image of the Fat Man holding his leg came to me. "How's Frank?"

"He's okay. They sent him home from the ER a little while ago. He wasn't happy about it, but really, the bullet just grazed the skin."

"Good. Good. All that blood, I thought it was worse," I said, then began to feel the pull of sleep again.

"You rest." She smiled and pushed the hair from my forehead.

"You're my angel," I said, and drifted off.

A while later, ignoring the dull ache in my neck and back, I sat up and looked around the darkened room. Carla was lying on my sofa. I waited for the dizzy jumble in my head to settle, then gingerly made my way over to her. I knelt in front of her, and gently kissed her forehead. She opened her eyes.

"Thanks for staying," I said.

"My pleasure." She took hold of my hand, sliding her fingers over mine.

"How about we get some dinner?" I asked.

"Sounds good."

"I know a great little Italian place not far from here."

"I heard they deliver," she said, smiling. There was a hint of expectation in her eyes.

I wasn't hungry, but I knew she probably was. She helped me sit on the sofa and we ordered pasta with tomato sauce and garlic rolls for delivery.

43

SINK OR SWIM

Frank sat his huge frame on the kitchen chair and held his cane at arm's length, both hands resting heavily on it. I stood by the stove and boiled water for tea.

"I don't adhere to an existential concept of the human dilemma," he said, raising his cane and prodding the kitchen floor with it, as if searching for some hidden room under the floorboards. "No, I believe we have purpose in a well-ordered world. Call me an optimist, if you will, but the chaos we see, it only exists because man is imperfect. If we lived in nature, with nature as the so-called natives had, we would be in harmony with the rhythms of the natural world and industrial chaos would be a thing of the past."

"I don't see you living in a tent," I said.

"Take the Big Bang…"

I glimpsed him out of the corner of my eye as I poured hot water into the teapot. Frank was in his glory. The bullet that pierced his leg, causing so much blood loss, had somehow invigorated his zest for life.

"Three things can be said of the Big Bang. As it goes, one: First there was nothing. That statement in itself is ridiculous. There never was, nor ever will there be *nothing*. Nothing simply doesn't exist. Every space in the universe is filled with something. Dark matter, presumably. Two: if nothing can't exist, either we are too dimwitted to grasp the idea of nothingness, or something always was. Right?"

He looked at me expectantly. I gave a non-committal shrug.

"Three: If something has always existed, and there is no such thing as nothing, as we comprehend it, then it is a fair assumption that we live in a world that has been created by something that we cannot comprehend. I've read, and personally like, the postulation that we are actually living in a very complex hologram. A designed universe."

"So, you believe in a god?"

"I believe nothing. I only speculate."

"Ah," I said, and set the teapot down on the table.

"But, Gus. I do believe we are all somehow connected. And that the connection can continue after death is irrefutable in my eyes."

"Your sister…"

"Yes, my sister." Frank spooned sugar into his cup and poured the hot liquid, inhaling the tea aroma.

"Scone?" I asked, and placed a box of berry scones on the table.

Frank's face brightened. "Don't mind if I do." He delicately lifted a scone and took a small bite.

"And this is what we will resolve today," I said. "Your sister and I will have a chat. If all goes well, she won't bother you anymore."

He took another bite of the scone, rolled his eyes in a way that said, *heavenly*, and sipped his sugar-laced tea. "Of course, the last time you made contact, she was quite well behaved for several days. But I can still sense her. I'm tired of it. She needs to vacate this realm for good."

"Okay, Frank, but you have to realize I'm not going to do that other thing you wanted me to do. That death thing."

"Follow her into death while in a Dream State, you mean? Pity. However, I'm now aware it was not a fair thing to ask."

"And," I paused for emphasis, "it's not what I do."

"Yes, yes, and I appreciate that. Not everyone can fully realize their potential."

I felt the flush in my cheeks. He was starting to annoy me again.

After a few scones and more tea, we sat down in my living room for what I hoped would be our final session, having every intention of doing a bullshit reading. I just wanted him to be settled and out of my life. I was willing to tell him anything to get him to leave me alone. I know it wasn't very professional, but I was desperate.

Frank sat in a low, stuffed chair in the corner of my living room. I seldom used that chair because of its proximity to the floor, and I wondered how the hell he would ever get his huge bulk up again. His shot-up leg was still quite tender.

I lay on the sofa and, for theatrical effect, placed a damp cloth over my eyes. The window curtains were drawn and a lit candle placed on the coffee table. "Watch the candle if you like, Frank. I'll have my eyes closed the whole time." I was half tempted to make moaning sounds, and suddenly had to bite my lip to keep from laughing. I didn't want to disrespect what I do, nor did I want to hurt Frank, but the whole setup was ridiculous.

"Now Frank, I need you to concentrate on your sister. Think about when you actually saw her last, near the pond, before she entered the water."

I took a deep breath. Frank took a deep breath. Annoyingly, I noticed our breathing was in unison, and I held mine in again to break that pattern.

I thought about Carla and how much I wanted to make her my girl. She was so lovely, kind and smart. I wondered why everyone wasn't in love with her, and a twinge of jealousy bit me. I concentrated on her and her alone. Her angelic face hovered over me, allowing me to go deeper into a relaxed state. Frank kicked a foot out and slammed his heel onto the floor.

I peeked out from under the cloth and saw he had his eyes closed, but was moving his fingers around on the handle of his cane in an erratic fashion. I turned back to my Carla visions, hoping I would soon doze off.

"No!" Frank yelled. "Leave me alone!"

I ripped the cloth off my face and sat up. "What is it?"

"I want it stopped. You're not helping me. I can't stand it anymore!"

"Calm down, Frank. I swear, we'll get to the bottom of this. Just…Let me do my work." Something in me relented and I decided to actually try to see what I could do for him. "Frank, give me something of yours to hold." He handed me an old, hand-tooled leather wallet, with the initials FC scrawled across the top. "Okay, now close your eyes. You're in good hands." I lay back down and rested the wallet on my stomach.

Carla's face again floated in front of me and I smiled. Just as quickly as she appeared, she was gone, and I was back at the small pond, pacing back and forth on the shoreline with Frank's sister. I was in a Dream State.

She's agitated. There's something she wants in the water and she can't reach it.

The grass and mud feels cold and wet on my bare feet. I'm about twelve, Frank's age at the time of the accident.

"Hey, Kate," I say. "Frank wants you to leave him alone. Why do you torment him?"

She walks in slow motion across the shore. Her hands are covered in mud. She sits and begins to make mud pies. I sit next to her. She looks intently at me, her round, blue eyes set off by blood-red petechial hemorrhaging.

"You know you're not supposed to be here anymore," I say.

"Who says?" She asks and holds a handful of mud out for me to take. When I refuse, she pastes her dirty mud pie on my bare chest. Pebbles and small sticks hidden in the mud scrape my flesh.

"Everybody knows it," I continue. "Why don't you leave Frank alone?"

"He's my brother, silly!"

Across the small beach, just beyond the tree line, I feel the darkness encroach. The same unsettling darkness as before. Unease grips me and I want to run away.

"You can go in the water," she says, smiling, her off-white teeth tinged yellow at the gum line.

"You have to leave Frank alone. He wants you to stop bothering him."

"I can swim far. Want to see?" She jumps to the edge of the black water and her eyes find me. "Are you coming?" She turns back to the black water and runs in, splashing cold droplets onto me, and washing away some of the mud from my chest. "I can go way out!" she yells, and plunges forward into the cold depths of the lake.

"Stop, Kate! You can't go that deep. Mom said," I yell.

I want to dive in after her, but she has already gone out too far. I am somehow in her body now and also in mine at the same time. I feel the drop-off below her feet. It is angular and deep, and the water grows instantly colder.

"Kate! Come back."

Panic etched on her face, Kate dog-paddles around in circles, getting nowhere. Hundreds of feet out, the space from shore is distorted and stretched in some cosmic rubber band.

"Kate!" My feet are trapped in the mud on shore and I cannot go to her.

She is underwater now. A hand comes up, the water swirls above her small submerged body.

I grab a large stick and pry myself free from the black mud. I run in after her. Hardly able to move in the freezing water, my legs ache and my heart pounds. I am swimming now, but can barely stay above the surface. I breathe in some water, choke and gulp it down, swallowing more water than air, but I keep going. I keep kicking and pushing, and I won't stop. I won't let her slip away.

I reach the steep drop-off and stop. Standing on my toes, I stretch out as far as I can, holding the stick out for her to grab. But she can't reach it. She's failing to stay afloat. Her hair swirls in the water, like ashen seaweed as she breaks the surface.

I feel the pull of the darkness on shore. It has moved closer from the trees, but I still cannot see who or what it is. "Help us!" I yell. "She's drowning!"

But the dark mass doesn't move. It stays partially hidden in the shadow of the trees.

I make another effort to stretch out with the branch. Kate sinks down, extending her arms, desperately spreading her fingers toward me, but she cannot reach me.

"I don't care if I drown," I yell. "I can't leave you!"

I step off the ledge and plummet into the deep void. The freezing water envelops my legs and seems almost to pull at them, drawing me closer to the frigid muck below. I pull the stick in with me and turn it toward the bottom. I hold my breath and probe below. I find a solid form. The soft bottom. I jab the stick in and pull myself forward toward Kate.

I see her, the yellow hues of her languid body in front of me in the cold depths.

I have a hold on her now. I pull, dragging her, kicking furiously, but she kicks away from me, as if to fight my every saving move. Gradually, we begin to make headway toward shore.

My head pounds, my chest aches. I am about to explode from lack of oxygen. I break the surface and suck in life-giving air, then I go under again. She breaks away from me and I reach out in the darkness. I pull at her and yank at her arm. Soon I can stand.

I am standing at the edge of the drop-off, reaching out into the void, pulling her into my arms. She breaks the surface, like a huge tarpon, caught and tired. Her body is pale and cold. She floats listlessly into my arms. I pull her face up to mine. Her blue lips are open. I turn her over and smack her back, then turn her back around and look into her dead eyes. They are deep pools of black. I blow into her mouth. I inhale huge gobs of air and force it down her throat. Then she coughs and convulses. Her eyes come alive, and she smiles. I smile back. She is alive, secure in my arms.

I look at the dark mass standing near the woods. It begins to dissolve. Like a mist at dawn, the shadow slowly dissipates into thin air, then is gone.

I awoke with a raging headache. My nose dripped blood. An out of focus shape stood over me, smiling. "Gus?" it said. I tried to sit up, but slid back down onto the sofa and closed my eyes. "Gus?"

"Yeah," I answered.

"She's gone."

I opened an eye and the out of focus shape slowly resolved into Frank and I realized what had happened. The glee on his face was unmistakable.

"She's gone!" he repeated.

"Who?" I asked.

"*She* is!"

"Are you sure?"

"Oh, yes. It's like a light has turned on above my head! I'm out of the shadows. I'm free!"

"Was that you in the shadows?" I asked, but his manic gaze indicated he didn't hear me.

"I can't thank you enough, Gus. What can I do to repay you?" He helped me sit up and held out the damp cloth for me to take. I thanked him and wiped my bloody nose with it.

"I guess we're done, then," I said.

"Yes, I guess we are!" Frank bounced around the room excitedly, removing and replacing his hat repeatedly, and barely using his cane to walk. "I've got to go. I've got to go!" he repeated gleefully. "Thank you, Gus. Thank you!" He stopped suddenly and looked dutifully at me. "Do you need anything?"

"No, you go on. I'm good."

"She's gone, she's gone!" He sang a few lines of, 'Ding-Dong! The Witch Is Dead,' then slammed the door on his way out. I heard his muffled, jubilant voice call out, "Sorry!"

I sat quietly, pondering what had just happened. Had Frank somehow been there to witness my dream? I was so relieved to have finally helped him; I almost didn't notice my cell phone buzzing on the coffee table.

"Hello?"

"Hi, Gus. How are you?"

I contemplated that question for a few seconds. How was I, exactly? I had no idea.

"Gus?"

"Hey, Carla, I was just gonna call you."

"You were?"

"Sure, I was thinking that, well, I miss you."

There came a tense silence, and for a second I wasn't sure if her lack of response was the last I'd hear from her. "Hey, how would you like a nice surprise?" she said, finally.

"Not sure I'm up for any surprises."

"Oh, you'll like this one."

"I will?"

"Dinner and maybe a neck rub?" she asked.

Another pause, this time because I was fighting the little lump growing in my throat. I swallowed hard and said, "Sure. That would be heaven."

"Good. See you soon."

"Wait. What are you bringing?"

"That's the surprise." She giggled and hung up.

I lay back on my sofa, thinking about the dark mass in the trees. *He's no longer in the shadows*, I thought to myself. I'd thought maybe it was me—my fear, standing in the shadows, but it was Frank all along. That part of him that somehow shared my Dream State.

I cradled the back of my head in my hands and kicked off my

shoes. A surge of happiness ran through me and I smiled. Carla was coming to bring me her surprise dinner, and with a little luck, maybe a whole lot more.

The End

Charles R. Hinckley is an author, audiobook producer, playwright and fine artist. His short stories and articles have been published by several online magazines and News America Syndicate. His plays have been produced regionally. As a producer/voice actor, Charles has several titles available through Audible and Amazon.